# *Marley*
## KNOTT'S
# MOUNTAIN

*Jesus loves you!*

*Pam Nester Cloud*

2-23

PAM NESTER CLOUD

ISBN 978-1-64028-601-6 (Paperback)
ISBN 978-1-64028-602-3 (Digital)

Christian Faith Publishing, Inc.
296 Chestnut Street
Meadville, PA 16335
www.christianfaithpublishing.com

Printed in the United States of America

In dedication
to
Jesus Christ
for his unfailing love
and
my daddy, Malcolm B. Nester, for being the storyteller in my life.

# CHAPTER 1

L ong before man came to live on Marley Knott's Mountain, it was foretold by a mountain circuit rider who came and held a tent revival down around the foothills of that mountain that God would use that mountain, as hard and thick as it was, to bring a multitude of people to the Lord. People had come far and wide to that revival, and witnessed the power of God to heal and deliver their friends and neighbors. Everyone but a few scoffers had received salvation. But the real mystery to them was the circuit rider's prophecy. How can this prophecy be true? No one even lived up on that big mountain, and the land so rugged they didn't see how animals roamed up there, much less people.

But God had a plan. Not long afterward, a man named Marley Knott brought in his bucksaws and his big draft horses and hewed but a road up through that mountain and built his family a small cabin on the north side. They lived there until they died, but no sign of any revival came forth. Thus, the mountain became known as Marley Knott's Mountain. This prophecy had been talked about for years. People speculated much about it, even called the old circuit rider a false prophet.

But God knew better. And slowly, ever so slowly, people began to build small shacks up in the mountain to escape progress. They were set in their ways and would not conform to change. The road that Marley Knott hewed out provided a way to get up there, and that is just what they did. They loaded wagons, often having to set some of their possessions off and come back later for them. But they nevertheless trudged forward, and families soon dotted the mountain. Some couldn't cut the harsh winters and moved back down, leaving but a remnant. Those who stayed battled the elements, often lacked food, and put down roots so far down in that mountain, they actually became part of the mountain, no less the rocky ground.

This is a tale as old as time. And yet, it never goes out of style, just a time much like today. When you are born on hard times, seems like that's all you know. But things are not always as they seem. God is the author of our lives. The Bible tells us He knew us while we were in our mother's womb. Sometimes, hard times will make us headstrong and determined, but make us unsure and out of place a lot of other times. But God knows exactly how to weave our lives carefully, bringing in and moving out circumstances that we become what He has intended for our lives. On the other hand, running away from God makes our life's path hard, rough, and rocky. This story has been passed down through generations of how one little mountain woman and a great big God brought a whole mountain to know the power of prayer, perseverance, and love.

Martha Rae Jenkins was born in the winter of 1912. She was a fighter from the beginning. Her mama, Sally Francis Ogle Jenkins, had been washing clothes on an old worn out scrubboard all day. That old scrubboard was falling on its last leg, literally. She had washed John Jenkins' old gallous, high back overalls twice and the water was so dirty she hated to put her things in that muddy mess. She thought she'd give them one more scrub and throw out that water when the leg on her scrubboard broke. It threw her sideways up against John's old oxen harness. She got up and brushed her scratched up arm off and it hit her. She bowed up double, knowing what was happening. She called for her man to come help her to the house. She lay there all that evening. Her husband John had gone down the holler to fetch the local mountain midwife, Sis. She had birthed nearly all the babies born on that mountain for the last twenty years. Finally, Martha Rae Jenkins was born, and this baby was to be her last. Sis caught the fever that winter and died.

Martha Rae was a born fighter since she was born. She was always little—born at just five pounds. One lady even asked Sal, "Were there any midgets in our family?" That's how little she was. But as time went on, she grew to be a whopping five-foot-two. But she was a five-foot-two package of guts, determination, and a love for the Lord that never wavered.

Four years later, her little sister Edna Sue would come. She was born on September 20, 1916. She was a fat little chunk of love. The little Jenkins family felt complete, although John always wanted a son. He loved his girls more than life itself.

Times were always a challenge for the folks up on Marley Knott's Mountain. Seemed like when they didn't need rain, they got a flood. It would run down that mountain and settle in the bottom below, creating nothing but a mud bog. If it was dry, all they could worry about was fire. They had seen what fire could do to a mountain. It could destroy what it took a lifetime to build. So to say life on the mountain was easy was an understatement, often spoken by those who had tried to settle on the mountain, the mountain got the best of them. Those who stayed were resilient. They became as tough as a pine knot, and could weather any situation no matter what. Little did they know that the storm that was brewing ahead in the realm of time would seem like a curse. But in all actuality, it would bring them to God.

It touched every family in the mountain, especially Martha Rae Jenkins' family. It would prove what she and her offspring were made of. Often, all she knew to do was put one foot in front of the other and walk hand in hand with Jesus. Sometimes she questioned, but most times she followed the lead of the Holy Spirit to show her every decision to make and pathway to follow.

# CHAPTER 2

The spring of 1926 was especially hard on the folks who lived up on Marley Knott's Mountain. But good times or bad times, Martha Rae Jenkins was the same. She could see the good in all things and in everybody. She had a song in her heart and a big laugh in her belly.

The folks who lived on Marley Knott's Mountain had gotten through a dry summer. Most got by with berry biscuits or squirrel, which was a delicacy to mountain folk. Mrs. Bright, who lived down past Marley Knott's Cliff, had sent word around the mountain to have a gathering. It would lighten the load off them for one evening. They all needed that. So they all decided to bring one dish per family and gather down in Sutphin's Bottom and have a picnic. Some thought that one dish was asking too much, since it took a lot of grubbing to come up with one dish of food. But all finally agreed, and they would gather in August to offer thanks to God for helping them get through.

Old man Charlie Sutphin had a fiddle that had been passed down to him by his grandfather, Oscar Sutphin. Seems that Oscar had ten grandsons, but only Charlie and Wallace took any interest in learning to play. So Oscar passed his fiddle to Charlie, and an old banjo to Wallace. Together, they could make merry the hearts of mountain folk.

The big day of the picnic finally arrived. The mountain was abuzz with excitement. It was to be the most fun that most had experienced in a long time. Sal and John Jenkins were gathering their things together to load the wagon and head down the road. Sal had fixed an extra dish, so there would be enough in case some family couldn't bring much. John had a tater patch that had done pretty good, so Sal cut up some new potatoes and boiled them up. Sal had to holler several times for Martha Rae to come on, that they were ready to go. Edna Sue was snuggled up between her mama and her daddy, playing with her baby doll when Martha Rae made her exit out of the house. John just stopped his fidgeting with the mule reins, and Martha Rae's mama's mouth fell wide open in what appeared to be pure shock. Martha Rae had adorned her jet-black mane of hair upon her head and somehow made a bow out of corn husk that she dyed with blackberries. She wore her Sunday dress, too. Her mama had made it for her last winter and it was only to be for church, but she looked so beautiful that she didn't have the heart to tell her to take it off. She soon realized her little girl was not so little anymore. John cut his eye at Sal and said, "You better keep an eye on that one. Somebody will want to snatch her up."

That was exactly what would happen. They finally made their way down the mountain. John had to stop a couple of times to move a limb or a tree out of the way so they could get by. He made the statement, "We goin' to have to do some clearing Sal." As they neared Sutphin Bottom, they could see all their dear friends and neighbors had already arrived. Charlie and Wallace had already started playing and there were several kicking up the dust.

Sal was so proud of her dishes she brought. She spotted her sister Mae and called her to come over. Mae and her family really had a hard time that year. Her husband Tom had died in an accident, and that left Mae and her little boy Roy by themselves. Sal handed Mae the bowl of potatoes to carry. Mae told Sal how good they smelled. Sal said, "This is what you brought." Mae didn't know what to say. She'd had started to tear up, but Sal held up her hand and told her, "No tears today, Mae. We going to have fun." So they went to where the ladies were gathered, chattering like doves. They were happy to be together.

John pulled the wagon under a big mountain maple, so old Dock and Burt could eat grass and keep cool. Martha Rae had hold of Edna Sue's hand, and headed toward where a little bunch of her girlfriends were. Edna Sue immediately spotted the creek a lot of children were wading in. So of course, Edna Sue ran right down to the creek. She was a normally clumsy child, and before Martha Rae could get the words out of her mouth, Edna Sue fell face first into that creek. She was kicking and screaming, not of fright but for the pleasure of playing in the creek. That just started all the other children and they all fell right in behind her, splashing and wallowing in that refreshing water. All was well, and the picnic was proving just what the anxiety-strapped people of Marley Knott's Mountain needed.

Martha Rae let Edna Sue have her fun. It really didn't matter to her, when she saw her best friends at the picnic. Mallie Tucker and some of the other mountain girls were swooning over some of the boys who were trying to show off their skills at playing horseshoes. Most of the boys, Martha Rae knew because, in one way or the other, they were kin, so they didn't seem interested in her in the least. She walked right by the game of horseshoes and didn't give them a second glance.

Toby Tucker had just stepped up to pitch. He was a tall, lanky, uncoordinated young fellow and he was also Mallie's brother. As he reared back to give the horseshoe a sideway pitch, it flew right out of his hand before he intended for it to. Martha Rae was going to be the stob, whether she liked it or not. Suddenly out of nowhere, a big arm reached right out and grabbed Martha Rae by her arm. That arm pulled her aside before the horseshoe flew right by her head. The girls started screaming. Mallie ran through the horseshoe game and almost caught a shoe as well. When she finally reached Martha Rae, it was clear she was shaken up.

A good-looking, sandy haired boy looked at Martha Rae, as if he could look right into her soul and asked, "Hey girl, you alright?" Martha Rae had never seen this young man before. She thought to herself, *who in the world is this?* Kindly stunned, she sheepishly said, "Yes, thanks for grabbing me out of the way." Caleb Moses and his family had just moved to the mountain about a month ago. His mama Corry had family on the backside toward the next county. The Hanks were little known. But one thing that was known was, they were a family of drinkers, mostly the menfolk. But it had been told, a couple of the women were not past taking a snort or two. None of the adults cared to come to the gathering, but Caleb was young, just turning seventeen, and he was wanting to see some girls besides his sister. So the day of the gathering, he put on his cleanest pair of dirty britches and his best shirt, slicked his sandy hair back with a little hog lard, and came to Sutphin's Bottom.

Martha Rae's mind and heart were going in a whirlwind. She thought she knew everybody, but here she was, face-to-face with the most handsome young man. And really, the only young man who had made her heart go flip-flop. She never had a loss for words, but Martha Rae couldn't even look him in the eye. She ever so shyly asked him, "What's your name?"

Caleb, as big and bold as ever, pronounced, "Why, I'm Caleb Moses."

All Martha Rae could say was "Oh." Mallie quickly nudged Martha to come over to where the other girls were, who were just dying to know where she got that beautiful hair bow.

As the evening wore on, everyone seemed to have the best time. The smaller kids had sack races, the older boys and men wrestled, and the ladies laid out a spread of food like most hadn't seen in quite a while. A few of the families had prospered a tad better than most. So those ladies brought cakes, sugar cookies, and ice-cold mint tea and sweetened, too. The rest of the families had everyday food— taters, beans, hoecakes, corn. From those fortunate enough to have a garden—tomatoes and apples that were always abundant on Marley Knott's Mountain. Everyone ate their fill, and most found a soft patch of grass and took a nap, while the ladies cleaned up the food and loaded the wagons for the trip home.

Martha Rae couldn't help but notice Caleb Moses was some- where close by every time she looked up. He'd be looking to see if she was looking back at him, and most times he was not disappointed. He saw the gathering was about to end, and Mr. and Mrs. Jenkins were loading the wagon. Edna Sue was still soaked to the gills, and Sal Jenkins was fussing at her for getting her seat soaked. "Get your hind end in the back," Sal would scold her. She was really after Edna Sue. She had creek sand caked in her bloomers where she had sat in the creek and played. "But Mama, I tried," said Edna Sue. "You hush up and get back there," her mama would say. Edna Sue slowly made her way to the back of the wagon. She had started squalling. Sal told her to hush up again. "I'll give you something to really cry about if you don't hush up." Martha Rae was taking her time getting over to the wagon, too. Caleb Moses had finally gotten close enough to her to ask, "Martha Rae, do you care if I come down to court you a little?" Martha Rae turned every shade of red there was and shyly told him, "Yea, I guess."

There was no more time for talk. Sal Jenkins had spied her talking to Caleb and really got after her, too. "Come on, it'll be dark by the time we get up the mountain." So Martha Rae left that day with something in her heart she hadn't ever felt before. Sure, she loved her mama, daddy, sister, and kin, but this feeling was different. Even different than the love she had for Christ. Her mama and daddy had a worried look in their eyes because they knew the bunch Caleb Moses was from. That bunch wasn't good.

John just sat there. He was afraid this would happen, but just didn't know how bad. "I want Martha Rae to have a good Christian man, and there is plenty here on this mountain who would be a good catch for her." So the Jenkins family left the gathering of 1926 with divided feelings. John and Sal had feelings of anger, fear, and especially the need for prayer.

On the other hand, Martha Rae was feeling light as a feather, and her head was going in a million directions. What would she wear when he came? What would she say to him? And most of all, what would her parents think and would they approve? Only time would tell what would become of Martha Rae Jenkins and Caleb Esley Moses. But one thing's for sure, Martha Rae could not have known what her heart was in for.

# CHAPTER 3

Martha Rae's parents were quite upset with her after they got home from the gathering. Sal told her, "Martha Rae, you might as well forget that Moses boy. He ain't coming around here." Martha Rae teared up, but wouldn't let her mama see her. It was Monday and wash day. Sal had not gathered enough water to wash clothes, so she sent Martha Rae down the mountain to Marley Knott's Cliff to get a bucket of water.

The Lord had always supplied the needs of the people on Marley Knott's Mountain, just as he did for the Israelites on their journey to the promise land. There was a hole in the side of the cliff where ice-cold, clear, clean water continuously came springing forth. Even in dry times, the water continued to flow. Someone found a pipe and stuck it in the hole so it would be easier to fill a bucket. Martha Rae just had put her bucket under the pipe when she heard Caleb call out to her, "Hey girl, wait up!" Caleb looked as if he'd been plowing the farm. His sandy hair was soaked, as was his bib overalls. He finally arrived to where Martha Rae was, and blew and exclaimed she was a hard girl to catch. Martha Rae was still shy as ever and could not look him in the eye. Finally, she looked up and said, "Yea, I guess, I am." Caleb ask her how she'd been after the gathering. He explained he hadn't been doing much, just hanging around home. That should have been a red flag to Martha Rae, but the love bug had bitten her and all she could see was that big handsome boy. As he talked, she was looking him over from his head to his toes. He had a scar over his right eye, scattered freckles that had faded a little, and the shadow of a beard that he had tried to shave with a dull razor. He was taller than her by about one foot. Being five-foot-two, almost everyone was taller than her except for her younger sister, and she was catching her fast.

"Did you like the gathering the other day?" Caleb looked intently at Martha Rae, waiting for an answer. Finally, she came out of her stupor and said "Oh. Oh yes, I loved it and hoping we will do that again sometime." Caleb reached down and picked up Martha Rae's bucket and told her, "Come on. I'll carry this home for you." Suddenly, the words her mama had spoken to her days ago rang in her ears again. *Martha Rae, that boy ain't coming around here.* What would her parents say when they see Caleb Moses coming up the hill carrying her bucket of water? She thought, *Mama will kill me after she kills him.*

But as they reached the top of the hill, her mama raised her head out from behind her newest washboard. She had worn out three since Martha Rae had been born. Nobody could say they didn't go clean. Martha Rae said her mama gave her one of her looks that she knew she was going to get it. But being a Christian lady, she knew if she showed her hind end, it would ruin her testimony. Martha Rae silently thanked God for being there to remind her mama whose she was. She knew her mama loved the Lord with all her heart, but she had an old adversary—a slue-footed devil, she'd call him, who pestered her. And if he rattled her cage long enough, she could make him look like a Sunday school teacher. Thank God, though, not today, or so she thought.

"Well hello! Where did you come from?" Her mama could put the biggest, fakest smile on her face and look to be the sweetest lady alive. Caleb wasn't afraid of Martha's mama one bit. He reared back and told her how pretty he thought Martha Rae was and he'd been watching her for a few days and she reminded him of an angel drifting around in the woods. Well, slue-foot got the best of her. Her face turned a beet red, and she grabbed the bucket of water he'd carried up the hill and dashed it right in his face. Caleb sputtered and spat and looked right at her, and said, "Why'd you do that for?" Sal pointed her finger at Caleb and said, "You get right back up that mountain and when you learn how to properly court a girl, you may come back and talk to me and her daddy about courting our daughter!" And she gave him one last word, "And not before." Caleb looked at Martha Rae. Her face wasn't red, but white. She looked like she could faint right in her shoes. He turned back to Mrs. Jenkins and said, "I am sorry to upset you. I surely didn't mean to." He then looked at Martha Rae and declared, "I will be back and I will court you properly." So off up the mountain he went. Martha Rae watched him go plum out of sight. She wanted to tear into her mama with her tongue, but knew better for number one and number two knew the Lord would not be pleased, so she ducked her head and said nothing.

Caleb went home with hurt feelings and mad as fire at Sal. His intentions were honest and he had never courted a girl, so he really did not know how to court someone properly. But one thing for sure, he would not be that easy to get rid of.

In the coming weeks, the air had begun to cool off. Martha Rae felt fall slowly moving in. One day, it hardly seemed like summer was leaving. But the next, she would awaken to the sound of crickets and would pull the quilt up a little closer around her chin. October was changing the mountain. The leaves had already began to take on a new color. Martha Rae felt in her heart, God was painting the mountains with all the brilliant colors in his huge pallet. She always loved the reds the best. It made the trees look like they were ablaze. It reminded her of the story of the burning bush in the Bible. That fire never consumed the bush, but these exuberant colors were consuming her heart, along with the fact she hadn't seen hide nor hair of Caleb Moses. She prayed, "God, please let me look on his face again." One day turned into two, and finally it was getting toward the end of October. Martha Rae had given up hope of seeing Caleb again.

Her and Edna Sue had gone down to a clearing everyone called the "back of the hill." There stood three of the tallest black walnut trees you ever saw. The green balls had begun to fall, and Martha Rae could see the maggots already doing their job. Martha's mama had told her to take an extra bag to carry some of the green ones home in. "I'm going to dye some flour sacks I've collected." Right then, Martha Rae knew what color hers and Edna Sue's spring dresses would be. *But the husk were a pretty green color*, she thought. The maggots had done turned a lot of the green balls black, and hers and Edna Sue's hands were a nasty greenish black color as well. They filled two small sacks, one for her mama to use as dye, but the other delicious meats would be dried and used for all sort of decadent Christmas dishes. Edna Sue said, "These nuts are making my mouth water." She knew all the foods that would be made better with these black walnuts. Martha Rae told her sister, "Come on! We'll be back in a few days. We can't carry but a few at a time."

Martha Rae took the heaviest, and her sissy the lighter sack. They had to stop several times going home. Edna Sue kept having to relieve herself. Martha Rae told her to duck behind a bush that still had a few leaves on it. Martha Rae found some mullein for Edna Sue to wipe on. She handed her the large soft leaves not once but twice. Martha Rae found the episode so hilarious, she had to sit down. She was laughing so hard. All of a sudden, Edna Sue came out from behind the bush with her bloomers around her ankles just a squalling. Martha Rae jumped up and said, "Good Lord above! What's wrong, Edna Sue?"

Poor little Edna Sue had stirred up a yellow jackets' nest. She was a jumping and waving her arms so wildly. The only thing Martha Rae could think of to do was run. She knew the wrath of yellow jackets because she had been caught in the same predicament that Edna Sue was in now. Yellow jackets would zoom in on you and chase you, so the only alternative was to throw water on them or run. And since they had walnuts instead of water, running was all they could do. "Run, Edna! Kick them bloomers off and run!" Edna Sue slung her bloomers to the side and took off like a bullet. They were near Sutphin's Bottom. Martha Rae yelled at Edna Sue, "Hit the creek!" They looked like two torpedoes when they finally got to the creek.

Edna Sue was still crying and her big sister wrapped her arms around her like a wall of protection and cuddled her until she calmed down. They slowly retreated to the creek bank. Edna Sue was looking herself over for stings. Turned out, she was stung a lot. The stings had begun to swell. Edna Sue suddenly began to vomit. Martha Rae got her over under a tree. She knew the signs Edna Sue was exhibiting were serious. She knew her mama kept herbs, but it would take probably an hour to get there and back and she had to leave her to get help. Martha told Edna Sue, "Stay right here. Do not get back in the water." Edna Sue nodded OK that she had heard, but Martha Rae was fearful she'd get back in the water. "Promise me, Edna." There was panic in her voice. Edna held up her little chubby hand and said, "I pinky swear."

Martha Rae took off running up the mountain to the house. All she could do was pray, "Lord, please let me get the help Edna Sue needs. Please don't let her die." She was already out of breath and knew it was a good piece to get home. Coming down Big Oak Lane was none other than Caleb Moses. It was truly an answer to prayer. Martha Rae stopped and could barely get a voice together to holler. But by the grace of God, she did. She called, "Caleb! Caleb, help us! Go get Mama. Edna Sue has been severely bee stung. Tell her to bring her herbs." Caleb never answered her. He just turned and shot up through the mountain like a spooked deer.

Sal Jenkins was sweeping the leaves that had fallen out of the path that led to her front door. The wind had blown the leaves up against her house and every time she opened the door, the now brown crunchy leaves danced by her feet and made a mess for her to clean up.

She just happen to look up when she seen Caleb Moses coming up over the cattle guard. "Now, you reckon what that rascal wants." Caleb made his way up to where Sal was sweeping and grabbed her by the arm and said, "You got to come. Edna Sue has been bee stung bad. They are down near Sutphin's Bottom. Martha Rae said for you to bring your herbs." Sal Jenkins grabbed her bag of salt and took out with Caleb as fast as she could.

Martha Rae had run back to Edna Sue. She had sat up and was leaning up against a log. Her chubby cheeks were dotted with multiple red whelps. Already, her eyes were beginning to swell and her arms and legs were dotted a little. *But her back side was really red,* she thought to herself and not to scare Edna Sue. She looked as if she sat down on the nest.

Martha Rae quickly got to work. She gathered up mud from the creek bank onto her apron skirt. She packed the mud on Edna Sue's bee stings. She had seen her mama do it a million times. "It'll pull that poison out" she would say. Martha Rae went to daubing Edna Sue with the mud. She made two more trips to fill her apron, when she spotted her mama and Caleb coming out into the clearing.

Her mama ran over to little Edna Sue and fell down crying. "My baby, my baby," she would say. She instructed Martha Rae to go wet the apron so she could wash the mud away, and just see how bad Edna was stung. Caleb followed Martha Rae down to the creek. He had never seen what bees could do to a body, and when he did, he was scared to death. "You reckon she'll make it?" Caleb said. "Let's not think that way, Caleb. She must make it," Martha Rae exclaimed. She wrung out the apron, but left it with some water so her mama could wipe off Edna Sue. Their mama was already praying for the Lord to help Edna Sue. She was praying for the Lord to give his angels charge over this situation, to bear them up in all his ways. Her mama grabbed the apron from Martha Rae and began to wipe all the mud off Edna Sue. *Yes, she was eat up,* it looked like to her. She grabbed Martha Rae by the arm and said, "Child, you likely saved your sister's life by daubing her up with mud. Now let me rub this salt on her and get her home. I think, she'll be alright." She raised those two muddy hands up to heaven and said, "Thank you, Jesus."

She looked at Caleb and said, "Now, boy, you go with Martha Rae home to get John to bring the wagon down here to get Edna Sue. Martha, you stay home. But Caleb, you come back with John." Caleb looked at Sal and matter of fact said, "Yes, ma'am."

Up through the mountain, Caleb and Martha Rae headed. As scared as he had been, it felt good to have Martha Rae walking by his side. Caleb chattered all the way up the mountain to her house. She barely could answer him when he would be asking another question.

Soon, Caleb and John Jenkins had harnessed the mules to the wagon and started down to Sutphin's Bottom. Edna Sue looked better this time when he saw her. Both eyes were swollen shut, but that mouth was going full blast. Sal told Caleb how grateful she was for him helping her baby. Caleb never heard praise from anyone, so he just sat there with his head hung down, grinning. She told him if he wanted to court Martha Rae to come by for Thanksgiving and they'd talk.

Caleb Moses already knew in his heart he was going to marry Martha Rae. His heart was so full of love for her right now. He told Mrs. Jenkins to set him a place for Thanksgiving that he'd be there for sure.

Sure enough, Caleb was there for Thanksgiving. He was spit shined from top to bottom. Sal had to go into the wood room to keep from laughing in his face. Not that he looked funny or anything, but that from the usual way he looked he was quite overdone. Just a clean pair of overalls and shirt would have sufficed. He had on a pair of dress pants that looked about two sizes too big, pulled up to fit him with a fodder twine. The ends of the britches were rolled up a least twice. She guessed these may have been his Pap's britches.

Martha Rae's mama instructed everyone where to sit around this meager Thanksgiving table. Her daddy offered up thanks to Jesus for the bounty they were about to partake of this year. Caleb ate heartily and praised Martha's mama's cooking, which put a smile on her face. Afterward, the family gathered in and around a good warm fire Martha's daddy had made and talked the evening away. Caleb left before dark, he didn't want to wear out his welcome. Martha's parents told him he could court Martha Rae a little—maybe once a month. So Caleb went home a happy young man, and Martha Rae was beaming.

# CHAPTER 4

C aleb Moses had been coming to court Martha Rae all winter. One could not say he was slack, because he came in snow up to his boot tops in pouring rain and sleet and howling wind. He had only missed one of his Saturdays. He had gotten up on a Friday morning with what felt like a bear sitting on his lungs. He knew he was fevered and was afraid to go down, for fear he would give it to Martha Rae. The fever had been going around up in the mountain and just figured he had caught it. He didn't believe he had ever felt this bad and didn't know really what to do for it. His Ma boiled up some onions and laid them on his chest. She said she often heard "it would kill you or cure you." Caleb just knew he felt bad enough to die. Seemed like when the fever broke, he set in to coughing up wads of corruption. He had coughed until his stomach was sore, and quite frankly, his Ma was tired of hearing all that harking and coughing. She slipped out the back door, and when she came back she had a little jar she called her homemade cough syrup. Caleb turned the bottle up and drank him a big swig. Sure enough, it did help him to quit coughing. He thought it tasted like his Pap's shine, but it was working and he rested enough to head down to see Martha Rae the next Saturday. They hadn't heard why he didn't come the Saturday he was supposed to. Martha Rae was worried that maybe he didn't like her anymore. Sal was praying that he didn't like her. But much to her disappointment, she spotted him coming down the mountain this Saturday morning.

"Well, Mr. Caleb, where have you been? We thought a bear may have got you," she said. She was kidding, but Caleb knew she wasn't. Matter of fact, she would have done a jig if she had heard he had.

He asked her mama where Martha Rae was. She told him she was down in the chicken house gathering eggs. He didn't even stop to say anything to Sal. He took off to where his beloved Martha Rae was.

Martha Rae had always loved these chickens. Not only did they supply food for their breakfast, occasionally, her daddy would wring one's neck off and they fry it up for their supper. She counted five, six, seven eggs today. She knew that was God's perfect number. Just as she was about to turn, something caught her eyes that looked an awfully lot like Caleb Moses coming toward her. By gracious, it was. She could hardly contain her emotions but knew if she broke any eggs her family would likely go without breakfast that morning. Caleb bounded in the chicken lot and grabbed her and kissed her hard on her mouth. He had missed his little dark-haired Raven, and his feeling for her got the best of him this morning. He was already choked up from the fever he had had, but this morning, he was choked up from seeing Martha Rae, and he knew he had to do some serious talking to her today.

"Here, honey, let me help you." He took the eggs from her apron and carefully laid them in her basket. He wanted breakfast this morning, too. He had already smelled some meat frying. He guessed it might be ham, as he noticed one of their hogs were missing. Martha Rae was glowing. She had missed Caleb and could not understand why he did not come last Saturday. He explained he had been under the weather and was afraid he'd give her something, so he stayed away till he felt better. That kindness just made Martha Rae's heart swell more for him.

Sal gave her one of her sideways looks when they came through the door. "Well, I see you found Martha. Y'all set the table. Breakfast is almost ready."

Edna Sue already had the plates and ran to get another plate for Caleb. Sal pulled out the biggest cat head biscuits out of her wood oven he believed he had ever seen. A big plate of ham was following close behind. She instructed Martha to hand her the eggs. She proceeded to scramble up a big skillet of eggs. There was blackberry jam on the table and good old cow's butter. He thought he had really died from the fever when he saw all the food they were having for breakfast. There was one thing about it John Jenkins never letting his family go hungry. He himself went without, but he was not about to see his wife and girls go without food and raiment. "Come on, young'uns," their daddy said. "Let's grace this food. I'm a starving." Caleb agreed because he had never had a breakfast that looked this tasty. John said the grace thanking the good Lord for all they had for breakfast this morning. He asked God to keep his hand upon Caleb and heal him completely. Caleb was just shocked. He could not believe they would bother to pray for him. He didn't think they like him much, but maybe they like him better than what he thought. He knew, after he talked to Martha Rae, it was likely they'd be praying for him to die, but he didn't care. He loved her and he was fixing to pop the question to her this evening.

Sal could always find more for Caleb to help her with than he cared to do. But he in order to get what he wanted, he would have to comply. He'd bet them one thing after he and Martha Rae married, they could find some other mule to do all the odd jobs. Sal sent them all down to carry in some stove wood John was splitting. Even though spring was not far from coming, the air was still a bit chilly. They carried wood for the better part of the day.

Caleb was getting tired and told Martha Rae come sit with him on the porch. She ran inside and got the shawl she had made from remnants of some of their old worn out dresses. She cut the good parts out and somehow made the prettiest shawl she had ever seen. She wrapped it around her and Caleb. She had never felt this cozy before. Caleb looked her square in the eye and said in his big bold voice, "Martha Rae, I love you and I can't stand being away from you as many days as I have to. I was just thinking—"

All of a sudden, Sal appeared out of nowhere and said, "Now tell us just what were you thinking, Caleb." Sal thought she could buffalo Caleb, but she had run up against one that was just as bold as she was. "I am going to marry your daughter! Well, if you all will agree." Sal looked like a chicken you had poured hot water on. He had just announced his intentions, and for once in her life she was without words. "John! John, come up here," yelled Sally Jenkins. "Hurry up!"

John Jenkins thought something bad had happened. He took out running just as hard as he could. When he got to the front porch, he was plum near out of breath. He was bowed over double, panting to catch his breath. "What in tarnation is wrong, woman?" "John, Caleb has announced his intentions of wanting to marry our daughter. Run him off, I said, run him off."

John Jenkins was a very wise man. He knew Caleb loved his daughter and that she loved him. There was no way he could change that. He hated to see Martha Rae get tangled up with that bunch as well, but his hands were tied. If he objected to her marrying him, she'd just run off. So he figured he would like to be there to help and guide her and Caleb. Maybe they would stand a chance at this marriage.

He also knew he would have to battle his woman. The best way to battle is to give it to the Lord. He knew that was the only way that this would work. They could pray and ask the Lord to save Caleb. If they stepped in the way, they could also run him off and he would take their precious girl with him.

He made Sal go in the house and calm down. She was ready to fight. She wished a thousand times over she had run him off before it got this far. The thought of her sweet Martha getting married at fifteen was all she could stand. She dashed back on the porch, her face red at fire. John wrapped his arms around her so she couldn't hit Caleb. "Calm down, Sal. You going to have a heart attack." She answered back, "Well, it's a heart attack or nervous breakdown."

All of a sudden, sweet little Martha Rae got some bearings and decided she could put a stop to all the commotion. After all, he had asked her the question and she was the only one who could answer it. She looked at her mama and daddy. They could already see the answer in her face. She then looked at Caleb Moses and said, "I love you, too, Caleb, and would be proud to be called your wife."

Her mama began to sob. Her daddy was hugging her and reminding her she was only fifteen when they wed. "I don't care. Martha Rae is not old enough to get married, especially to that one." John took Sal in the house and told Caleb to get on home. "Come back in a few days when this idea has settled in our hearts and mind and we will talk about all this." So Caleb got up and hugged Martha and told her, "I will be back. I love you, girl." She just, like him, assured him she loved him and always would. She watched him go plum out of sight. She hated to face her mama and daddy when she went in the house, but that's all she could do was face the music. She knew in her heart what she wanted, and nobody could talk her out of it. Her daddy wanted her to pray about it, and she told him she would. But at this point, she wouldn't let God nor her mama and daddy talk her out of it. She would be Mrs. Caleb Moses or bust. And before things turned around, she busted more times than not.

Martha Rae rose up early the next morning. She had a lot on her mind. Why on earth had her parents objected to her marrying Caleb? She just could not wrap her brain around the answer. He had done everything they had asked him to do. Did they not care about her feelings? Back when she was younger, Martha had a special place in the mountain to go to when she needed to talk to Jesus. She had not visited this place in quite a while. But this morning, she knew she desperately needed some time by herself, so she could talk to her Maker. The brush and leaves had not put out their leaves yet, so everything looked naked to her. She spotted her rock. It was a funny looking rock. She thought often it looked like a chair but with no arms. She often thought that God had often told her to pull up a chair and talk to him. Today, she had much to discuss with him. She climbed over some limbs that had fallen from the heavy snow that they had the month before. Finally, she was there. It was a place of comfort, and she always found her answer when she came here. As soon as she took her seat, the tears of hurt and sorrow began to flood her lap. This should be a time of great rejoicing, but instead, it had turned as sour as buttermilk. Finally, she looked up through the trees and said, "Lord, I need your help. I love Caleb Moses very much, but my mama and daddy are totally against me marrying Caleb. Lord, I need an answer. I hate to go against my parents, but I don't think they really know Caleb like I do. He is kind to me and loves me, he told me so. I know times are hard, but I believe in my heart we can make a go of it."

She sat for what seemed like hours, waiting on God to talk to her. She looked up and saw her daddy coming down behind her. She knew he was worried and she didn't want to be a thorn on his flesh. "Come on over, Daddy. I just needed to talk to the Lord." Her wise old daddy sat down by her and took her by her hand. "Martha Rae, first I just want you to know, me and your mama love you and only want what's best for you. We also know we can't tell you who to love. I have talked to your mama and we both agreed to let this be your decision. We have nothing against Caleb, really, just the fact he wants our baby girl. It would be no different if it was another boy." John knew he was lying, but what could he do? He was between a rock and a hard place. But he knew the Rock, and knew God could change Caleb. In all of, his days he had been a praying man. He remembered the Lord touching Sal when she was about to lose Martha Rae in childbirth. She had always been a born fighter. Although small she was, he loved her and her sister Edna Sue, and could not stand the thoughts of any kind of hardship in their lives. And that was what he was afraid of. He felt if Martha Rae married Caleb, her life would be hard and he just did not want that for her. But it was Martha Rae's decision to make. So to be the good father, he told her they would give them their blessing. He also made an offer to help Caleb fix up her grandparents old place. Martha Rae jumped for joy and grabbed her daddy around the neck and said, "Thanks, Daddy. A bushel and a peck and a hug around the neck."

Seemed like all she wanted was her daddy's approval, and up through the woods she ran. She and Mama had to make some plans. Just as she topped the hill, the Lord spoke to her heart and said, "Martha Rae, your path will be a hard one to travel, but you can make it. Trust in me only for the help you need." That was it. God had just given her the OK, and so it was settled she was to be wed to Caleb Moses soon. She dismissed that the Lord had told her the path would be hard. She knew Caleb would make a great husband and father to their family. She remembered telling her mama she loved Caleb good enough to eat him, and how her mama answered back, "And you'll wish you had before it's over." Her mama didn't know everything, and Martha Rae was sure she was wrong on this. She would show them that she was right all the time.

She could see her mama sitting on the side of the porch, playing babies with Edna Sue. She herself had always wanted to be a mother and she had settled on four children. Two boys and two girls; that would be the perfect family. Sal Jenkins heart was broken, but she knew she could not allow Martha Rae to see her despair. So she greeted her with a big smile and told her that they would talk wedding plans as soon as Caleb was made aware of their approval. Her beautiful daughter who she had so many plans for was stepping into something that she feared would be the end of her. But not today. Today they would begin talking about a dress for her to wear that she would sew for her. She wanted it to be a happy time for the two of them, so she would have to fake it and try to make the best of the circumstances that were about to take place.

Sal Jenkins had been saving a piece of cloth for this very occasion. It was a pretty piece of cotton that she had bartered Mrs. Banks for. She had agreed to iron her washing in exchange for enough of that beautiful fabric to make her girls a dress. Little did she know, it would be used for a wedding dress. She often thought it would be pretty Easter dresses for them, but never got around to getting them started. So she would make her daughter a wedding dress fit for a queen. Really, she only had one pattern she used for all of their dresses, but she would embellish it with some buttons she had saved and a special ribbon she had gotten for Christmas herself one year.

Martha Rae was just about to pop to let Caleb Moses know they would get to be married. They needed to set the date and invite all the people living on Marley Knott's Mountain to her wedding. It was so much to do, she began to tire just thinking of everything. The main thing to do right now was to get word to Caleb Moses to come back down to her house. She would have gone to his house, but she had never been there so she really did not know the way. She would just watch him go up the mountain out of sight, and where he went after that, she did not know.

Much to her amazement, here comes walking up to her house the answer to her prayer. Jonas Dalton was headed up to their house as hard as he could get there. He was looking for John about some wood. John had agreed to bring Jonas a load of wood, but with all the commotion, he had completely forgotten it. Jonas lived by himself down by the road that took you to Sutphin's Bottom. He was quite a character. He could talk, but if you got him excited, he couldn't say two words right. "Hey, Jonas," Martha Rae called. "Come here. Do you know where Caleb Moses lives?" He scratched his head and said, "Yea, I-I-I believe I do." Martha Rae began telling him all the exciting news of her getting married, and she needed him to go tell Caleb to come to her house. Poor Jonas was really stuttering then. She knew he'd never get out what she wanted him to tell him. So she did the next best thing she knew to do. She got a piece of paper and pencil and scribbled out "Come to my house soon. Love, Martha." She handed it to Jonas and told him to get it to Caleb as soon as he could. Jonas took out like a scalded dog. His feet were making tracks up that mountain, and she knew it wouldn't be long until she'd see Caleb and give him the good news.

Caleb was sitting on his front porch, reared back in one of his grandma's cane bottom chairs. He was still stewing about how Sal had acted toward him. He knew he didn't know much about book learning and not a whole lot about farming, but what he knew for certain was he loved Miss Martha Rae Jenkins and he would try with everything in him to make her happy. He had just started in the house to get him a bite of something to eat when ole Jonas came bouncing upon the porch. "Mr. Caleb, Miss Martha Rae said to give you this." Caleb unfolded the note that Martha Rae had written. He hoped it wasn't too much writing for he could barely read. He knew in his heart that the Jenkins would never let Martha Rae marry him. He must have been an idiot to think otherwise. But he would go get the news straight from her lips; that way, he could accept it better.

He grabbed an old coat that belonged to his Pap and started down the mountain to Martha's house. Jonas was right behind him. He was so torn up, he couldn't even put a sentence worth understanding together. Finally, Caleb just turned around and told him to hush. Jonas hung his head down, but stayed right with Caleb all the way to the Jenkins's home.

Martha had hoped he would come tonight. She did not think her heart could hold this information till morning. Martha was in the house with her mama when Caleb jumped upon the porch. It sounded like a horse had jumped up there. But when Martha Rae looked out her window and saw it was Caleb, she made a dash toward the door, and when she saw him, she jumped right into his arms. "My parents said yes, Caleb. Yes. Can you believe that?" He said, "Well, I ain't marrying them. What do you say sweetheart?"

"Like I told you before, I would be proud to be your wife." Caleb got the biggest grin on his face that ever was. He did not believe he could be any happier. She told him they would need to set a date. "Daddy said we could live in my grandparents' old place and he'd help us fix it up as time went on." Also, she let him know they would need some time to get her dress made. Caleb told her he would need to get some dress clothes too. Nothing was too good for the happiest day of his life.

Sal and John Jenkins welcomed Caleb into their family, and after a whole lot of discussion and some back and forth, they all decided June 4, 1927, would be their wedding date. That was to be a little over a month and a half, and it would be pushing that to get everything organized.

After Caleb went home and everyone was in bed, Martha Rae was pondering on the day and everything in it. She thought about what the Lord had spoken in her heart and what kind of hard road would come for her. She could not even think of anything, maybe miscarriages or money or probably lack of it. She also remembered the last word the Lord gave her—to trust in him only. Would she have others that would try to gain her trust? Her head was swirling right now, and all she wanted to do was sleep and dream of her knight in shining armor. Tomorrow would bring another day. She silently said her prayers and drifted off to sleep, unaware of the changes that were about to take place in her life.

# CHAPTER 5

The big day had finally arrived. There had been much preparation to do to get this day together. Martha and her mama had worked endlessly on her dress. It really had turned out to be the finest piece of work Sal Jenkins had done. The bodice was very modest. Just because her daughter was getting married, that did not mean you let yourself go. The neck was about halfway up her neck with a pretty piece of lace to trim the edge. Three small pearl buttons came down in a row to meet the bodice. The skirt was gathered at the waist, and the sleeves were probably the prettiest of the whole dress. Sal Jenkins had worked very hard to make this day special for her daughter. She had visited the local mercantile in town and found the most beautiful piece of lace. She knew she could not afford that but she was a cunning barterer. She asked if they had any work she could do for them in exchange for a yard of the lace. The lady of the house came out to talk to her and she asked Sal if she could bake. Well, that was like asking "does a pig like slop?" "Yes, indeed, I do. What do you need?" Come to find out, they needed some baked items to sell in their store. "Can you make cookies?" "Law, yes I can make cookies. What kind do you want?" So she and Mrs. Banks decided on a cookie menu. They gathered all the supplies she would need to bake these wonderful cookies and sent her home with a load of ingredients and a yard of lace.

Just as soon as she got home, she went to putting the sleeves in the dress and any other final touches it needed. She hollered for Martha Rae to come in where she was sewing. "Come on, try your dress on." Edna Sue watched every stitch that was put into her favorite sister's dress, really the only sister she had. She couldn't wait to see her in it.

Martha Rae very carefully unbuttoned the back of the dress and stepped into her mother's masterpiece. She looked like a princess to Edna Sue. Her mother was so overcome with emotion, she just broke down and cried. Her daddy was about to come into the house as well for a drink of water when Sal warned him to stay out. He did not need to see her until the day she got married which weren't going to be a long time coming.

June 4 was right on Caleb's heels. He knew he needed some clothes for his wedding, but did not for the life of him know where they were going to come from. His Mama and Pap had done told him they would not be able to come to his wedding, but his sister assured him she would not miss it for the world. Matter of fact, his sister asked him, "Caleb, what are you wearing to the wedding?" Caleb hung his head down and said, "To tell you the truth. I really don't know." "Come on," she said. She had her a boyfriend in that mountain, too, and she knew he had a suit of clothes he would let Caleb borrow, but he would have to give them back the same day he got married because these were his church clothes.

They took out down the mountain to Boyd Baker's house. He had a son the same age as Caleb and just about the same height. Caleb was just a tad taller. Caleb tried on his suit of clothes and it looked like they were tailor-made for him. "Boy oh boy, don't I look good. First suit I have ever had on." Mrs. Baker told him, "You take it on with you today. I am coming to the wedding tomorrow and I'll get them then." Caleb took them off and folded them ever so neatly. He thanked his neighbors, and he and his sister Ocie Jane left that day better than they came.

The whole mountain was buzzing about the wedding they were going to. They knew everybody would be there, except for Caleb's parents. Reverend Vass was coming from Carroll County to marry them. He had baptized Martha Rae when she was a little girl, and he always felt God had placed a calling on her life. He sure hoped she was doing the right thing, and would be sure to send up lots of prayers for her and Caleb.

Sal had done told Caleb to stay away from her house until the day of the wedding. Martha and Caleb would be married in her front yard and she wanted everything to be just perfect. She had saved her eggs for several days to make a wedding cake. The cake had come out beautiful. This was a treat they were going to get to have early this year. Usually, they only get cake at Thanksgiving. The next day, Martha Rae woke up early. She almost seemed sick on her stomach, but knew she was nervous and emotional so it quickly passed. Her mama helped her with her hair. She gave her the pretty ribbon that had been given to her from her mother to put in her hair. She made Martha promise she would keep it and pass it on to one of her girls if she and Caleb had children. That's all it took. She burst out crying and fell over on her baby's shoulder and cried to the point she almost had the snubs. But she washed her face and composed herself. She would not spoil this day for her girl.

Martha Rae's daddy put on his newest pair of overalls and his Sunday shirt to wear to the wedding. He was usually a very strong man, but this had brought his heart down and he slipped off down to see about his mules, and he prayed to God that he would put his blessing upon Martha Rae and Caleb.

It was getting just about time for the wedding to begin. All the friends and family had gathered together. Reverend Vass was standing in his place. All that was left was for John to walk Martha Rae out of the house and give her to Caleb. He walked in to get his sweet daughter, and her beauty just about took his breath. She looked just like her mama at that age. He kissed her on the cheek and ask her, "Baby, are you ready?" To which, she replied, "Anytime you are, Daddy." If she really knew the truth, he would never be ready to give her away. She had been his firstborn girl, and he had spoiled her silly when she was smaller and done a pretty good job of it right up to today. But this was her day. He knew this day would come sooner or later; wishing for later, but it was way too soon. He gently got her by the arm and she locked hers into his and they made their way out to where the preacher was.

Caleb could not get over how beautiful his bride was. She was overwhelmed as well when she looked at Caleb. He was so sharply dressed today. This made her proud. She knew he didn't have much and family wasn't as important to him as it was to her, but he had really outdone himself today. She looked around at all her friends. There stood Mallie, her best friend. There was Mae, her mama's sister, and Little Roy. All the Sutphin boys had come with fiddles and banjos in hand. They would be making music after the wedding. And finally, her little sister Edna Sue. She loved this girl so much. She had asked her to be her maid of honor. Edna was the prettiest she had ever seen her and when she got close enough, she leaned over and kissed her on her cheek and said, "I love you, Edna Sue, with all my heart." That done it. Edna Sue cut loose in a wailing cry that they probably heard in town. Her mama ran over and wiped her face and told her, "Stop that crying, little girl. I am going to need you to help serve cake, and we can't serve cake with you crying and all."

As Martha Rae stepped beside Caleb, the preacher asked, "Who gives this young lady to wed this young man?" Her father looked straight into the eyes of Caleb and said, "Her mother and I." Caleb knew he was serious about this, not just saying it because they told him to. He had every intention of honoring his daughter as his wife. Nothing on this earth had made him so happy and determined to be a good husband, and maybe a father one day. Not like his Pap but more like John Jenkins, whom he had grown to have much respect for.

After the wedding vows, he kissed Martha Rae right there in front of everybody. She was blushing so much, she thought her face would bleed. Edna Sue and her mama were serving cake and mint tea. Everyone was wishing the couple much happiness. The men were shaking Caleb's hand when out stepped an acquaintance Caleb had not seen in some time. All of a sudden, his hands became sweaty and he told Martha Rae he was going to go get them a glass of tea. Martha was quite alarmed at Caleb's rudeness to this man. He introduced himself to her as a longtime friend of Caleb. In fact, they had grown up together before his family moved. He told her he would catch him in a few minutes to congratulate him on his marriage. Martha Rae thanked him and thought, *he never even told me who he was?* She thought that was very strange, but would not let it ruin her day.

Caleb was over getting him and Martha a glass of tea when his old friend approached him once again. "Well, well, well, Caleb, I never thought I'd ever see the day you would marry anyone. I'll be by to see you in a few days and we will talk of all the good times we had together." Caleb wanted nothing to do with this man. He had shown Caleb he could be a very dangerous man, and he wanted nothing more to do with him and told him he was married now and had no time for that kind of living. He walked off and left him standing. If Martha Rae knew what he and this man had been into in the past, she would run from him as fast as her legs would carry her. He hoped he would just go back to where he came from and leave him alone. He had started a new life now, and all he wanted was to make Martha Rae happy and Conrad Cox was not going to spoil this for him. He and Martha Rae and all the folks on Marley Knott's Mountain danced the evening away with the Sutphin boys playing that sweet mountain melody with the instruments that had been passed down to them a long time ago.

John and Sal Jenkins even seemed to enjoy all the merry this marriage was bringing. *Maybe, just maybe, it would be OK,* John thought. Sal, on the other hand, never intended to take her eyes off of Caleb Moses for one second.

And so the lives of Martha Rae Jenkins and Caleb Esley Moses became one. In the eyes of God, they were one now. She was where she wanted to be, in the arms of Caleb Moses dancing to the hillbilly version of "The Man I Love." Life was perfect right now, but there was a storm on the horizon that she could not see right now. It was a good thing too, if she had seen this storm, she would have ran as fast as she could away from Caleb Moses.

# CHAPTER 6

The weeks and months that followed Caleb and Martha's wedding could have not been anything other than heaven. Her mama often said, "Did two adults get married or did they just find a playmate for themselves?" Where one went the other was not far behind. Caleb had never been happier, although he found the role of a working husband to be dull and dreary mainly because he didn't know how to do much manly work. He couldn't chop wood. Martha Rae's daddy had tried to show him for what seemed like a thousand times, but he just didn't have the knack for it. He would rather just go into the woods and gather sticks and limbs that had fallen. That's the way his Pap did and they didn't freeze to death, so he thought it would be good enough for him and Martha. John tried to explain you needed big wood to keep the house warm, but it usually went in one ear and out the other. John was so concerned, he talked to Martha Rae, but she didn't seem to care either, so if she didn't care, why should he? So he just left them alone.

Sal Jenkins was another story. She ranted to John to go get after Caleb to do this and to do that. Finally, he told her, "Mind your own business, Sal. If they need our help, they will ask." So she hushed for a while. And then if something didn't look like it ought to, she was after John again to say something.

Long about October, Sal Jenkins was looking up toward Martha Rae's home as she did a lot of times. What in the world is wrong? It looked like Martha was on her knees with her head hung down. Had that dumb cluck dared to hit her daughter, especially this close to her house? She shot out the back door and ran up to where Martha Rae was, only to meet Caleb coming out of the house with a wet rag.

"How do you do, Mrs. Jenkins? Seems like the weather is cooling off." "What is wrong with Martha?" said her mama. "I could care less about the weather." Caleb was trying his best to be nice to his mother-in-law, but with all that was going on this morning, he just lost it. "Well, for your information since you are such a busybody, I might as well let you be the one to announce. We are having a baby! Not me, you, and Martha, but me and my wife. I would appreciate you staying out of our affairs."

Now that did not go over so good, as anyone could guess. Caleb and Sal Jenkins were going at each other with their mouths, while poor little Martha was vomiting her guts out. John Jenkins had heard all the commotion from down where his mules were and ran up to Martha's house to see what was going on. He expected to see Martha Rae and Caleb into it, since they had been married long enough to have a big fuss. But much to his shock, it was his wife and Caleb going at it like professionals, and it looked like Sal Jenkins was going to take it up with her fist before long.

John got there at the nick of time." Settle down, you two. Martha, what is wrong honey?" She got up off the ground and wiped her mouth off with the rag that Caleb had brought her and said, "Well, Grandpa, let me think!" Her daddy's face went from anger to a joyous smile. He hollered loud enough that some close neighbors heard and came up the mountain to see if things were OK at the Jenkins's place. He began to jump and grabbed his wife and said, "We going to be grandparents, Sal. Can you believe that?" She got to laughing at the way John was carrying on, and felt like a fool for jumping on Caleb. She immediately turned to Caleb and apologized for acting so ugly. They got their daughter a chair and asked her how she knew she was expecting. She told her mama she had peed on wheat and barley seed and the wheat sprouted, so they were look-ing for a baby girl. Why that was a surefire way to know! Her girl must have been paying more attention to her growing up than she thought. "Come on down to the house. Let's all get us a bite to eat and talk about this baby."

Caleb could get over any rile when it came to food. He wasn't going to miss any opportunity to eat. He knew Sal Jenkins was a good cook, and his mouth was watering already. Martha Rae told Caleb, "You go on down and eat with Mama and daddy. I am going to lay down and rest." She felt like she might have to vomit again and wanted to be close to home when she did.

Caleb went on down to his in-laws to eat, and Martha Rae went and laid on the bed. It was exciting and scary at the same time. What kind of mother would she be? She knew she would love her baby and teach her the godly values of being a good girl. But what kind of dad would Caleb prove to be? He had not had the love and nurturing she had had, and it really might be challenging for him. Her dear sweet daddy had tried his best to show Caleb a few things he desperately needed to know but had not had much success. One thing for sure, Caleb needed the prayers of everyone if this marriage would succeed.

Martha's pregnancy was difficult, to say the least. Her morning sickness seemed to never subside, not her appetite. She was constantly hungry. Caleb did his best to see that what she wanted she got. But that in itself was getting harder and harder. Just the bare essentials were getting hard to get not only for him and Martha, but the Jenkins family as well. Most everybody on the mountain had a special knack for saving. God always left handfuls on purpose for them and they gleaned that mountain for everything. But the summer had been dry and hot, the people had already began to talk. What in the world will we do this winter? Seemed like everything around them was scarce. Martha herself thought it would be a hard time to bring a child into this world, but her mama assured her "if you wait on a good time, you will die childless," so Martha Rae put away all her fears into the hand of Jesus and relaxed.

The end of her pregnancy was better than the beginning. Even Caleb's parents seemed to be excited about a new baby. One evening along about her seventh month, Caleb's Ma and Pap came down to see them. They had never been to their son's home. They had excuses for what seemed like everything they did or didn't do. Caleb had seen them coming and ran to meet them. Even though they were not the best parents, Martha could see Caleb loved them in spite of everything. "Come on in, Pap. Let me get you and Ma a seat." Martha Rae came into the room beaming. She would show her husband's parents the best hospitality she could. She asked Caleb to go get them a good jar of that cold mountain water. They immediately grabbed a jar and drank like they had never had any water. Martha then asked, "Would you like a biscuit with some of my mama's blackberry jam she made this year?" Both nodded yes, and she brought out a plate with biscuits for all of them. Were they hungry? Was this the reason for the visit? She would make sure they would go home that afternoon with their bellies full even if it was just biscuits. Martha found out that they were different. Perhaps this was the reason for Caleb's lack of ability.

Mr. Moses was very proud of the fact that he had been out in the woods all day gathering firewood for his wife to cook with. Anyone knew you needed real wood, tree wood, not limbs and brush. His Ma was a strange looking-person, period. She had an old rag tied around her head. Her hair did not look like it had been kept for days, and both had rotten teeth almost to the gums. Martha had to dismiss this from her mind or she felt like she might vomit any minute.

Their visit was brief and they sauntered back up the mountain. She could hear them talking, as it was echoing back down to her. She could not help but laugh. They thought she was a rich woman and that Caleb had done real well for himself. Little did they know, they were as poor as field mice, but very rich in the things that mattered. Love for each other, the love of the Lord, and love for their neighbors. After all, that was what Jesus had called the greatest commandment. She felt good in her heart and good in her belly, although this child had become very still in the last few days, she wondered if things were OK.

The days lingered on. Winter was really hard this year. They had eaten enough pumpkin and leather britches that they could not wait for spring to arrive to get a good mess of greens. Martha's grandmother always said, "You need a good mess of greens." She called it her spring tonic and it was, but you never get intoxicated with hers.

Sal Jenkins had just got a big pot of spring greens off her cook stove. They probably could smell them from the top to the foot of this mountain. The smell was not very inviting. It really stunk to most folks. But to Sal Jenkins, it smelled like heaven. She was just about to holler for John and Edna Sue to come eat a bit, when Caleb busted through the door with a look on his face that told them he needed help. Sal jumped up, "What's wrong Caleb?" It was a stupid question to ask because she herself knew Martha Rae's time was coming soon. She just about knocked him down, took out her door, and up the hill she ran.

Martha Rae was in hard labor, and Sal was as afraid as Caleb after she got up there. "Law goodness, who do I need to get?" She hollered for John and Caleb to go get Old Mrs. Moles and hurry up. They soon had Mrs. Moles loaded up on their wagon and headed up to the Moses's home. About the time they rounded the chicken house, they heard it. It was the clear distinct sound of a newborn baby, letting out its first cry. Mrs. Moles said, "Welp, I guess we are a little late, don't you think John?" Caleb shot off the wagon and ran to the house. He started in where Martha Rae was, but Sal tried to get him to wait until things were cleaned up a little better. But nothing doing him, he gave her one of those looks that she'd love to smack off his face and went in anyway. "Oh my baby." He didn't really know what had taken place nor did he realize how much Martha had suffered to get this beautiful black-headed little girl in the world, but he did know his heart was might near about to bust. He finally got closer to Martha and his new daughter, although he was so scared to touch either of them. Sal came and asked him to go out until they could clean up Martha and the baby. Mrs. Moles remarked what a great job Sal had done birthing that baby.

Martha was the most tired she had ever been in her life, but she was also the happiest she had ever been. She and Caleb had talked about what her name would be. She would be called Angela Delilah. Angela because she would be Caleb's angel, and Delilah after Caleb's grandmother. Right at that moment, they did not know what their future would hold, but she had the never had this much love for another human being in her life. She loved her sister Edna Sue and knew she would be the greatest aunt to her children, but nothing compared to the love she had for her very own daughter. Sal and John each took turns holding their first granddaughter. Caleb had not yet gotten the nerve to hold her, but he finally did and he rocked her to sleep, cuddling her in his arms. It was a picture of peace.

Martha hoped all would continue to be good for them. She knew it would be foolish to think that they would never face trials, as her mind drifted back to what the Lord had spoken to her last year. Love covers a multitude of sins. Martha was too tired to think. She would talk to God soon. But right now, all she wanted was to cuddle her little girl and sleep.

# CHAPTER 7

L ittle Angela was the apple of everybody's eye. Martha did not have to worry about having help. All the neighborhood women loved to hold her. They all remarked that she looked just like her mama, that black hair was no mistake. But Martha knew she favored her daddy every other way—temperament and all. She was hungry all the time. She could drink twice the milk that Martha Rae's body produced and it was beginning to show. Her little legs were filling out and she was going to be chunky like Edna Sue, she thought. Her mama had been cooking up some apples to feed her some solids," she said. That's the reason she is so hungry. She believed her parents had been feeding her gravy; otherwise, she wouldn't be getting so heavy. It wasn't long till Martha Rae noticed she was getting up feeling sick. Food just wasn't settling on her stomach very good, she thought. All this stress of motherhood was taking its toll on her. Her little Angela was already six months old and was sitting up and chewing on everything. Her grandpa had brought her a piece of leather for her to teethe on and said, "It will help get them teeth through. Put a little jam on it, she'll go to town after that and those teeth will soon be through." Martha Rae did just exactly what her daddy told her to do, and sure enough, a little corner of her first tooth appeared.

Caleb had not been too good of help. Sure he would play with his angel, but taking care of her physical needs was something else. If she needed changing, she did it. If she was just fussy, she was handed to her as she wants her mama. He never got up with her when she had the colic, just rolled over and looked at Martha Rae and said, "Honey, you do it. You are so much better at it than I am." Martha

Rae had never spoke of Caleb's lack of duty with his daughter to her parents. Why, they would have hung him in the backyard. There wasn't anything her daddy didn't help her mama with. He often would scrub those dirty diapers on the scrubboard himself, seeing they only had a few and babies go through a lot of diapers that first year.

Martha finally confronted Caleb about his laziness with little Angela. He dismissed her off by just saying he didn't know much about taking care of babies. She stormed back at him, "Well, ain't nothing wrong with your knowing how to get them. And by the way, since we are on the subject of babies, we are going to have us another baby next year. So you need to get off your stool of do nothing and learn how to do something besides keeping me pregnant." She was ready for bear and was not backing down to Caleb Moses one bit. He looked at her and he could see Sal Jenkins coming out in her and told her as much. "Well, I am honored to be called just like my mama." She knew she could lay into him about how he was like his Pap, but there was no need to just keep this racket going. She ducked her head, and out the door she went with her baby in her arms. *Where was she going?* she thought. She knew she needed someplace to go sit and talk to Jesus. All the stress of having to do everything was eating at Martha Rae's soul. And she knew if she didn't get away for a day or two, bitterness would likely settle in. She would go stay with her Aunt Mae a day or two. Maybe Caleb would get the message and straighten up. Her emotions were shot this evening, and she knew the pregnancy was not helping any either. Mae would welcome her in and ask no questions. If she had went to her mother's house, she would have asked her every question she could think of, and then go barreling up the hill and jump on Caleb. Maybe that's what he needed—some of Sal Jenkins what for. She knew if someone dare mistreat her daughter, she would indeed take it up. But on the other hand, she knew her and Caleb would need to fight their own battles between them. If she brought her parents into the fight, likely he'd leave, and she did love him and desperately needed him. So a day or so at Aunt Mae's would surely give Caleb some time to think and all would be well. She needed to hurry because it was getting dark and she wanted to get to her aunt's house before then.

As she was going down through the woods, she had a feeling someone or something was watching her. The thoughts of a bear or some other animal made her feet go just a little bit faster. There had been a lot of mountain people tell of seeing a big bear roaming through the mountain lately. She had completely forgotten about that or she would have never taken off. *That's what happens when you get angry,* she thought. *Your head is on backward.*

Anyway, she held her baby a little tighter. *If we can only get to Aunt Mae's, we will be OK.* On down through the mountain, she trailed. She was almost to the clearing down near the bottom of the mountain when she saw something move just ahead of her. Her heart was already beating out of her chest, and her knees were so weak she feared she might faint from fear. But something arose up in her, it was the mother instinct that the Lord had instilled in her. She stopped in her tracks. She was going to see what was tracking her. Why, it was that man who had come to her and Caleb's wedding. Conrad Cox, she remembered as being his name. She bet he was looking for Caleb. She yelled, "Hey, Mister! You looking for someone?" Conrad looked shocked. He had never expected her to call him out. He would have to pretend and go along with her to keep her suspicions up. "Yes, ma'am. I was looking for Caleb. Do you know him?" He knew exactly who she was, but pretended not to. "Yes, he's my husband. I remember you at our wedding. How have you been?" "I've been doing good but I need to talk to Caleb about something. If you could direct me to his house, I will be on my way and quit bothering you." Martha Rae assured him she was not being bothered and told him a shortcut up the mountain to her house. She did ask him one favor, "Please, don't tell Caleb you saw me. We have had a little spat and I just needed to get away from him a day or so." "Oh, don't think nothing of it. I won't utter a word of seeing you." She told him good-bye and was on her way to see her Aunt Mae.

Boy, that was that a relief off her. At least she knew it wasn't a bear. Her aunt was out in the back, getting some clothes off of a tree limb that she had hung up to dry. She saw Martha and thought,

*Wonder why she is coming down here at this time of day? Sure hoped nothing was wrong.* She began to wave an old pillowcase at her so she would see her and she did. Martha had Angela wrapped up in a shawl, and it was getting on late in the evening. Mae knew something had to be wrong. She ran over to Martha and grabbed her by the shoulders and said, "Honey, don't tell me something else bad has happened. I don't believe I could stand any more bad news." Martha by this time had cooled off and felt foolish for bringing her troubles to Mae's house. She knew if she told her about the fuss her and Caleb had, it would just worry her. She was nervous about things anyway, and it would just worry her to death if she thought something was wrong. "Oh no, Mae. I just had you on my mind." She knew that was a flat out lie and asked the Lord to forgive her; she meant no harm. "I just wanted you to see Angela's first tooth." "Well, child, you could have waited until tomorrow. It's almost dark. I have been hanging my clothes on a limb to dry. One of these days, I am going to get me a real clothesline like your Ma has. By the way, how has Sal and John been doing?" You could tell she was lonely for adult company because she did not stop talking to Martha Rae. She wanted to know about everyone who lived up in Marley Knott's Mountain.

Finally it, dawned on her it was dark, and Martha and Angela were still at her house, so she offered for them to stay overnight and go home in the morning. Martha told her she thought that would be a good idea. Caleb knew she was coming down the mountain, so he would probably know she was at her aunt's house. Boy, did she have a lot to answer for to Jesus and Caleb. Why on earth didn't she just take a walk and go home? She silently thought, *I hope I ain't getting like my mama, hotheaded and mouthy.* But regardless of what had happened, she was here and would have to spend the night. Mae fixed her and Angela a pallet on the floor beside her little Roy. Martha thought poor little Roy ain't got no daddy and really needs a man in his life. *And here I sit with Angela and she has a daddy and I have run off.* She felt so ashamed of herself. Maybe Caleb would see she needed him to help her. She would get up first thing in the morning and head up the mountain and apologize to Caleb. *Lord, please, forgive me,* she whispered. *Help me to be the wife and mother to my family that I need to be, and submit to my husband.*

Caleb was really getting worried about Martha and Angela. Where in the world had she ran off to? He knew if he went down to her parents they would blame him for everything, so he thought he would just go off and hunt her himself. It was getting dark but he wasn't afraid. Many a night he would travel through this mountain alone. He just about had every path memorized and there were not many places she could go and him not find her. He grabbed his coat and started out down the mountain. He figured if she wasn't down at a neighbor's house somewhere, he'd head out down toward some of her kin. She might go to her aunt's house. He knew she loved to visit there and would be welcome to. He felt a briar go in his foot, these old boot soles were just about off and they flopped every step he took, so it wasn't any wonder. He sat down to see if he could get it out when he heard someone walking close by. Martha Rae, that had to be her coming home. But as he watched the figure coming closer, he saw it wasn't her but a young man. He seemed to be in a big hurry and wasn't letting the grass grow under his feet. As he got closer, he recognized his old acquaintance, Conrad. *Yea, wonder what that slue-foot wanted,* he thought. Caleb hunkered down. He wanted nothing to do with him. He was married now, with a baby and another on the way and had no time to fool with this joker. He was trouble and he knew it. He looked like he might be going up to their home, so he didn't want to be there when he arrived. He sure hoped Martha Rae and Angela were not there either, because no telling what he might try. He was not above anything, and he knew it. He was afraid to venture any farther. He would follow this bird to see where he was going and if it was his house, he would make sure if Martha and Angela had come home he wouldn't bother them. Sure enough, he headed right up to his house. He knocked and knocked, but no one came to the door. Conrad almost opened the door anyway, but looked up and Mr. Jenkins was coming up the hill to his daughter's house with a gun in his hand. He approached Conrad and asked him, "Boy, what can I do for you?" The word "boy" struck a nerve in Conrad instantly, but since he was on the wrong side of the gun, he would mind his manners. He explained he was a childhood friend of Caleb's and had been at his wedding, but never got to really talk to him and was in this area and decided to stop by and see him and all. He had heard Caleb and Martha had a baby girl and he was just wanting to catch up with him. Martha's daddy told him he didn't know where Caleb and Martha Rae were. They might be off visiting some neighbors, seeing how everybody loved Angela. Conrad told him to tell Caleb hello for him and he'd be back another time. John thought it was odd. Instead of going down the mountain the way he came, he went up the mountain. Something told him to watch that boy. He did not have a good feeling about him.

Caleb had watched the whole thing take place. Thank God for his father-in-law, maybe there was something to all this God talk this family did. He just hoped his wife and baby were OK. John Jenkins already knew they were not home, so he would track back down the mountain and find Martha.

Mae had fed Martha Rae a good supper. She had some pinto beans that one of her husband's family brought her. She cooked them up with a piece of hog jowl. Martha thought it was delicious. Mae brought out some fried apple pies she had made the day before. Roy told Martha, "Them is the best pies I ever eat in my life." They all got a big kick out of him talking. Martha was getting sleepy and Angela had already gone to sleep. Her aunt, she thought, could talk all night. She knew she needed to visit her more often. It was so sad that her she was all by herself, with a sweet boy to raise. She prayed the Lord would send her a good man to be her companion and help her raise this little boy. They all got quieted down when they heard a loud bang on the door and Martha Rae knew it was Caleb. He was hollering, "Martha Rae, you in there?" Her aunt Mae looked alarmed. She didn't know if Caleb would hurt Martha or what. But Martha assured her it was OK, and she went to the door herself to talk to him. She opened the door and he pushed it the rest of the way open. "What are you doing down here, honey? I have been worried sick about you. Now you get Angela and we all are going home." Martha hung her head and went in and told her aunt she guessed she'd just go on home with Caleb. She wrapped Angela up in a blanket her aunt gave her, and all three made their way home.

Caleb talked, of course, the whole way. He told her he was sorry and would really try to do better. Martha was just mostly listening. She would talk herself the next morning. She had a whole lot she needed to tell Caleb Moses. Right now, all she wanted to do was get her baby up this mountain and snug her into her little cradle and crawl herself into the bed beside her husband. Caleb made no mention of Conrad nor did Martha Rae. Martha Rae wondered what he wanted with Caleb, and Caleb wanted nothing to do with this character. As much as Martha Rae wanted things to be OK, she felt in her heart it was going to be a hard life living with Caleb

CHAPTER 8

Martha Rae was helping her mama wash clothes that morning. She had not been feeling very well these last few days, but she dismissed it on her heavy pregnancy and the fact that she was twice as big carrying this child. She called for Caleb to please run down to the cliff and bring them another bucket of water. That way, she could rest a little before starting rinsing her clothes. She sat down on a stump that had been there for as long as she had, when it hit her. She knew from the last time what was beginning to happen. She called out to her mama. "Mama, please come here quick. I think I'm starting labor." Her labor with Angela was quite quick and she hoped this one would be, too. Sal Jenkins came a running while hollering for John to run and fetch Ellen Moles. Martha really wanted to have this child at her house, but she did not think that would be possible now.

John had hitched up his two ole mules and started down the mountain when he ran into Caleb and told him, "You'd better hurry up. You fixing to get yourself another baby here before long." Caleb dropped the water and ran all the way up to his in-laws' house. Martha wasn't really in hard labor right now, so she had instructed what she would need from her house and would he run get if for her. He took out with a mental list of what he needed to bring. After he got there, the mental list was gone so he just got what he thought was best. She won't be concerned with this list in a while and it won't matter then anyway.

John got back with Sis Moles' daughter Ellen. She had taken over after her Ma's death and had done quite well. All the mountain women trusted and respected her. She was the first one they called when things get difficult for the mama. Martha Rae was having some hard contractions, but progress was not taking place. She had gripped Caleb's hand until it had turned white. Caleb had not really been with her when Angela was born. He just sat on the porch. But today, he was with Martha and he was very uncomfortable with this situation. He finally told John, "I just can't take this, seeing her in all this pain. I got to get out of here." So he took off through the mountains. His mind was going in a million directions. This would be the last child he would father. Martha Rae just was too small to have all these babies. He finally got himself calmed down enough to where he thought he could stand a little more, and as he was headed back up the mountain, he could hear Martha Rae wailing at the top of her lungs. He had big tears come in his eyes, and if he ever prayed, it was today. "Lord, help my raven-haired wife. All of a sudden, he heard what he had been wanting to hear. The sound of his baby crying. He was really excited now. He had wanted a boy, but if it was not to be, he'd love another little girl just as good. Just as he got up to the porch, he heard Ellen yell for Sal to get in there. Sal pushed the anticipating crowd away and ran into where Martha was and shut the door. Shortly, a little timid cry came forth. Caleb looked at John like, *what has happened?* John returned that same look back to Caleb, and soon Sal opened the door to where Martha was and said, "Caleb, come on in here and see your children." Caleb felt like he was about to faint. "What do you mean children?" "Just like I said, you have a big bouncy boy and a tiny petite little girl. What do you think of that?" He let out a yell so loud, John bet his Pap probably heard the announcement up there where they lived. Martha was out of it. She felt like she had been in battle all day. But when she found out she had twins, she had a smile come on her face that would melt the heart of a bear. "Twins, twins," she just kept saying that over and over. "What will we name them? Caleb," she said. "You name the boy then I'll name the girl. How about that?" Caleb reared back and said, "His name will be Laymon Cornell Moses. Now, what will you be naming that little girl?" Martha Rae beamed and said, "Lilly Jean Moses. Laymon and Lilly." All of a sudden, their family had gone from three to five. She did not even want to think of what or even how they would raise all these babies, but one thing she did know for sure, the good Lord would see them through.

She had done heard of talk going around the mountain about something they were calling the Great Depression. She couldn't tell any difference in the way they were living. It was early in the depression, and Caleb and Martha had not even experienced how really hard life would get. All they knew right now was their family had grown quite a bit, and she had made her mama a happy grandma.

Martha Rae proved to be a very fertile girl. For the next four years, she had another child every year. Violet Alverta was born in the biggest snowstorm that they had seen on the mountain in a long time. Caleb Esley Jr. or CJ came the same year only eleven months apart. Susan Francis was born the next year around Christmas, and Little John, who would be the last baby, was born down at his Grandma Jenkins's place. Labor came so quickly that Martha could not even get back up the hill to her house. Her mama, in fact, had to deliver him. When he came, she could see something was wrong, so she called for John to go get Ellen for she thought something was wrong with Little John. Sure enough, Ellen confirmed it was Down's. Sal Jenkins or Martha Rae neither had a clue as to what she was talking about. "What do you mean, Ellen, by Down's?" "Well, honey, we will just say he will need a little more attention than the others, and will go at a slower pace. But he will prove to be the most loving child you have." Ellen told her the best she could that Little John would be mentally slow. Martha didn't care. She loved this beautiful little boy and she didn't care if he didn't look exactly like the rest. He was hers, and that was all that mattered. Caleb was the one who was having the Great Depression. He was overwhelmed most of the time, instead of taking up his responsibilities and working to see his family had food and raiment. He just fell right into his Pap's lifestyle.

Martha Rae, as strong a woman as she was, just did not know how to handle Caleb. She found herself on her knees more now than ever. "Lord, I need your wisdom and guidance. I have seven mouths to feed and very little to feed them. Show me your ways, Lord, and help me to walk in them." As bleak as it often seemed, Martha and her children always had food to eat every day. Even if it was only one meal, it sustained them. She would not let her children see the despair on her face, so she would make games up and they would go foraging in the mountain to see what handfuls on purpose God had left for them.

One evening, she and her children had found enough blackberries, so she had decided to make them a blackberry cobbler. She had sent Laymon down to get a little sugar from his grandma. Laymon Moses was Sal Jenkins made over. He was hot-tempered and could speak his opinion whether you wanted to hear it or not. But his grandma recognized that in him and he was one of her favorites, not that she'd ever admit she had any favorites. "I love them all" she'd say and she did. But she always hid Laymon a piece of cake or pie she just so happened to have left, and call him down for some crazy reason and just happen to have him a piece of cake. Martha was busy putting the cobbler together and waiting on Laymon to bring the sugar when she heard someone at the door and assumed it was Laymon and hollered, "Hurry up and bring me the sugar. These kids are getting hungry." She looked up and saw Mr. Conrad Cox coming through the front door with a big grin on his face. He blurted out, "Well, I have a little sugar but it don't go in no pie." Martha's face turned so red, she was embarrassed and didn't quite know how to answer him. Instead, she just asked, "What can I do for you, Mr. Cox? You looking for Caleb?" Conrad became embarrassed then at himself and he didn't expect Martha's sudden confidence. He thought, *she has surely gotten brazen since I saw her in the woods years back.* He told her he was up this way and thought he'd drop by and see ole Caleb. He heard he was quite the father. Martha just threw her head back and laughed saying, "I guess, that's a good way to put it. Caleb's quite the father, but he's not here at the moment. Most likely he is up as his Pap's house. Do you know where he lives?" "Oh indeed, I do," Conrad said. "I just go up there. You take care, and maybe I'll see you again one day."

Martha just got a sinking feeling in her gut. He didn't want to see Caleb for nothing. They were going to get into something and she knew just exactly what it was, shine for sure. Caleb had become a drinker, but could not be classified as a big drinker because he had little to no money to buy any. Ellis Johnson was his uncle on his daddy's side, or rather half uncle. He was a bastard child, never knew who his daddy was, but he sure did look like the Tatum men, if there could be any guessing. They had always heard, if you didn't know who your daddy was, you could blow into the mouth of a child with thrush and it would heal it. Only thing was, Mr. Ellis had the worst breath odor anybody could smell and it was not a secret. All the people in Marley Knott's Mountain likened it to an outhouse. So most people just kept their mouth shut and said nothing about thrush.

But everyone knew Ellis Johnson could sure make some of the best shine in Marley Knott's Mountain. Caleb knew he would sell him a drink at a time. He often traded chores of carrying firewood for Ellis, or being a lookout for him if he had some business to take care of. If anybody worked any harder to get out of work than Caleb Moses, there was none to be found as lazy as him. He would get to missing his sweet little raven-haired Martha and go home to see her a few days and all them young 'uns. But to say he was a good family man just wasn't in the mouths of the fine people who lived in Marley Knott's Mountain. If anything, it left a bad taste if his name was spoken.

Laymon had brought the sugar just as Conrad Cox was leaving. He asked his ma who that man was and what did he want. Laymon was the oldest son Martha had, and he was very protective of his mama. He resented the fact that his daddy had left her with a big family to raise on her own, but she was the perfect picture of a godly mama. He respected her and was proud to let people know who his mama was. "Oh honey, that was a friend of your daddy's. Did mama have any sugar to spare?" Laymon quickly thought of what he went after and handed her a little bowl about half full. Martha Rae looked at it and thought, *This is probably all she had. God love her soul, but it will be better than nothing. The berries will be sour as gall, but at least it is something to fill my babies' bellies.* All her children were in the yard playing with a ball of string.

Martha was just like her mama, she saved everything. She used that string to mend things or tie up something that had fallen over. Her mama asked her, "Why in the world, child, are you letting them play with the only string you got?" Martha laughed and told her, "Well, they needed something to play with, and since I can't afford play toys, I guess if they want that old ball of string, that would be okay." Angela would always take the younger children and make up a game to play. Today, they were playing catch, and who ever had the ball of string when she got to ten was out. The winner would be the last one standing, which often was Little John, because his brothers and sisters adored him. They would just let him win. Violet suggested they play hide and seek. There were all kinds of good places to hide in the mountain. "Laymon, you be it," she said. He reluctantly agreed, but told her, "I ain't going to do this but one time. Then, I get to hide." He started to count. When he got to fifty, he lit out hunting everyone. Little John was not ever hard to find. He would always be giggling when you got to near he was. "I see you, Johnny, my boy." Out comes Little John, running as fast as his little legs could carry him. Laymon always had a special spot for Little John and let him beat him back to base. Laymon would pretend he was upset with himself for letting Little John beat him, and it would cause that little fellow to laugh even harder. "I see you Lilly. You are behind Papa's old wagon. Come on out." Lilly stomped her feet. She thought she had the best hiding place of all.

Laymon was looking around for all the other kids when he saw Jonas coming up the mountain pretty briskly. "Wonder what that stutter box wants?" he said. He could see in the distance that another person was coming, too. As she got closer, he could see it was a finely dressed lady. *Who in the world is this?* he thought. He headed back to his house to tell his mama of the lady who looked like she was following Jonas to their house. "Mama! Mama, come out here, we are having company." Martha Rae stepped out on the porch to see what all the commotion was when Jonas jumped up on the porch. "M-m-mrs. M-m-moses," he stuttered. "This here l-l-lady wants to s-s-speak to you." Martha Rae had just made a batch of biscuits. She told Angela, "You go on in and take Jonas with you and fix him a bowl of berry biscuits." Old Jonas was smiling from ear to ear when he heard her say that. By the time the lady made her way up to Martha's porch steps and sat down, she was so out of breath she could hardly speak.

She held up her hand as if to say "wait a minute." Martha sent CJ into the house to get this lady a dipper of water before she sat there and died. CJ came back and the woman hesitated when she looked at the dipper because she knew everyone in the family drank from this same dipper, but she was so thirsty she turned it up and drank the bottom out of it. Martha let her catch her breath a minute or two, and proceeded to ask her what she was doing so far up in these mountains. They hardly ever seen anybody new. Townsfolk wouldn't dare venture off up in here, so it had to be something serious for her to come all the way up to her house. She began by introducing herself as Mrs. Ella Patterson. She and her husband Sid bought the mercantile that Mrs. Banks had previously owned. Mrs. Patterson began to tell her about all her bad luck at bearing a child. She had been to many doctors and the last one told her she most likely would never be a mother. That's when she began to cry. And not only a few tears, she had a gully washer coming down her face. Martha Rae was speechless. She told her of all the work of having so many children, and how she had to wash twice a week and carry the water to do so. And then, there was feeding them. Those boys sure do eat a lot. She was running out of things to say when Mrs. Patterson jumped in and said, "Well, I heard you had a houseful of children and I know times are hard, so I was just thinking, maybe you could just give me one of yours?" Martha Rae felt the blood drain out of her face. She had never had anyone ask for her children. She looked at the lady and said, "Well, let me see." She called all seven of her children. Angela was still in the house trying to save some of the berries for the rest of the young 'uns. Jonas was just about to eat them out of house and home, and that in itself would not take long. Laymon was leaned up against one of the post on the porch with that Sal Jenkins look on his face that said you better not even think about it. Lilly was down at her grandma's where she stayed most of the time anyway. Violet was drawing pictures in the dirt with a stick, and CJ thought it was about time for a trip to the toilet, out of sight out of mind. That left Susan and Little John, and they all knew Little John wasn't going anywhere. "Well, let me see Mrs. Patterson." She looked at all her kids several times and finally turned to Mrs. Patterson and said, "I just don't see a one I can do without." Mrs. Patterson commenced bawling so hard, Martha Rae tried to console her but with no luck. This ladies heart was broken. Martha Rae began to tell her about Hannah in the Bible, and how she prayed for a child and God gave her one. She cried that much harder. She really thought she would go back down the mountain with a child. Martha Rae finally said, "How about me just letting you borrow a child for a day or so? Violet, you go get your Sunday best and something to sleep in and go stay with Mrs. Patterson until Sunday. You can show her where we are meeting down near Sutphin's Bottom for church." That seemed to satisfy Mrs. Patterson. If she couldn't give her a child, a loan would have to do. Violet was so happy, she had never been anywhere but this mountain. It would feel like what she heard was a vacation. Mrs. Patterson got her little sack of belongings and grabbed Violet by the hand and off the mountain she went a happy lady. Martha Rae went in the kitchen and Jonas had eaten every last berry in the bowl. She thought, *I ought to kill him but I guess the poor old soul was hungry, too.* She and the rest of her children ate butter biscuits that evening and discussed who could go stay with Mrs. Ella Patterson next.

aleb dragged home Saturday evening. He was a sight for sore eyes. Somebody had given him a black eye and it was still quite swollen. All his children gathered around him and was asking him, "What happened to your eye, Daddy?" All but Laymon. He could care less, and what's more, he probably deserved it. Martha was in her kitchen, cooking up something that smelled mighty fine to Caleb. She had done enough ironing for Mrs. Patterson to acquire a good size piece of beef. Caleb's eyes grew big at the size of it. Surely, that would feed them for a day or so. "Honey, where in the world did you get that big hunk of meat?" Martha replied that she had worked for it. Mr. and Mrs. Patterson, the new owners down at the mercantile, had hired her to do various jobs, one being to keep her and her husband's clothes ironed neatly. They were in the public eye and needed to look nice. Martha thought she was just doing it to help her seeing how they did not get much trade with the depression and all going on. But it was going to feed her children, so she never questioned or disagreed with her. Martha turned away from her cooking and saw Caleb's eye. "What in the world has happened to you, Caleb? Who beat you like that?" All Caleb could do was hang his head. He never acknowledged her question nor gave her any answer. Martha was so upset with him. She asked him, "What are you teaching your children, that it's OK to fight? Talk to me Caleb!" She was really getting aggravated with him now, but in an instant remembered all the little ears listening and knew it was best to hush. "We will talk later if you are still here after a while and I strongly suggest you to be." Caleb knew he was in the big doghouse now, and he had better walk Martha Rae's fine line or he'd be out on his head with nowhere to call home anymore.

She called her children to come and eat. They had been smelling the meat cooking all day, and it had been so long since they had actually had any that they were talking about it as if it something they were getting for Christmas. Martha spread the table with her pot of stew. She knew how to make the beef go further. She added a few onions her daddy had sent up to her, and she had herself grown a fine bushel of potatoes and added enough to make this a fine stew. She pulled out a big pone of bread out of the oven. Her babies would eat good tonight. She called all of them in and asked Caleb to say the grace. He just sat there and looked at her. She finally said, "Little John, will you say grace?" Bless his little heart, if any one of her children had her heart it was her baby. He folded his little hand and said, "Jesus, we thank you for this food 'cause we ain't had much in the last few days. But thank you, we do now. Please bless my daddy and help his eye to get better and help him to want to stay home with all of us 'cause we love him." Caleb's good eye teared up and he just went to the porch and sat. Martha got everybody some food on their plate and she went out on the porch to talk privately to Caleb.

"Caleb, where have you been? I saw that friend of yours the other day, Conrad, and knew there was no good going to become of his visiting you. Was he the one that done this?" Caleb never uttered a word. He was so ashamed, he could not face Martha or his children. He felt like he was good for nothing. What Martha spoke to him next just about tore his heart out. She told him, "Look me square in the eye, Caleb." He slowly raised his head and looked at her. He thought he would see anger in her face but it wasn't. She told him, "Caleb, we are a family and you are my husband. I took those vows we made before God seriously. I love you and always will. I just wish you cared for us as much as we care for you. Please, stay at home with us. We can work all of this out somehow."

Caleb began to speak. He had almost forgotten how sweet his little Raven was. He knew he was mixed up with the wrong crowd and he had tried to stay away. But for the life of him, it got the best of him every time. "Please forgive me, Martha, and if you would pray

56

for me, I need it more than any of my family." Martha pulled him over to where she was sitting and kissed him on his cheek and told him, "You dummy! There is not a day that goes by that I don't pray for you. Now, let's go in and eat some of that good stew." Caleb tried to tell her he wasn't hungry, but she knew he had to be. After much nudging, he went in and sat down with his family and ate. He told Martha he didn't believe he had ever eaten as good a stew as what she put before him tonight. All the children chimed in the same. Martha Rae felt so happy to have her entire family together. She didn't know for how long, but she would take what she could get.

The next morning was church. They had been meeting down at Sutphin's Bottom for a very long time. They could only meet there when the weather was warm. They had a brush arbor, and when it got cold they just had to have church at their homes. Reverend Avery Banks had been preaching for them this past two years, and they really didn't know who they could get if he left. He was Mr. and Mrs. Banks's son who used to run the mercantile and since they had moved they were afraid he might follow them. Reverend Banks had tried to get them to build a more permanent place to worship, but with times being as hard as they were, people just didn't have the means to pitch in to help get a church built. So they did what they should have been doing to start with—pray. Celeb reluctantly agreed to go to church with his family the next morning. When he asked where Violet was, Martha told him she had went down to stay with Ella Patterson and would be at church and come on back home afterward. John and Sal loaded all the young 'uns up the next morning and was surprised to see Caleb ready for church, too. Sal remarked about his black eye, and Little John took his daddy's side and told her he got it bumped. Caleb found that amusing and it even brought a smile to his face. Martha told her parents she and Caleb would be walking down. They needed to talk. Sal Jenkins said under her breath, "He needs more than a little talk." But no one heard her. John clicked his tongue and his old mules took out down the only path they had ever known to get out of this mountain.

Martha looked at Caleb and said, "You ready to head out?" He answered, "Yep, I guess so." As they walked down through the mountain, Martha could not help but see how the mountain was changing seasons. She remembered Edna Sue's bee stinging episode and laughed out loud thinking of it. Caleb looked at her and said, "What is so funny?" Martha reminded him that it was along this time of year that she had met him, and what seemed to really set their relationship off was the fact that he had helped rescue Edna Sue. "I really don't believe Mama would have let you come see me if it hadn't been for you running up to our house to get help. But she did and look at what all we have now, Caleb. We have a home together and seven beautiful children. We are rich, not with money, but with love." Caleb looked at her and said, "Yes, we are, Martha, but you can't feed them kids on love. They need real food." Martha felt like she was making some progress convincing Caleb how this family needed him. He even said so himself. "I am going to try harder, Martha. Really, I am. I have good intentions, but that seems to be all that ever becomes of it: intentions." Martha grabbed him by his hand and said, "Come on, honey. We are almost at church. Let's pray as a family today. I feel that in my heart, God is fixing to move in this place in a great way. I can feel it in my heart."

They ducked down and sat on a few stumps that some of the men had managed to move in, mostly the womenfolk and old people sat on them. But today, it didn't seem like there would be many who came out. Sid and Ella Patterson were there. They had been coming faithfully these last few weeks, and Violet was the best thing that had ever happened to this family. They loved her just like she was their daughter. When she went home though, they never forgot the other children either. They sent each one a little sack of candy that had some peppermints and a new penny in each sack. They so looked forward for Violet to come home, for they knew she had with her those special little sacks of goodies that they would otherwise not get to smack their lips on. Even as big as Laymon was, he took his bag of candy just like the rest and hid it. He had managed to save over fifteen cents so far. He was saving for something he had always wanted but it was to be his secret.

Reverend Ave, as they all called him, called up Lilly to lead the congregation in *Victory in Jesus, my savior forever.* Sal Jenkins looked like she swelled up big enough to bust with pride every time Lil got up to sing. *He sought me and he bought me with his redeeming blood.* The power of the singing that morning had stirred the hearts of some of the congregation. "Sing it, Lil!" came a yell from the back of the people. Everyone looked around and to their surprise, it was Caleb. He was standing beside Martha, clapping his hands just as hard as he could. "What in the world has gotten into him?" said Sal Jenkins. John just looked over at his wife and said, "I believe I hear Jesus knocking. Don't you hear it, Sal?" He just cut loose a shouting himself. He had those long arms raised and praising the King of kings Jesus. Reverend Ave felt the spirit moving himself and stopped the singing and said, "If there is anyone here today who would like to step forward and give their heart to Jesus?" All of a sudden, two feet walked the aisle. It was Ella and Sid right behind her. They were just a squalling. "Preacher, come help us pray. We have never did this before and don't know what to say." Reverend Ave fell down between the two sinners that morning, and had one hand in Ella's hand and the other hand in Sid's hand. They went down one way but came up another. All the ladies hugged Ella, and the menfolk shook Sid's hand so much, he laughed and made the statement he hadn't had his hand shaken so much. That brought much laughter from everyone, including Caleb. Martha had watched him thinking he might take the walk this morning, but she saw conviction in his face and would just have to keep on praying for her dear Caleb to get saved. Until then, they would just keep trusting Jesus, for without him, she knew they would never make it in this world or the next either.

Ⓐll the mountain folks who lived up in the mountain and those who lived close by knew that winter was approaching fast. They could feel it in their bones. It was going to be a hard winter. The leaves had fallen off the trees earlier than usual, and it had gotten cool enough to wear a jacket. Sid and Ella Patterson were already dreading the winter because it would take away their time to spend with all the folks at church, and they knew Violet may not come as much. They had already seen to it that she and her brothers and sisters had the coats and shoes they would need for the upcoming winter. They had the money to buy things that most people only wished for, but that wasn't what made them happy. They loved Martha Rae and her family. They didn't know anyone else on that mountain who would lend, so to speak, a child to a family who had none. And for that, they were truly indebted. Martha Rae never asked them for anything except their friendship. She still insisted on working for her pay, and they knew in their hearts she needed to feel like she and her children were not charity. It made them feel worthy, and her as well.

It was to be the last Sunday at the brush arbor until spring. The whole little arbor was standing room only that day. Reverend Avery told the congregation that he had a big surprise for them that day. All the ladies had been talking among themselves and felt like Reverend Avery Banks would be leaving their church to take another church up around the hollow, seeing how he had met a pretty, young girl by the name of Bess. She had started coming to church with him in the last few weeks, and they could see how much he seemed to like her and some even felt like he would most likely marry her. They sung

*I'll Fly Away* and a chorus or two of *Just As I Am*. They just didn't have the joy of the Lord with them this morning. Martha and her children were all together this morning. Caleb had taken off on one of his escapades, and she had not seen him for a number of days. Ten, in fact. Her heart was heavy, too. She had prayed her heart out for Caleb Moses and she could not see any difference in him. He still shunned the responsibilities of a father and husband. She was so thankful though, she had not gotten pregnant in several years. She thought, after seven you learn a few things about being with child, and she knew for sure she could not raise any more babies by herself.

Reverend Avery stood and motioned for the congregation to have a seat. "Ladies and gents. Today, I have some very exciting news." They all dreaded to hear it because they knew they would be looking for a new preacher soon. "Me and Miss Bess back there have decided to make it official. We will be married in the spring." All the congregation clapped but not with joy. He went on to call her up to the front with him. "We also have some more good news. Someone has so generously offered to put us a church under roof in the spring. They have asked us to not reveal who they are, but the thing we will need now is willing hands to build it. Do I have a show of hands right now?" Every living soul in that church jumped up and raised both hands; hands in agreement for the building of the new church and hands of praise for answering the prayers of the faithful people who had prayed their hearts out for this very thing. They all knew it was the Pattersons who would contribute the materials for the new church, but they never let on because they knew God would bless them for this sacrifice. Reverend Avery Banks gave a good sermon on giving this last Sunday and told the church, "Next year, we will have a building to worship in good Lord willing." A big shout went up, and they all left knowing they had all winter to talk this out. Plans had to be made, and Reverend Avery and Miss Bess Hawkins would be the first to be married in the new church. All was well at the time for the folks in Marley Knott's Mountain. God had richly blessed all of them in spite of it being a depression. They knew in their hearts it wasn't what they owned that made them rich, but it was the blessings that fell from above and knowing Christ Jesus was their savior who kept them from falling into utter despair like so many other folks they knew. Caleb had been up to his Uncle Ellis's for at least three or four days. He really could not keep count of the days anymore, but he knew in his heart it was too many. Everything had become such a blur. Life itself had become that way, too. Even the numbness of the alcohol was wearing thin. He thought of his family every day, but thought was as far as it went. His uncle called him over, "Get up, you pile of lazy bones." That cut Caleb to the very core. His uncle had a sharp tongue and it spewed out words that cut him to the bottom of his soul. Caleb crawled out from under a blanket his Ma had given him. He knew this was going to be the last batch of shine before winter. Ellis was getting old and his body just couldn't take the chill anymore. Ellis looked at Caleb with a look that made Caleb cringe. His uncle was near about the ugliest man he knew. He didn't know if all the liquor he had drank had caused this ugliness or it was the way he was born. "Come here, I said." Caleb knew in his heart he wasn't anything but a coward. He feared his uncle. He had a mean spirit that some say had put men in their grave. "What you want, old man?" That fired Ellis up, "Shut your mouth, and I mean shut it up." Caleb tried to be brave but that old coot got him every time. "I am going down the mountain to deliver some of this shine to some of the local boys and spread the word we may have a potent batch coming before winter." "How in the world could you make moonshine more potent than it already was? Now, how you going to do that ole man?" Ellis just smiled, "Us moonshiners know tricks you don't know nothing about." He threw his ugly head back and laughed the most evil laugh Caleb had ever heard. It scared Caleb like nothing else he had ever witnessed. "Now get over here and keep this fire stoked." Caleb dropped his head. He often thought of the times he helped Sal Jenkins get her firewood carried up to the house. John would bust big loads of wood. He needed to keep his girls warm in winter. He would also bust enough for Caleb and Martha and their brood. A tear came into his eyes. He thought this was the hardest work he had ever done. But if he had it to do over, he would carry all that wood and more. He had it good and did not even know it.

After about a month of not seeing Caleb, Martha had begun to get really worried. "Do you reckon he's dead?" she asked her daddy. To be truthful about the matter, John Jenkins had thought the same thing. Martha had been ringing those prayer bells a lot more here lately than usual. "Lord, I don't know where my man is or what he has gotten into, but you never put this bad feeling in me for nothing. Look after Caleb, Lord, 'cause he sure ain't got enough sense to look after himself."

All Martha Rae could do now was pray and wait. She remembered the Lord speaking to her long before she married Caleb to trust only him. She thought, were there others who would try to sway her in their direction? So she knew she would have to really seek the Lord for more direction herself. "God, help me. I feel like I am up against the Red Sea. Make a way, Lord, for me and all my family. Change Caleb. I know only you can, Lord." Martha still felt a storm was coming to the mountain and it was about to hit her family hard. All she knew she could do is pray and believe God for an answer.

# CHAPTER 11

I t was getting on down closer to fall. Martha Rae had already begun keeping a fire. It was early morning; the dawn had not even broken the day. She had felt a stirring in her heart to get up and pray. She arose out from under one of her mama's older quilts that she had given her and Caleb when they got married. She looked at each and every square that had been so lovingly stitched together. There was a piece of her grandma Lilly Francis's old apron that Martha Rae remembered that pulled a lot of delicious food from her wood stove. It also served as a handkerchief that wiped many a baby's nose and mouth off. And there was a piece of her daddy's shirt that Sal had made him one year for Christmas and he wore it out. Her mama often remarked "liked to never found a piece big enough to put in my quilt." There was also a square from Edna Sue's dress that she had on the day the bees got her and Martha. That made Martha laugh. So many good memories in this old quilt. She cherished this quilt. And often on days that her heart would be so burdened from life itself, she would sit and reminisce about good days gone by and she'd have the strength to make one more day.

Somehow today, she could not reminisce her troubles away. She had never had such a burden on her heart as she did this day. Martha got on up and went to her place that she had called her "just a little talk with Jesus" quilt. Her children knew never to disturb or move anything that she had placed in that quilt. She had placed prayer clothes in every nook of that old quilt. When her children had sickness, she placed a cloth in her quilt. When they lacked food, she placed a cloth in that quilt. Caleb had so many in it with his name on it, it just about made the quilt fluffier. This morning she knew she must ask the Lord to lead, guide, and direct her. To be with Caleb wherever he was and direct his footsteps home. Something came over her and she began to weep, not just shed a few tears but her heart was shattered. "Lord, I don't know how much longer I can hold on to this marriage. I have tried with everything in me, but Caleb just doesn't seem to care about me or his children one bit. I know what I said the day, I married him for better or worse and I take all that I said that day very seriously, but worse is getting harder and harder to bear. Jesus, please intervene and help me." She sat up on the old quilt and the Lord began to speak sweet words to Martha. "Trust only in me, Martha." These were the same words he had told her when she and Caleb married. "Lord, what does all this mean? Lord, I will trust you. Direct my path and guide me to the place you have ordained for my life." Martha slowly got up and wiped her face. She heard Little John calling and she knew her babies would be hungry, so she went to her cupboard and had enough flour and lard to make them all a biscuit this morning.

All of a sudden, Little John came in from using the toilet and had in his arms a sack of apples. "Mama, look what I found over by the tree in the yard. It's almost full. Look!" he cried. Martha Rae took the sack from Little John, and sure enough, it was a big sack of apples. *Where in the world did this sack of apples come from?* she wondered. *I bet Daddy had been down in Sutphin's Bottom looking over where they might build the church. He probably brought these up. I will thank him after a while when I go down for this good surprise.*

Caleb sat up in the mountain and watched Little John get the apples. He knew one of his children would come out early and find the sack. At least his children would have something to eat this morning. Tears filled his eyes. He wanted to do better, and he promised himself after this last batch of moonshine come off he was going home and staying home with his family.

Ellis had already had his last batch of the season going. He'd stand and rub his hand together and say, "Boy, this going to be a humdinger batch." Caleb really didn't know anything about moonshining. All he knew was, he had to watch out for revenuers who might be snooping up in this mountain trying to smash a still. Ellis was hollering for Caleb, "Stoke the fire, hurry up! You are pert near good for nothing, you know that, boy?" Caleb just kept stoking the fire. He actually felt he hated Ellis. He had done nothing but use him all his life and he didn't have enough sense to see it. *I'm getting out of this mess one way or the other,* he thought. He heard Ellis talking and looked around to see Conrad Cox standing there. "Hey there, Caleb. I never dreamed I'd see you up here. I figured you'd be down there with that pretty little wife of yours. If I knew you were up here, I'd stopped by and gave her a little sugar for her breakfast." Conrad reared back and hollered and laughed. That was all Caleb could take. He took a dive and tore into Conrad. He was about eight inches taller than Conrad and his long arms were no match for the short, stubby little man. He beat the living daylight out of him. Even old Ellis seemed startled. He had never seen Caleb this mad before and really didn't care to witness this wrath any more. "Get on out of here, boy," Ellis told Caleb. Caleb was done. He took off through the mountains. He was so angry, he was afraid he'd kill Conrad if he stayed any longer. He wasn't sure where he would go from here, but he was leaving this crazy bunch and was not looking back.

Caleb finally got himself calmed down. He thought he'd go up to his Pap's a few days and get his head together and go on home. His Pap told him, "Come on in and stay the night. I told you to leave that crazy brother of mine alone. He ain't right, you know, but he sure did not get it from our side of the family." Caleb found a rug and laid it down beside the stove. He wished he had a blanket because he knew the fire would go out up in the night and it would be cold in the morning. But besides all that, he wished he was beside his little Raven. How his heart ached for her right now. He meant what he promised himself, he was going to make things right for his family, somehow some way.

Next morning, Ellis got up. He had stayed around for the last few nights. He knew it was getting close to coming off. Conrad was hanging tight, too. Ellis had started in on Conrad just like he did Caleb, calling him lazy and stupid. Only difference was, Conrad did not take it as well as Caleb. Really, he wasn't going to take it at all.

He'd shown that bunch who he was. He had a plan and he knew by the time he got through with all of them, they'd be lucky if they didn't bury them under the jail.

# CHAPTER 12

It was a cold crisp morning the day the shine was ready to come off. Mrs. Bright had slipped up the mountain early this morning to get her usual quart for doctoring this winter. Ellis had saved her a quart from the batch before this one. He knew his last batch would be very potent and didn't think this sweet little old lady needed something this stout. He thought she'll never know the difference anyway, but the truth was he always had a crush on her and obliged her with some hooch. Ellis told Conrad, "We going to get this shine moving today." He had already been talking of what he would do with his shine money this year. He had been saving all year and he was thinking about moving anyway. Conrad listened to the old man talk and thought, *Yea, you going to move alright but it ain't where you want to go.* Conrad was a slick man. He knew if Ellis kept talking, he would tell where he kept his money. He thought he could use a little extra money himself. Sure enough, Ellis just kept running his jaw when he accidentally let it slip and didn't even realize he did it. Old Conrad had it made now. He had a debt he owed several in this mountain, and he was going to repay them good. He would slip out and nobody would know the difference. Ellis told him he was going to relieve himself, and when he got back they'd take the run off. Conrad knew this was his chance. Ellis slipped down through the woods and while he was gone, he pulled a little bottle of something out from a sack that he had with him when he came up the mountain. He poured it into the shine and threw the bottle down through the woods. Old Ellis came back. He told Conrad, "I'm feeling good about this batch. I've done sent word through this mountain that this would be the best of the best." They slowly and carefully began to fill every mason jar they had with the shine. Ellis even poured off the first pint. "Just to be on the safe side," he said. They worked and finally processed about five gallons of the finest shine they had seen. Ellis told Conrad, "Here, let's get us a little sip." Conrad declined saying, "I had been a little sick last night and don't think my stomach can take a swig this early in the morning." Ellis told him, "You know what, I think I'll wait, too. My stomach was not into good a shape this morning either. We can deliver this shine and come back here this afternoon and indulge ourselves." So they loaded up a wagon full of fifteen quarts of moonshine. Ellis knew he had it sold and the first stop would be his brother Pap Moses. He told Ellis he wanted the first quart he sold this time, because if he went down in the mountain, he might not get back with him a quart, so he wanted his first.

Pap was out messing with his old cow when he saw Ellis coming in his wagon. That was a sure sign that that the hooch was ready. His mouth was beginning to water already just thinking about it. He waved his arms so his brother could see him and not go to the house. His old lady would drink it up if she got to it first. He would hide it somewhere in the barn and she would never know where his treasure was. Ellis had seen him and turned his old horse toward the barn. When they got there, Pap saw Conrad was with him. "My boy really gave you a good whipping the other night, didn't he?" Conrad was embarrassed, and just turned his head and mumbled under his breath. Ellis asked him, "Where in the blue blazes did he go?" Pap told him, "Ah, he took off. I think he went back home." All the time, he knew he was in the house with his Ma. Ellis took Pap's money. He only had enough to pay for half, but told him he would give him a ham out of a pig he knew some of the neighbors were killing soon. He laughed and said, "I get the five finger discount, you know." Ellis didn't care how he got it. He could use some fresh meat this winter and it was a good trade.

By the end of the day, Ellis and Conrad had delivered all the shine to the menfolk that drank in the mountain. Ellis could not wait to wrap his lips around a good swig of moonshine. He had saved him a gallon of it. He was going to be sure he made it through the winter. Conrad knew he had to be swift. "Here, Ellis, let's taste of this hooch." Ellis poured him and Conrad a taste. He lifted his pint jar and looked at Conrad and said, "Yehaw, boy! Let's drink up." Conrad pretended to drink his, and every opportunity, he got he poured it out little by little until Ellis was so drunk he staggered and fell down, passed out. Conrad ran to the place that old Ellis had said his money was, and sure enough, there it was, just waiting for him to take. He then ran back to Ellis and took what he had in his pocket. *This is the easiest stealing I have ever did. And no one will ever know that Caleb didn't do it.* Conrad ran off that mountain, slipping by some of their recent customers' home so they would not see him leave. If the authorities came and questioned him, he'd tell them he left before Ellis went back up the mountain. That Caleb Moses had been hanging with Ellis all month and he was the only one that probably knew where Ellis kept any money. Conrad ran like a scalded dog. He had to be quick and get himself an alibi as to where he was the last day or so. He had a lady friend that owed him a favor and he was sure he could get her to help.

Caleb had not seen his pap all day. Sometimes he would just take off with his dog and shotgun and ramble the woods all day to see if he could kill a squirrel or rabbit. Caleb had really had a heart-to-heart talk to himself and decided it would be best if he went and talked to Martha Rae and see if she would let him come home. He had missed his children more than he realized. He even thought he might take up a little of Bible study if she would help him. He told his Ma he was going out toward the barn to see if his Pap was anywhere around. He had gone and told her he was going home to Martha and she was glad. He had near about ate up all her food she had managed to get, and she knew she'd never make it through the winter if he stayed with them. "Pap, Pap," Caleb called. "You anywhere around here?" Caleb looked in every corner of the old barn when he saw his daddy's feet dangling up in the loft. "What are you doing up there, Pap? Get down here a minute." His daddy's feet never moved, so he climbed up the ladder and there laid his daddy. He looked like he was dead. Caleb shook the daylights out of him. He roused a little, thank goodness. He thought, *he is just drunk.* Pap was more than drunk, he had been poisoned. Caleb did not really know what to do. He ran home and got his Ma, and both of them together got him down and into the house. All they knew to do was let him sleep it off and hope for the best. Pap Moses groaned and mumbled all night long. By morning, he should be sober. Caleb sat by his Pap all night. He even said a prayer or two for him. It was getting daylight when his Pap came to himself. "Caleb you there?" Caleb answered, "Yes, what you need? Cut the light on so I can see." Caleb thought, *so you can see why? It's daylight outside, why can't you see?* when it hit him, his pap was blind. He had forgotten that bad liquor could blind you, but he never thought it would hit so close to home. Caleb questioned his Pap, "How much did you drink, Pap?" His pap told him he just took a few swigs. Ellis had told him he was going to make a potent batch this time, and he felt the effects with the first swig and didn't want to drink too much at one time. Caleb could not believe what was happening. Would his Pap get his eyesight back? He didn't know. And what about Ellis? How much did he drink? Then, reality hit him hard. How many people in this mountain had Ellis delivered this poison to? He knew he needed to get down to where Ellis was and see how he was doing. He took off running as hard as he could go. When he got there, he didn't see Ellis at first, but soon saw his lifeless body lying slumped up against a tree. He was dead as dead could be. Caleb was in shock. All he could think to do was run, and run he did. He knew that everybody knew he had been up there with old Ellis. He knew he would likely get blamed for all this. Tears began to fall down Caleb's face. He had brought all this upon himself. Here he was, fixing to straighten up and then all this happened. He almost wished it had been him instead of his Pap. He didn't know where he was going, but all likelihood was, he probably would never see Martha Rae and his children again. This mountain had dealt him a cruel blow. Only, he was not the guilty party this time. No one would believe him for one minute. So to keep all this away from his wife and children, he would just have to disappear. As he got to Sutphin's Bottom, he turned around and looked. There was the brush arbor still standing. For the first time in his life, Caleb went into the little brush arbor and kneeled and prayed for Jesus to please forgive him and not let his family suffer because of all his shortcomings. It was almost like the mountain was speaking and it was. All the menfolk who had drank the poison shine was either dead or blind. Their families were weeping and wailing. It echoed off the mountain. Caleb cried that much harder. He didn't know where or what he was going to do; but one thing for certain, he would be a wanted man.

# CHAPTER 13

Sal Jenkins had yelled up to Martha Rae about noontime for her to come down for just a few minutes if she had the time. That was all Martha Rae had—time. Time was sometimes her worst enemy. If she had lots of chores to do for the day, she was constantly in a race with time. But if she did not, she had way too much time to dwell on her circumstances, and often had no answer to offer herself. But today she had more to get done than she probably would, so time would most likely win the battle.

Laymon had been asked if he would come down to the Barrett place this morning and help bust up some wood. The whole mountain could feel an early chill, and all were preparing for some cold days ahead. Mr. Barrett had promised Laymon a load of wood as well, which would be so good to have. His papa had allowed Laymon to take his wagon with him today to haul their wood up the mountain. Martha Rae always worried when Laymon took off with his Papa's wagon. The road home was rugged and it took a skilled hand to handle those mules. Lilly was cleaning the house. Martha Rae knew it would be spit shined when she got through, she took that after her Aunt Edna Sue. Violet was still down at the Pattersons', and the rest of her brood would create enough mess that it would take them two days to clean up. Martha could not shake the feeling of something bad going to happen. Anyway, she headed to her mama's. *She had something she wants me to help her with,* Martha thought. She bounced into her mama's house and tried to put forth a smile on her face, but Sal Jenkins could read her like a book. She saw the wrinkled brow and her eyes had the look of worry. It almost appeared she had a mask on. This was not her daughter who radiated joy most of the time. And she knew the news she would tell her would only magnify her worry. "Come on over here, honey. Sit down and I'll get you some coffee." Martha Rae knew something was wrong. Anytime her mama offered to get her some coffee and ask her to sit down, it usually wasn't good. "Mama, just tell me. Do you think I don't know when you have something to tell me and nine times out of ten it is not good?" Her mama looked at her daughter. She was so young to be carrying the burdens that were laid upon her. She did not look like she was in her twenties but more like forties. And she knew the news she had would only make her heart that much heavier. Sal Jenkins just could hardly bear to tell her sweet daughter this heart-wrenching news. She had wrung her hands till they were red as fire. But nonetheless, she had to know. "Honey, there has been a tragedy that has taken place in this mountain. There are at least five men dead that we know of, and several more blinded. Seems like they got some shine that had methanol added to it." She paused. She didn't know if she could finish the worst part of this news or not. *Where was John at?* She knew he had a way with words and could deliver any blow with a cushion. Martha's face turned to a pale white. She knew in her heart the worst was yet to come. "Finish it, Mama. You know what I want to know. Was Caleb one of the dead?" Her mama looked at her with such sadness, and slowly spoke the words that would tear Martha Rae's heart the rest of the way out. "No, child. He was not one of the dead or blind, as far as we have heard. But he is nowhere to be found and some are thinking he was the one that may have poisoned the hooch. His pap is blind and Old Ellis Johnson is dead. It's his fault for making the devil's brew to start with." Martha Rae was in shock. Her insides were reflected on her face. She had a look of disbelief and belief at the same time. "Several others who live down through this mountain are blind or dead. I don't yet know who all of the others are." The tears just would not come. Martha felt like not only had her husband abandoned her but God had, too. Why was all this happening to her? She just did not know if she could go on. She really felt like if she was locked up in some asylum where the world could not touch you would be a good place to be right now.

All of a sudden, Little John burst through his grandma's back door. He had caught a baby rabbit in one of his Papa's rabbit traps. He did not see supper, he saw a pet. "Look, Mama! I have caught me a buddy." Martha Rae suddenly was back into reality. She had seven children looking to her to be the parent who would guide them through life, to have supper on the table, to learn to deal with circumstances that were not always good, but most of all, she needed to instill the love of Jesus into their hearts for she knew he was the only one who could move this mountain in her life right now. She instantly asked for forgiveness and looked at her mama and Little John, and said, "We need to pray right now, so let's hit the prayer room, Mama, and ring those prayer bells. This mountain needs help, and I don't know of anyone else who will pull us through all this than God himself." Her mama agreed, so Sal, Martha, and Little John held on to each other and sent up a prayer that would cause Satan to tremble. When Martha arose from that prayer, she felt like the mountain had been lifted off her heart. Good would prevail. What Satan had set for evil was going to backfire in his ugly face. That was an assurance that the Lord had placed in her heart. She would not be defeated or moved, for in Christ Jesus she was anchored. "Come on, Mama. We must get armored up for battle." Little John looked at his mama with a puzzled look on his face. "Where we going to get our armor, Mama?" Martha Rae had something arise in her that she had not felt in a long time. "Baby, we are going to put on the whole armor of God. He has enough for all of us." She had a defiant look on her face, and it was coming straight from the throne room of God. "We will get through all this by letting Jesus lead us all the way." Sal Jenkins cut loose shouting. She felt a stirring of the Holy Ghost, and out the front door she ran, praising God for she knew who was in control of this terrible ordeal. If the local people had seen her praising God in her front yard for all that they were going through, they would have locked her up or may have joined in with the praise.

Martha Rae and Little John marched up the path home. She would see that the little rabbit got away. But for right now, Little John needed this little pet. "What you going to name this critter, Little John?" asked his mother. "Hmmm, I think I'll call him Bill."

That caught Martha Rae off guard. "Bill? Where did you come up with that name?"

"Well, it's really easy to say, and if I ever get another brother, I would like to name my pet Bill after him." That was the funniest thing Martha had heard in a long time. She laughed so hard, she had to stop and sit down. "Mama, what's wrong? Why do you think this is so funny?" She finally just said, "I think it's just a funny name for a rabbit." It seemed to suffice for Little John and he began laughing. "I think so, too, Mama." She would make no mention of the news her mama had given her to her children. She knew they would likely hear of it soon anyway. You can't shield them forever, although she wished she could. But for a little while longer, she would try.

When she got home, Lilly was in the process of dusting all of the whatnots that all her children had dragged in over the years. She didn't really have any that was store-bought, so she decorated her home with all the little treasures that her children had brought in.

CJ was a wood-carver; it was a gift. He could take an ordinary piece of wood and make the most beautiful things out of it. He often carved out animals he saw run through the mountain. He could detail them to make it an exact replica. She had many crosses he had carved, and probably her most loved piece was the crucifixion of Christ. Not that it made her happy to see that, but it often reminded her what a price he paid for her sins. Martha often told him he ought to take them down to Ella's mercantile and see if she could sell some for him. He just always told her, "I'd just as soon give them to you, Mama." That melted her heart, so she had placed all of them around her house and adored every one of them.

Little John was a rock collector. He brought home some of the prettiest rocks from that mountain anybody had ever seen. He also brought some in that were ugly, too, but the family always told him how beautiful each rock was. He took a few to his Papa, which had a good knowledge of rocks and they would sit and talk for hours about rocks.

"Where is Violet? I told her to sweep the front porch off," said Martha Rae. Susie spoke up and said, "She finished that and took off down to Mrs. Patterson's." That made Martha kindly mad. She knew she would get down there and hear all the bad news that was going on in the mountain. Martha thought for a few minutes. *I need to know myself. I'll just go down the mountain to and see what all I can find out.* She knew Reverend Avery would be busy talking to all the families, and Martha Rae couldn't help but think from the look of those clouds there may be some snow fixing to fall. She instructed her children to listen to Angela. She would be in charge until she got back. They loved Angela to take care of them because she could come up with the best games to play and they always had a big time. "Angela, you stir these young 'uns up something to eat. Put on a pot of leather britches and make some bread. That will be good for supper, too."

Martha Rae grabbed her shawl, and down through Marley Knott's Mountain she went. She may not get all the answers she wanted but she bet one thing, she'd know more when she came back. She went down through the rugged terrain. She stayed away from the road that had been hewed out. More than anything, she didn't want to run into anyone she knew. She knew the rumors, and they would be pointing fingers at Caleb and figure she knew where he was and maybe even think she was hiding him. So until she got some facts, she would stay away from people as much as possible. She rounded Marley Knott's Cliff and saw the Reverend Banks's buggy he and Miss Bess often traveled in. They were at the Harris' place.

Everybody knew he was a drinker, and probably wondered if he was in the group of dead drunks or blind drunks. She would cut around by Mrs. Gratts' place and make tracks on down to the mercantile. When she arrived, there was Violet behind the counter filling up the glass container that held all the candy bars and penny candy. She looked like she had seen a ghost when she saw her mama come in. Martha Rae looked at her and said, "Don't be scared, Violet. I knew you were down here. Just wish you would start telling me when you are coming down here." Ella came through a curtain she had hung up to separate the front of the store from the back. "Well, how do Martha? Come on back here. I have something to show you." Martha Ray knew she had nothing to show her but some information she wanted to share privately without Violet's ears hearing her.

"Come on back here where the feeds are." Martha Rae followed her to the very back. You could tell it was the feed room. The smell of corn prevailed, and the hog chop came through quite strong as well. "Listen, I know you have heard what has happened," said Ella. "How many dead from this mountain?" Martha asked. Ella Patterson looked her right dead in the eyes, "I am afraid, seven, and six have been blinded." Martha felt her spirit drop within her. All she could say was how sorry she was. Ella looked at her and said, "You know they are looking at Caleb for doing this. Do you know where he is at?" Martha looked at Ella and said, "You know me, Ella, and know I would not lie. Not for Caleb or any of my family. I haven't seen Caleb Moses in over a month. Last I heard, he was up at his Pap's and was helping Old Man Ellis get his last batch of moonshine going. I guess it really was his last batch 'cause they found him dead leaning up against a tree as well." Ella let out a blow and said, "No one mentioned Ellis, so that makes eight dead. I just thought I'd let you know, the officials are here now, and they will most likely be coming up your way. I thought I'd just let you know, and maybe you can prepare your family for what's to come. Martha, they will think you are lying and try to trick you into telling them where Caleb is. Of course, if you don't know, you can't give them any information. They will be watching you and your family like a hawk. Keep your children close by home, if you possibly can. If they see you leave, they will think you are going to take Caleb some food or something he might need. If you would like Violet to stay here till all this is resolved, that is fine, and any of your other children as well. We will open our door to as many as you want to send." Martha Rae felt tears starting to well up in her eyes. "Ella, I can't think of finer people I'd rather have watch my children than you and your husband. I will send Susie and Little John down here, too. They are my least ones and they wouldn't understand all that is going on. Thanks so much for helping me. What should I do next, Ella, to prepare if it was Caleb?" Ella looked away because she had started crying herself. "Martha Rae, I have never had a sister or a brother, but you come as close to being my sister as I've ever had. I just want you to know, we are here for you for whatever you may need. Don't hesitate to ask, because it will be yours. We will be praying for you much, and don't worry, we will take care of your little children. Now go get them children back down here. Bring them a few clothes and shoes. Also, bring their coats because it looks like it may start snowing this afternoon." Ella reached over and grabbed Martha Rae around the neck and they both sobbed on each other's shoulders. "Now get out of here before you get yourself caught in a snowstorm."

Martha Rae took out of that little mercantile almost running. She looked at the sky, and for sure, it looked like snow would be on the ground before morning. She would get Laymon and her daddy to get the children down here in the wagon. Those old mules had been used to traveling in bad weather. She also knew she needed to hurry home to her other children as well. They needed to be filled in on what was happening, too. She wanted no surprises for them either. Her head was spinning in a million directions. All of a sudden, she heard the voice of the Lord remind her to only trust in him. "Thank you, Lord, for assuring me once again that you haven't left me. I will seek your face for the answers I need and follow the direction you give me. But for now, let my feet go up this mountain fast and deliver my babies to Ella Patterson, bless her and Sid for being the allies that I need so badly right now."

# CHAPTER 14

I
t had started to spit snow when Martha Rae left the Patterson's mercantile. Martha Rae had so much on her mind that she hardly even noticed the snow picking up the farther and farther she got up into that mountain. She could not believe Caleb had something to do with this, but it was looking more and more like he was connected with every report she got. If she could have gotten hold of him now, she was sure she might turn his sorry hind end in herself to the authorities. But in all reality, she knew she couldn't because deep down in her heart she had to admit, she loved him. She jolted herself back to where she was at and knew she must hurry. By the time she got to her house and got her children prepared to go to the Patterson's and loaded her Papa's wagon up with young 'uns, it would be almost dark. "Lord, help me" was all she could mutter right now.

It was snowing so hard she could barely see. She had gotten up to Marley Knott's Cliff. All of a sudden, her feet begin to slide. The water that ran freely out of that mountain had frozen, and her feet was in a race to see which one could withstand the impending fall. *Whommp!* She hit the ground and rolled backward. The white ground had come up to meet her face-to-face. She scrambled around and got hold of some branches that had not shed their leaves and got back up to her feet. She looked all around to see if she could find a stick to steady herself with the rest of the way home, and miraculously she did. It almost looked like it was custom-made for her. She trudged and plowed through the snow when she saw smoke coming from her little home. *God bless, my daddy,* she thought. *He had been up there and built me a fire.*

Laymon was the first to move. *I think I heard something.* He pulled back the curtain and said, "It's Mama!" He opened the front door, just as Martha Rae stepped up on the porch. "Boy, you are a sight for sore eyes, woman!" He had never spoken to his mother like that, but he had been so worried about her. He was just about ready to take out looking for her. Martha had the look of anguish on her face. She could hardly speak. "Laymon, honey, go down and tell Papa to get the wagon hitched. You and he are going to have to take Susie and Little John down to the Patterson's to stay a few days." Laymon knew exactly what had happened, and so did Angela and Lilly. CJ was big enough to understand, and she would talk to him in the morning. He had already laid down and went to sleep. "Now hurry, honey. It's snowing hard and I don't want you all out in this all night." Laymon immediately took down to his Papa's and told him what was going on. "I think your Ma is doing the right thing right now," said John. "Let me get my overalls and a coat on. Laymon you help me get the mules hitched up." Sal Jenkins was frantic. She did not want her babies out in this snowstorm, but she also knew it was for the best. The government officials would be up here probably tomorrow, and it would scare these little children to death. They would be safe and sound down with Ella and Sid. She would spoil them rotten while they were down there.

Martha Rae gathered up some clothes for her babies and kissed them good-bye. "Now you all mind your manners and listen to Sid and Ella. I'll be down in a few days to get you all. But in the meantime, have fun." She tried with everything in her to put joy in her voice and a smile on her face, but you can't disguise fake. Even her children could tell the difference. Little John ran back and gave her one last hug and said, "I love you, Mama. I'll take care of everybody." That broke Martha Rae's heart right there. She swallowed hard and bit her lip and said, "OK, honey. You're in charge." To be such a young woman, she had carried a lifetime of sorrow in just the last few years. Her mama was afraid it would get the best of her daughter, but she didn't know that the Lord was equipping her every day to withstand this great trial. Sal watch John and Laymon go out of sight and saw Martha Rae go into her own house. "Lord, when will this trial be over? You promised to not put more on us than we could bear. I see her bending with this trial, Lord, give her your strength and guide her. Guide us all, Lord." And with that, Sal shut her own door and cried.

Martha lay awake almost all night. She had gotten up a few times to see how much snow had fallen and it looked about eight inches to her. She thought about her babies but she knew they were in good hands, and she thought of all the men who had died and those the shine had left blind. They would have to delay their funerals until this weather broke. *This weather*, she thought. *It was very unusual.* They would get snow in late November but it was late October, all the leaves had not fallen off the trees. It felt like God sent the snow to cleanse the mountain of all the death and hurts that had gone on in the last week. And then there was Caleb, what in the world could he be thinking? Was he crazy? She knew he suffered a lot of emotional abuse from his family and he may have just snapped, but why take out all the other men? They were good, moral men; good to their families and had been good neighbors. They seldom came to church with their wives and children, but they all had prayed that one day they would accept Jesus Christ as their personal savior. She hoped they did. Oh my goodness, she hoped they did. Finally, she just got up. There was a little coffee left in her pot from yesterday. She set it upon her stove to warm, and instead of kneeling upon her prayer quilt, she wrapped herself up in it. "Lord, today I need you to wrap your arms around me. Speak for me when the authorities come, and most of all, Lord, give me peace." She watched as steam began to come out of her old coffeepot. She had maybe a cup or two in that old pot. She had actually found that old thing down in the mountain. Someone had obviously thrown it away. But when she saw it, she knew it was much too good to let it lay there, so she had brought it home and washed it up and had used it ever since. At that instant, the Lord began to show her that the old coffeepot was a reflection of Caleb. His family had more or less thrown him away. They looked upon him as no good, but she had picked him up for she saw something in him that no other saw. She brought him home and instilled all she knew about the goodness of the Lord. Evidently, it was of no effect, for look what he had done even with the words "Trust only in me for the help you need." Those words had been echoed in her head before, and just when she would forget them, the Lord would remind her again of his promise. *OK, Lord, I'm listening.* She sat still as a mouse and felt nothing else come from God. *Those nine words looks like to me, Lord, you could tell me more than that.* But she heard no more. But she had a confidence this morning that she hadn't had in a while. Her heart was no longer burdened. The Lord had truly come and refreshed her, and for that she was truly grateful.

She got up, stoked up her fire, and got some breakfast going. Laymon was the first to get up. "What you doing, Mama?" he asked. "Oh, you all aren't hungry this morning?" Martha Rae replied. "Well yea, but I figured you'd be too upset too upset to cook." said Laymon. "Well," she replied. "You ain't too upset to eat, are you? Look, Layman, we have to go on. Life goes on. I have seven children who I dearly love. Whether or not your daddy did this terrible deed, I do not know. But what I do know is, I only want the best for my children. I want you to be able to read and write better than what me and your grandmother have tried to teach you. There is a world outside this mountain that I want you all to journey to. I may never leave from up here but you all can. One thing I want you to remember, that Caleb is your daddy whether he did this or not. His blood runs through you and your sisters and brothers. Don't ever disrespect him because of that fact. He was never nothing in the eyes of his parents and people. We all need to pray for him. If we never see him again, we must never deny who he is to this family. Now get the rest of this bunch up and come on in here and eat. We have a lot to do today."

Laymon hollered at Angela and Lilly. CJ stumbled on into the kitchen just like his daddy did when food was involved. Martha Rae asked them to bow their heads and she said the most humble grace over the breakfast that morning. They were as grateful as if they had a full course breakfast, but biscuits and gravy were good enough for them this morning.

Martha had just cleared the table and was telling Angela to wash up the dishes when she heard a commotion outside. She went and pulled back the old feed sack her mama had made for her curtains, and there sat two law officers on the backs of the biggest horses she had ever seen. No guessing here, she knew exactly what they were here for. She slowly opened the front door and slipped out on the porch and said, "I have been expecting you, men. Won't you come in and have a seat? I have a good fire going and you can warm yourselves." Just so happened, her daddy saw the men ride up and took off up to Martha's house. He was not about to let his daughter go through this alone. He knew how vicious these men could be, and if they thought she had no one to stand beside her, it might even be worse. He knocked on the door gently and proceeded to go on in.

"Hello, gentlemen. My name is John Jenkins, Martha Rae's father, and you are?" The two officers arose and removed their hats and introduced themselves as Howard Sult and Jim C. Long, officers of the law for Russ County. They cordially shook hands with Martha Rae and her daddy. They talked briefly about the cold spell and early snow, and then got right to why they had come. Mr. Long had a deep voice that would cause anybody's knees to buckle. And as he began to speak, he spoke with much authority. "Mrs. Moses, as you know, your husband Caleb Moses is alleged to be in a partnership with his uncle, the now deceased Ellis Johnson, in the processing of illegal liquor. Is that true to your knowledge?" Martha Rae cleared her throat to speak and her daddy quickly told her, "Honey, speak all that you know yourself, not what has been rumored throughout this mountain." As she looked at her daddy, he could see the fright in her face. He knew she would not lie, but she did not want to say anything that would incriminate Caleb as someone he was not. She looked squarely in the eyes of Mr. Long and addressed him. "Mr. Long, Caleb had been away from this family for well over a month. What he did or didn't do, I cannot honestly tell you. I have heard the rumors just like you all, but I cannot truthfully tell you what he was doing in the time he was away from his home." Mr. Sult then asked, "Have you seen him or know of his whereabouts since the said incident?" By this time, she was getting upset. Why didn't they go up to where this all took place, talk to the families who had bought the moonshine, and were either were blind or dead? Why did they want to bring any more sorrow to her family? She opened her mouth and she couldn't believe herself what came out. She had always been taught to respect her elders and those in authority, but today it just wasn't happening. "Sirs, I mean no disrespect, but why have you all not been to the place where all this took place? I mean, have you questioned Ellis Johnson's kin? They would be the ones to ask. They frequently visited Ellis at his still. By the way, what caused all this to happen anyway?" Her daddy then spoke, "It was well-known fact that Ellis Johnson was an experienced moonshine maker. And I know for a fact, he was as careful about how he made it. He always poured off at least a pint jar before he let anyone take a drink including himself." Mr. Long asked him, "Well, Mr. Jenkins, you sound as if you might know more about this process than you are letting on." John squared his shoulders and his voice became stern, "If you all think I could have been involved in this, you are crazy. I am not going to tell you all, I have lived a perfect life. I have drunk a snort or two in my day, and it usually came from Ellis Johnson's still, I'll have you to know. But I have been a church-going man for longer that you two have been on this earth. My little girl has not had time to go chasing her man all over this mountain to see what he was into. She has seven mouths to try to feed by herself. Now, if you all will excuse yourselves, we around here have work to do." They nodded in agreement and told Martha Rae they would most likely be in touch, and if she dare see Mr. Moses anywhere up in this mountain, she must notify authorities. They mounted their horses and took up the mountain. Martha guessed they were headed up to Pap Moses's place. He most likely had all the answers, but she doubted he would tell these men anything.

Her daddy hugged her tightly and said, "We will get through this, Martha. Hold on to that unseen hand, he will lead us to the truth." The tears begin to flow. She had tried to be strong and have a positive attitude, but all this today settled into her heart that she might never see Caleb Moses. If he was caught and tried, he would most likely be executed. The thought of that, she could not bear. Suddenly, she thought, *I will give these men time enough to get away from up at Pap's and I'm going up there myself and talk to him. Blind or not, he's going to tell me if Caleb was involved.*

# CHAPTER 15

I t had been several days since the authorities had visited Martha Rae. The snow had been slow to leave, and it had warmed up a little since the snow. Violet, Susie, and Little John were still down in town with the Pattersons. *Today, I will go down and see about my babies. I know they are fine, but I surely do miss them.* Sal had mentioned she would like to go with her when she decided to go, so Martha thought today will be a good day to walk down there. *Me and Mama can go together. It will seem like old times.* They had received a letter from Edna Sue that she would be coming home for Thanksgiving. Martha was so proud of her little sister, she could hardly wait to see her. She had been gone for about six months to nursing school. She was staying at the school and she had to adhere to their strict rules, so that meant very little visits home. Thanksgiving and Christmas were the only two holidays when they were allowed to come home. She, too, had heard of all the trouble that Martha Rae was having to go through, and she hoped if anything, she could raise her sister's spirits during the holidays.

Sal was wrapped up good. She had just gotten over what she called influenza and, she did not want a back-set on this mess. So she had her head wrapped up and a quilt wrapped around her shoulders. When she got to Martha's house, she looked comical to her. She couldn't help but laugh and tried not to in her face. But the way her mama looked, she could not hold it back. "Well," Sal said. "Are you going to be able to get down to the mercantile without busting your britches?" That made Martha laugh that much harder. "Come on in, Mama, and I'll be ready in just a minute." Martha went into her kitchen. When she came out, Sal knew exactly what she had done. She had baked her babies some cookies. Where she got all the ingredients, she did not know. But sure enough, she had cookies. "I declare, child, where did you get the ingredients to make cookies?" Martha Rae just smiled and said, "Oh I guess, a good neighbor." Sal knew that Ella had been up there the other day and she probably had brought them some supplies. Good Ella, she was a saint. There was not a better friend to her daughter than Ella Patterson. She prayed the Lord would send her a child of her own one day, for she truly loved Martha Rae's and Caleb's children as if they were her own. "Come on then. Let's head out. I don't want to stay long. I must get back and tend to my supper. You all coming down tonight to eat with us. John killed a good mess of squirrel, and I'm frying that up and stirring up a pan of squirrel gravy." "Mama, you are making my mouth water now, and yes, we will for sure be down."

Martha Rae and Sal headed down the mountain. They had talked for what seemed like a good hour. They discussed the quilt that Mrs. McPeak was making. Sal remarked it was absolutely beautiful. She thought she and Martha Rae might try their hand at one of those pretty quilts this winter instead of the usual crazy quilt she always made. Martha agreed she would help her. And before they knew it, they were in sight of the mercantile.

The walk down the mountain didn't seem as long today. She guessed because she had her mama to keep her company and they had talked all the way down. She could see a little face in the window of the mercantile. Little John ran to open the door for his mama and grandma. He had been watching some rabbits hop through the snow and had seen them coming. "Mama! Mama, I have missed you so much!" About that time, Susie heard her mama talking and dashed into her arms as well. Sal looked at these two and said, "Where's my hug?" Little John and Susie both jumped into her arms together. "Hold on, you two. Let's not get carried away and fall." By that time, they had Sal laughing so hard she was snorting. "Where's Violet?" asked Martha Rae. She looked up and Ella was motioning her to come over to where she was. "Look," she said. "She can run this place as good as me and Sid." Martha peeped around the corner, and sure enough, there was Violet waiting on a customer. Ella said,

"She's a natural, personality and all. They all love her here." Martha was taken back. She could never have thought one of her children could actually run a store. But here was Violet, doing just that. Ella went on to tell Martha, "She had been working on her math skills with her for a long time. It has come so very easy for her, and she is a big help to Sid and I. We have time to work on ordering things we need and balancing our books. And, oh yes, a little more time together as well. Sid has suggested we all take one evening and read a book together." "Oh my!" Martha exclaimed. "What book are you reading?" "It's a book by Louisa Mae Alcott called Little Women. We are looking forward to it so much, we have set aside two evenings instead of one. Little John and Susie love it, too." Martha was just without words. Here, not only were Ella and Sid taking care of her children, they were educating them as well. It kindly made her feel like in some way she had let her children down. Down here, Ella and Sid had given them food and clothing and a warm place to sleep. When, if they were at home, all these things they were enjoying would be scarce. Ella read Martha's face and knew immediately what she was thinking. "Martha," Ella said. "These are your babies. They love you dearly. They tell me every day how much they love you. Little John even told me the other day, 'Your biscuits ain't as good as my Ma's.'" That made Martha Rae laugh. She knew her children would come back home soon, and she would allow them this time with Ella and Sid. This was as good for them as it was for her. They then chatted about any late developments on the case. Martha told them about the authorities coming and questioning her about anything she might know. She asked Ella, "Had any of the families of the men who died been in?" Ella told her, "Yes, a couple had been in and were asking for credit." She told them she would help as much as she could. "They were distraught and didn't know how they were going to make it. Mrs. Edwards told me that Nate her husband had bought shine off of Ellis for years and had never had any problems. She even said they would use it medicinally in the winter for colds and coughs. She also mentioned a young man who was with Ellis she had never seen before." Ella cut her eyes over her glasses and asked Martha, "Caleb knew all these mountainfolk, didn't he?" Martha Rae said with a puzzled look on her face, "Who do you reckon that young man was? Caleb knew all these folks. I have got some praying and some investigating to do. As soon as this weather breaks, I'm headed up to Pap Moses's house and see if he knows anything. You did hear he was blind, didn't you?" Ella answered her she had, and told her she would be keeping her ears and eyes open. If she heard anything interesting, she would keep her in touch. Martha Rae asked her if she could get a little flour and some beans on credit. Ella said, "You silly woman, you know what's mine is yours."

With that, Sal and Martha Rae headed back up the mountain. She told Ella she would be back down in a few days and get some ironing Ella needed doing. All the way up the mountain, Sal was talking non-stop, Martha was nodding yes, and acknowledging, "Yes, I know, Mama." But her mind was a million miles away. Sal finally told her, "It's hard to have a one-sided conversation!" Martha stopped and said, "What do you mean by that?" Her mama laughed and told her, "Did you know you just agreed to put britches on our old sow hog so she wouldn't get cold this winter?" Martha Rae exclaimed, "I did not." "You did so," Sal said. "You have not listened to anything I've said. I know you have got a lot on your mind." Martha sighed and said, "I guess I have, Mama. I think I will stop by my prayer rock before heading up the mountain home. Will you be able to make it on up?" Martha said. "Oh yes, I'll be OK. You just go ahead and pray and send one up for me and your daddy. Go on now, I'll be fine." With that, Martha kissed her mama on the cheek and took the path that would take her to her prayer rock.

It didn't take long to get there, and Martha Rae could see her rock in the distance. Nobody but her mama and daddy knew where this place was, and how special it was for her. When her heart would be so burdened or broken, or if she needed guidance from the Lord, she would venture down through the woods to this special place to pray. Seems like lately, though, she was here a lot. Martha sat down in the chair as she called it. She had to admit she was a little weary from coming home from the mercantile today. As she sat resting, her mind went back to the many times she had visited here. It was a place where she could unload her burdens before the Lord. Today, she had much to pray about. She knew she needed answers and she did not know who to ask the questions to. "Lord, if I ever needed you, it's now. I have so many unanswered questions and don't know of anyone but you to give me the answers I need. Lead me, Lord, to the truth in this mystery. Help me, Lord, to show your grace and not let anger or bitterness take up residence in my heart." She sat there for a long time and finally said, "Lord, I love you with all my heart and I also love Caleb, so please Lord, I need to know he is alright and safe. Lead him, Lord, for we need him in our family." She picked up her flour and beans and headed to her little house on Marley Knott's Mountain.

The next morning, Martha arose earlier than usual. She had a lot to get done today, and every minute she had would need to count. Her daddy had brought her a mess of sausage from one of the hogs he had killed. If it wasn't for her mama and daddy, she didn't really know what she would do. They supplied her with milk and butter from their cow, and had hogs and a few chickens. It was what had sustained her and her children for the last few years. She owed so much to her family. She just hoped one day she would be able to repay them for all they had done for her.

CJ had kept her wood box full ever since his daddy left. He and his papa John had been down in the mountain cutting wood for about a month now. They both knew winter was coming fast, and they needed to go ahead and get as much wood cut as they possibly could. They could rest later, sit by a good, warm, crackling fire, and nap or read some from the Bible. CJ had even busted her up some kindling wood to make it easier on his Ma. She opened the stove door and shoved some kindling wood. She then proceeded to pour just a dab of kerosene onto the wood to get it going good. She struck her match and threw it into the fire, and poof, it gulfed up but she was used to that. She added more wood until she had a good hot fire going to cook their breakfast on. She patted out seven good size patties out of the sausage this morning. She knew her boys could eat more than one. They often never had much, so she wanted to fill them up this morning. She mixed up a batch of biscuits and was scrambling eggs when Laymon got up to see what was going on in the kitchen. He could smell the aroma of sausage, and it just drew him up and into the kitchen. "My, oh my!" he said, as his eyes feasted on the big breakfast he was going to get to partake of. Martha looked at him and winked, "Now you go get the rest of our bunch up 'cause everything is just about ready." The last thing she would have to do was stir up the gravy. "Lilly," her mama said. "Set the table and make sure we have enough jelly for this breakfast." Lilly set the table, all the boys on one side and her and Angela would sit next to their mama. Sal had been busy making jelly out of the mountain berries this year. She loved to can better than anyone they knew, and it was a good thing, too, because they knew she would share with them. After they all had sat down and eaten, Martha Rae told them, "While I have you biggest children with me this morning, I might as well let you know about all that has been going on with your daddy." She proceeded to tell them what Mrs. Edwards had told Ella at the mercantile, that there was a stranger with Ellis when he came to deliver the shine. "I'm going up to your Pap's house today and talk to him. Surely he will know something. I want all of you to keep your ears and eyes open and mouths shut. Don't let on that you know anything at all. If we are to find out the circumstances surrounding all these deaths and blindness up here in this mountain, we have to be sharp and outsmart who is behind all this. I'll keep you all informed but let's keep this in our family. No talking about this outside of this house." The children all nodded in agreement. She had so much to sort out, but she was going to be ruthless and relentless about finding out the truth.

# CHAPTER 16

A ngela was cleaning up the breakfast table when Martha Rae came out of her bedroom. She wasn't sure exactly how to get up to Caleb's parents' house, because she had only been up there once and that was when Caleb went to get his clothes after they married. *Poor fellow*, she thought. Her heart was nearly breaking, He hardly had a small box of belongings to bring down with him. Life was hard, she knew that, but it seemed to her his Ma and Pap were happy to see him leave. And she would bet they were just as unhappy when they saw him coming back home. She had never had to deal with anything like this. Her parents had always loved and welcomed her and her children to their home. She couldn't get it in her head how insignificant Caleb had to be feeling. "Angela, you take care of things a while today. Remember, no talking about what we discussed." Angela assured her she would keep quiet about everything and wouldn't even open the door unless it was her grandma and papa John.

Martha wrapped up good in the best she had and started out the door. She looked back at Laymon who was fixing to head down to his Papa's house. "Laymon," she said. "If I don't come back down by this afternoon, you come looking for me. I don't foresee anything hindering me, but with all that's going on, you can't ever tell. Pray for me, young 'uns."

The climb up the mountain was not easy. The higher up you got, the more rugged the terrain was. She had not followed the path she and Caleb had taken, thinking this was a short cut. It was really grown up and she was getting scared when suddenly, she stepped onto a small clearing. Immediately, she knew where she was. She was at Ellis Johnson's still site. *So this is where all this took place.* She thought to herself. *Well, since I'm here, I might as well look around a little bit.*

She looked over Ellis's still. She had never seen a moonshine still before, although she had heard a lot of stories. She just didn't see how this contraption made liquor. She spotted some quart jars that Ellis probably would have used next year. Next year for him would never come. She walked around the site thinking when her eye caught a glimpse of something under the leaves. She reached down to pick it up and it was a small glass bottle. *Wonder what this is doing laying here?* It didn't look like it was weathered, the label was still torn half off. As she got to looking closer, it had the letters "ol" on it. What could have been in this bottle? Probably something Ellis used or maybe nothing, but she would take it with her just in case it was a clue of some kind. *Now which way do I go, Lord, you lead the way. Up, I guess, is the only alternative.* So she began to climb on up the mountain. *Why didn't I stay on the road?* Martha thought. *But it's too late now, so I'll just continue to climb up higher.* She saw a few rabbits and deer on her way up, and in the distance, she saw the shack that she and Caleb had visited a few years back. She believed that the old lady in the yard was Caleb's Ma. She looked so old and she knew she couldn't be as old as her mama. Maybe if she combed her hair and seen to her hygiene, it would help her appearance. Anyway, she was not up here to judge her mother-in-law. That sounded so strange to say. They had never felt like what Martha Rae had envisioned a mother-in-law to be, but nonetheless she was.

Martha began waving her arm so she would see her and maybe welcome her in. As she got closer, her face revealed this woman was not glad to see her. "Mrs. Moses, how are you and Pap doing?" Mrs. Moses frowned up her withered face and pointed her finger at Martha Rae and said, "You think you are something special, don't you?" It took Martha Rae by surprise. "Why on earth would you say such a thing as that for?" "I'll tell you why. You ride up here with that sorry boy of mine in a big fine wagon, looking down your nose at us. Then go in my house and snub your nose at Caleb's belongings. Don't lie, girl, you know you did." Martha Rae could feel the anger rising in her. She couldn't let her feelings get in the way of why she came here in the first place. As calmly as she could speak, she looked at Caleb's mother and said, "I have not come up here to fight and fuss with you. I have come to see about Pap and see if he knows anything about what they are accusing Caleb of. I cannot believe Caleb would be so mean as to poison his own father and people in this mountain. Now, if you would be so kind and take me to where Pap is at, maybe I can help you all somehow." Corry Moses bowed her head. She knew Martha Rae was not going to back down and she didn't have a leg to stand on anyway.

"Come on, then," said Corry. "He's up here in the house, blind as a bat." Martha Rae followed her mother-in-law into the house, and she could have almost cried when she saw Pap sitting in a chair. "Who's there with you?" Pap asked. Martha Rae didn't give Corry time to answer. "It's me, Pap, your daughter-in-law." She held out her hand and touched him and he grabbed her hand and kissed it. Tears began to well up in his eyes. Martha had never thought she would ever see this man emotional. "Pap, what can I do to help you and Corry? I am as hurt as you are. You know they are trying to blame Caleb for it, don't you?" "Yes, I've heard. The authorities have been up here questioning me and Corry, but we had no information to tell them." "Good," Martha Rae said. "They also have been to my house. I know Caleb was helping Ellis with his moonshine, but can't imagine him doing something this mean." Pap's voice began to tremble, "Caleb had been up here with us for a couple days before all this happened. Him and Ellis had a big falling out, and he told me he was fixing to go home to you and his children. The day Ellis brought me the moonshine, he had that boy Conrad with him. Caleb had beaten the socks off of Conrad. That's part of the reason he came home. Ellis gave me a quart of moonshine. I was his first customer. I knew that this would have to do me all winter, it's the only reason I didn't drink too much. I would have been one of the dead had I drank another swig or two." Martha felt her heart melt for this man. She had not liked him all that much because of the way they had treated Caleb, but he was reaching out to her and she could not turn him away. She ask "Has a doctor examined you?" Pap hung his head, "Nope, we have no money to pay a doctor, so this is the fate that I'll have to live with. I have gotten a little of my sight back. I can see shadows, but cannot make out who or what it is." "Pap, I found this little bottle down by the still with the 'letters ol' on it," Martha said. Pap said, "Let me smell that bottle." She handed the bottle to Pap, and one sniff, he knew exactly what had been in it. This bottle had methanol in it. "I have smelled this smell lots of times while down there with Ellis. He'd sometime add a little to his hooch, you know to make his shine have a little more kick. My guess is ole Conrad poured the whole bottle in. You need to take this bottle to the authorities and tell them what you told me. They would believe you, Martha Rae. Well, you would have to talk to them as well you saw him with Ellis the day they were delivering the shine. I'll tell you what, I'm am going to talk to some of the other people that their family members were taken blind or dead. If that Cox boy was with Ellis at every stop, we may have something." "You all got food?" Martha couldn't leave without asking that. Corry even softened her voice when Martha asked that. "Well, if you could bring us some more of those good biscuits and jelly, we would be most thankful." "I'll do it. I'll send Laymon back up here maybe tomorrow, if that's OK?"

Pap thanked her three or four times for coming up to see about them, and even Corry walked with her out on the porch. "I know I was kinda harsh a few moments ago, I thought you were going to rub all this in our face. I am sorry, child, that's all we know." Martha reached out her arms and embraced Corry for the first time ever. She wondered how long it had been that anybody hugged her. And if she could guess, a long, long time.

She'd hurry home and send Laymon up here with some biscuits and jelly, and maybe her daddy would send a piece or two of ham, she hoped. She felt true sorrow for her father-in-law. Sure, she could say he brought it on himself and he had, but it had brought him to a place where she felt she could minister to him and Corry about the love of Christ. Wouldn't Christ do the same as her? She was sure he would; his word taught as much. The air felt like it was getting cold. Martha Rae hoped it wasn't going to snow today. She had much traveling to do in this mountain. She would get her daddy to take her down to the neighbors in his wagon. That way, she would drop by the mercantile and see if Ella knew anything, and most especially, if her babies were all right. She'd made extra biscuits for Little John, since he thought her biscuits were better than Ella's. Her children could always lighten her load with just a thought of them, and Little John always added a smile as well. Ella had mentioned some ironing, and she would pick that up as well. What on earth would she have done without her friend? The Lord had worked all this out before they even knew each other. That, she was sure of. She had gotten in sight of her house and seen something that made her jaws drop wide open. *The very nerve*, she thought. *The very nerve.*

# CHAPTER 17

Martha Rae had just gotten past the chicken house when none other than Conrad Cox was walking up the path to meet her. *Keep your head, girl,* Martha Rae thought to herself. "Well hello, Mr. Cox. What brings you up in these parts today?" said Martha. She knew she must not wear her feelings on her sleeve, so she spoke in the kindest voice she could muster. He must not know that she had a tad of a thought that he had something to do with all these tragedies. Conrad cleared his throat to speak and spit before he could get a word out. "Oh, I just got word a few days ago about all that had been going on in the mountain and thought I'd see how Caleb and his daddy were doing?" He was as nervous as a cat in a room full of rockers. That was very easy to see and his bold, confident demeanor had shrunken to cowardice. Martha knew she had this in her favor. "Well, Mr. Cox. What is it that you heard?" Conrad would not even look her in the face. He had his head hung down and was taking the toe of his boot and kicking dirt back and forth. "Uh, Mrs. Moses, I heard that there had been a lot of people dying up here in this mountain and came to see if I knew any of the dead. You know, to pay my respects and all," Conrad said. "Is Caleb around?" Martha felt a bolt of anger surge through her and it hit her right in her heart. She knew if she talked for much longer, he would get to see a little of her mama come out of her. "Oh, no. He's not here today. He's out hunting." She did not want to tell a lie. But in all reality, he probably was hunting for food and somewhere to sleep, and especially somewhere to hide. "Well," said Conrad. "I didn't know if he had drank any of the shine or not." "Really, Mr. Cox. So you think it was shine?" That caught Conrad off guard and it showed on his face. He looked like he had just gotten caught with his hand in the cookie jar, or the liquor jug in this case. He knew he had spoken too much and backtracking would only make him look worse. So he immediately changed the subject. "Well, I hope you all have a good Thanksgiving and tell ole Caleb to not eat too much." Conrad let out a little snicker and turned to head on up the mountain.

Martha Rae was flabbergasted. She thought he was fishing for information, that she was sure of. But why would he head up the mountain to Pap's house? That had to be where he was going, because Pap and Corry were the only family who lived up higher than they did. CJ had seen his mama coming and just about broke his neck to get to his mama. *For only a young boy, he could run the fastest of all her children,* she thought. "Mama! Mama!" he called. "We were getting worried about you. And then that friend of Daddy's was down at the house trying to talk to Angela. But Grandma came up and told him to leave. Don't worry, we never said anything." After getting that mouthful out, he gave his mama a big hug. "I love you, Mama. I just don't want anything to happen to you." Martha Rae was taken aback. She had never seen CJ so emotional before. He had always had a nature like his daddy, keeping to himself and his feelings on his sleeve. But today, he was sincerely worried about his mama. *There was more to this boy than meets the eye,* Martha thought. *And I must remember that.* "Come on, son. Let's get to the house and see what we can stir up for supper." CJ placed his hand in his mama's hand and told her, "I'm going to hang on to you so I can make sure you get there OK." Martha Rae wrapped her fingers through her son's fingers and exclaimed, "CJ, you are growing up. Look! Your hand is almost as big as mine. Soon, you are going to become a young man. Follow the Lord, son, with all your heart. That is the only way we can make it in this life."

The rest of her clan were waiting on the front porch. Angela had a good fire still going, and Laymon and Lilly Jean had made them a game of checkers with rocks and drawn the board on a piece of wood their papa John had given them. Martha Rae worried that all that was going on in this mountain would have a negative effect on her children, especially the older ones since the younger ones were down at Ella's. She unwrapped herself of the quilt she had worn up to Pap's and it hit her like a ton of bricks! Was Conrad going to do harm to Pap and Corry? He knew they knew all of the details of that horrible day. "Laymon!" Martha screamed. "Go get your papa John's wagon and hitch up the mules! Tell my daddy to please come up here quick." Laymon shot out the door running. He did not have a clue what had went through his mother's head, but he sensed the urgency in her voice and knew he had better make tracks.

John had been packing up the wood box for Sal before it got dusty dark when Laymon ran through the back door. "Papa, please come! Mama sent me down to tell you to please come." His papa felt his knees get weak and his heart begin to pound. "Tell me, Laymon, what's wrong?" said his Papa John. "I don't know," said Laymon. "But from the sound of Mama's voice, it is not good." With that, John Jenkins dropped his last load of kindling in the wood box. He didn't even bother to tell Sal where he was headed. She was cooking them some supper herself and pushed her pots off to the back of her wood cook stove and followed John up to Martha Rae's. "Wait, John! I'm coming, too," said Sal. John hollered back, "Where have you been? Come on! I ain't got time to wait on you. Something's happened up at Martha's and I got to get to her."

When her daddy reached Martha's house, she was already on the porch. Laymon had just pulled up in the wagon and she was reaching for his hand to help her in. "Martha, honey, what's wrong?" her daddy asked. "I think Conrad may be headed up to Pap's and Corry's to do them harm." "Yes, your mama ran him off, didn't she?" said John. "Daddy, I would love to discuss this but we haven't time. Get in. Did you bring your gun?" said Martha. "Shucks no. Laymon never said nothing about no gun," said her daddy. CJ was standing on the porch with his sisters Lilly and Angela, who had already started to cry. "CJ!" Martha yelled. "Do you know where Papa keeps his gun and ammo?" "Yes, I do, Mama!" cried CJ. "Then you run down to their house and get it for us and hurry please!"

By the time Sal reached Martha Rae's house, CJ had already retrieved his Papa's gun and ammo, and was running up to give it to his Papa. "Y'all be careful, Mama. I love you." Martha Rae blew her children and her mother a kiss, and the last words she spoke before heading up the mountain was "Pray for us." Sal put her hands together as if she was praying, and lifted them up in the air so Martha Rae could see them. "Oh Lord! Oh Lord!" was all Sal could muster.

"Come on, children. Let's get in the house. I'll stay with you till they come home. Now let's take hands. We have some praying to do," said Sal. With that, Angela, Lilly Jean, and CJ took hands and Sal Jenkins prayed a prayer from the bottom of her heart. "Dear, Lord, you see we try to be obedient servants to you and we offer charity to every soul in this mountain. Please put your angel around my family and Pap and Corry, too. We have seen enough death and destruction for one lifetime. Help us to have mercy for Mr. Cox as well. Again, I say Lord, take care of my loved ones. In Jesus's name we pray, Amen." With that, all said "Amen" in unison again. The girls were crying, and CJ had a scared look on his face. He stood up and told his sisters, "Let's get some supper going so when mama and the rest get back, we can have some supper." Sal looked at him and said, "Why, boy, you are becoming quite a little man." And proceeded to look at the two girls and say, "Get up. You heard your brother."

Sal left that evening to see about her own supper. CJ squared his shoulders just a little prouder that evening, too. He had felt so insignificant to his family and neighbors. His daddy had brought shame to the family, and he knew they were looked down upon because of it. But tonight, God lit something in his heart that let him know he was not his daddy. Although he carried his name, he carried his mother's heart. And for that, he felt like he was ten feet tall.

Laymon was pushing the mules as hard and as fast as he could without causing them to overturn the wagon. The road up to Pap Moses's house was the worst road in the whole mountain. Most folks had worked on the road that led to their place, but not Pap. He said, "Let 'em get here the best way they can." And that was most of the time by foot. When they arrived at Pap's, nothing out of the ordinary was going on. Martha Rae and her daddy got down and slowly walked to the house. John tapped on the door with his gun. He could hear them on the inside talking, and Corry finally came to the door. It was quite evident that they had retired for the night. Corry had on a gown that had the bottom ripped off. She had tried to cover it up by putting on one of Pap's old shirts. Pap was lying beside the stove. He never even heard them pull up in the wagon. "What's going on Martha?" said Corry. "We hate to disturb you all tonight, but Conrad Cox was at my house this afternoon asking all kinds of questions about Pap and Caleb. He was nosing around, wondering if Pap or Caleb had got into some of the shine. He tried to play it off as he was concerned about all the men that had died, but I know better. When he left, he took off up the mountain. I knew you all were the last family past ours in the mountain, and I was afraid he came to do you all in." "Do us in for what?" said Corry. "To maybe kill you and Pap. He knew you all knew he was with Ellis the day the shine was being delivered. He probably thought Pap and Caleb would drink enough to kill them. But his plan did not work out." You could see Corry's expression change right before your eyes. Her eyes began to go back and forth. She was thinking the same thing now. "Here y'all come on in. I'll get Pap up." Martha Rae and her daddy stepped through the door of the Moses house and the stench would knock you down; it smelled so bad. Martha even wondered if they were keeping animals in the house. She never saw any come forth, so she knew where the stink was coming from. Pap and Corry probably hadn't had a bath in a month of Sundays. Corry had Pap by the arm guiding in to the front room. She put an old chair behind him and told him to be careful and feel for the chair and sit down. When Pap finally got into the chair, he spoke up. "So y'all think Conrad may be coming up here to kill us? What makes you think that?" Martha Rae began to explain why she thought Conrad would want to harm him and Corry. He was listening to every word she spoke. "Well," Pap said. "You may be right. That rascal had a debt to pay us, and I reckon he don't want no jail time. So sure enough, he may want us dead. What y'all reckon we ought to do?" All eyes then went to John. He ducked his head because he knew the only answer, and it was not one he wanted to do. John finally grunted and took his hat off and said, "Corry, you know how to shoot a gun?" "Why law! Yes, I can shoot and you better believe I'll lay him out if he comes snooping up here." "Thank you, Jesus," John whispered under his breath. "What's that you said, John?" Pap didn't have eyesight, but he could hear better than they all knew. "Oh, I said thank you, Jesus. You got a good woman there. Any woman that can shoot a gun is worth a pound of gold." Pap had a big smile come across his face and so did Corry. "Yep, you said that right," said Pap. John talked to Corry a little more, and told her not to open the door for anybody and try to bolt her back door a little better. She had an old heavy trunk. She told him she could scoot across the door if Laymon and him would help her. John looked at Laymon and said, "Come on, boy. Let's help your grandma bar this door." They took hold of the old trunk. Laymon said to his Papa, "As heavy as it is, I believe she already has stashed some gold in here." "You may be right," said Papa John. They got a big laugh out of that. Martha was calling for them to come on. John was giving Corry some last instructions. "We'll check back on you all in a few days. If you need anything, just let us know."

They all got back in the wagon when John noticed something in the dirt. "Hey, Corry!" he hollered. "Come out here." Corry stepped out on the porch and asked John, "What you need?" "Do you or Pap smoke?" asked John. "Well, we used to but had to quit. It was too much money. Once in a while we may take a little chew, but that's about all." "Well, look here what I just found. Somebody has been here that smoked." Corry walked over and told John, "Let me see that." John handed her the cigarette butt and she looked it over. "Nobody I know smokes nothing like this. Everybody I know has to roll theirs. This one looks like a city smoke to me." "All the more reason to keep your doors locked and be on the lookout. Conrad may have been by here and you just didn't know it." With that, John tipped his hat and told them all good-bye. Martha assured them she would be back to see about them in a few days.

Back down that rough road, they retreated. Laymon fussed all the way down. Martha rolled her eyes at her daddy and he just laughed. "There is more excitement up here in this mountain than Dodge City," Martha said. And she got to laughing as well; something she hadn't done in quite a long time.

aleb Moses had been on the run for almost two months. He was tired of running and being hungry all the time. But most of all, he missed his wife and children. And as hard as it was for him to admit, he missed that old hard, rugged mountain. Tonight would be no different. He had found him a cave that was nestled in the side of a creek. It was cold and damp, but at least he was out of the rain and soon the cold. The best he knew, nobody ever saw him. He knew they were probably looking for him, but they would never find him here. But the truth was, he was tired of this cave by the cold creek bank. Even if he went to jail, they would have to give him a trial. *Surely they couldn't hang someone without one,* he thought. Then, he would get to thinking about jail. He'd probably be locked up for the rest of his days, or even worse, hung. The thought of his neck being stretched scared the daylights out of him, so he believed the cave was going to have to be good for now. Caleb knew in his heart who committed this horrendous act, but he had no proof. Conrad was slick as a snake. He had proven that to Caleb in the past. His fingers had always been sticky, and he would always try to point the blame at him. "What an idiot I have been?" he said out loud. "I tried to fit in with that low life to be popular, and look where it has gotten me?" His mind quickly went to Martha Rae. He loved her with everything in him, but he just couldn't seem to fit the mold as husband and father. Not that he ever had any teaching, but that was no excuse. If he got caught, he just has to face his punishment although he was not responsible for all those deaths and men losing their eyesight. *Poor old Pap,* thought Caleb. *It's a wonder he ain't dead. I guess he never drank enough.*

It was getting dusk and this is the time of night Caleb would get out and prowl. He often raided someone's garden but that was just about over. A few turnips or greens or a pumpkin or squash was about all he could round up this time of year. But he knew of a farm down the creek, and surely they might have an egg or two still in the nest. That's where he would hit tonight. He made sure he had gathered enough wood for a small fire later tonight, and he lit out to try find him some food.

Joe Lambert had just finished mending one of the holes that his cows seems to always get out through. He had been walking his fence lines for a couple of days. He had a small farm with about fifteen heads of cattle and a few pigs and chickens just enough to get by with. He loved farming and his animals but when they started causing problems, he gets to thinking about selling out. Today was one of those days. Every day for the past two weeks, he had to go hunt some of his cows that would get out. He'd been to his neighbor's farm and brought four home day before yesterday, and here was another hole and it was no telling where these had gotten off to. He raised up from nailing the barbed wire to the post when he saw someone in the distance coming down the creek. It looked like a young man to him. "Hey, boy!" Joe yelled. "Come over here for a minute." Caleb's ears perked up. He thought for sure no one would be out at this time of evening, especially fixing a fence. He should be home with his family. Not wanting to risk getting caught, he darted through the woods. Briars and limbs were beating him in the face. It was almost like he was in a fight. Finally out of view from the old man, he kept walking toward the fields that had the pumpkin in them. He was so tired of pumpkin, he didn't know what to do. But at least he wouldn't starve. Maybe he could steal a chicken and roast it tonight over his open fire. *First, I'll hit the chicken house. I'll wring that thing's neck and head to the pumpkin field.* By the time Caleb got to the chicken house, it was dark. He could hear the old hens cackling but paid them no mind. About the time he went around the hen house and gently opened the chicken house door, he heard a click. Caleb froze because he knew exactly what that click was. It was the sound of someone pulling back on the hammer of a gun. When he turned around to see, there stood the old man who had yelled at him earlier. "Yep, I figured this was where you might be headed," said Joe. Caleb felt like he might faint from fright, but he would try to explain to this man why he was in his chicken house. He was starved. "Come on. You are going to my house until I decide what measures need to be taken." Caleb hung his head. He never thought he'd get caught in a chicken house. Most likely, this man would turn him in. He didn't care if he did. He was tired of running and hiding. So whatever would be, he would accept.

Joe led Caleb to his house and called for his wife to step out on the porch. "Mabel, you still up?" said Joe. She poked her head out the back door and said, "Yes, honey. What you need?" "I caught me a boy in my chicken house about to wring one of my good hens' neck. Set a place at the table for him and pour him a big glass of milk." Caleb could not believe his ears. He felt so ashamed of what he had done. He hadn't wrung a chicken's neck tonight, but he had the other night right out of this same man's hen house. Joe nudged him with his gun, "Come over here, boy, and wash your hands. Pull you a bucket of water out of the well and clean up." Caleb proceeded to turn the rope and brought him up a bucket of water. His first instinct was to drink him some. He cupped his hands and drank some of the best water he had tasted in quite a long time. The only water that was any better was the water upon Marley Knott's Cliff that freely ran out. He washed his hands, then washed his face. For a moment, he forgot that the old man had a gun in his back. That didn't matter. He surely appreciated all this good water. "Now come on, boy," said Joe. 'By the way, what's your name?" Caleb knew better than to tell him who he was, for he feared the authorities probably had put his name out far and wide. "James is my name. Yes, James White." "OK, Mr. White. You go on in front and we will head around back to get into the kitchen." Caleb walked as carefully as he could. He didn't want this old man to get any ideas he was running. No, sir. He wasn't about to miss out on some good food. Caleb opened the door, and there sitting on the table was the finest spread of food he had seen in a long time. The only other spread he had seen like that was down at Martha Rae's mama's house. He kindly thought of Sal Jenkins. She could make him the maddest of anybody he had ever ran into, but she sure was a good cook, he would give her that.

Mrs. Mabel had set out her half runner green beans she had canned this past summer along with a pone of cornbread, a pint mason jar of pickled beets, and some deviled eggs. Caleb had not eaten in days. He had nibbled around on some pumpkin and had found a chestnut tree loaded down, but he ate very few of those. The husk had been hard to break and his fingers were sore to the point that they bleed. Caleb didn't want to seem over anxious, so he politely asked Mrs. Mabel where she wanted him to sit. "Oh, honey! You go ahead and sit right there where I put your plate. Me and Joe have already eaten." Caleb didn't let the grass grow under his feet. He sat down and she began to put food onto his plate. He had never been treated this well, especially when he was intending to steal a chicken from their coop. Caleb ate till he was just about to pop. "Boy, Mrs. Mabel," he said. "This is some of the best food I've eaten in a long time." He knew how to flatter her to maybe get dessert. Sure enough, she turned around with the biggest piece of chocolate cake he had ever seen. He had only eaten chocolate cake one other time in his life, which was at the gathering when he first met Martha Rae. "Do you think you can hold this?" Mrs. Mabel asked. "Well, I'll sure give it a good try," said Caleb. He ate every bite and then proceeded to take his finger and dab the crumbs. "Mrs. Mabel, that was simply delicious," Caleb said. "Well, thank you, honey. My Joe liked it, too." She cleaned up her dishes and bode the two men a goodnight. "See you in the morning. Sweet dreams, dears. Oh and 'James,' we would love to have you join us for Sunday services tomorrow. How about it?" Caleb just about declined the offer when visions of that chocolate cake danced before his eyes. He wanted another slice tomorrow. If he declined church services, he might get run off or turned in to the authorities. "Why yes, ma'am. Ain't nothing I'd like better." "OK, it's settled then. See you dears in the morning." Caleb thought, *Well, that was easy enough.*

Joe came over and sat at the table with Caleb. The expression he held on his face let Caleb know he would not be as easy as his wife had been. "Boy, who really are you? You ate like you were starved to death and you probably were if the truth were known." Caleb just sat and stared at Mr. Lambert. "Well, sir," he said. "I really don't know where to begin." Joe just looked at Caleb and said, "We got all night. Now get to talking." Caleb coughed and swallowed hard. "First thing, my name is not James." "I figured that from the get go," said Joe. "What is your name? And don't tell me no more lies, boy, or I'll call the law." Caleb knew it was time to fess up. He was sick and tired of running and sleeping in that damp cave and nearly had starved to death. "OK," he said. "My name is Caleb Moses. I am on the run from the authorities. I have been accused of spiking some moonshine with methanol, and several men died and some are blind, including my daddy." Joe looked him right in the eyes, "Well, did you do it?" he asked. Caleb hung his head. What a mess he had made of his and Martha Rae's life. He didn't know if he could ever make it up to her for all the shame and disgrace he had caused his family. Not to mention his seven children who needed a real father figure in their life. "No, sir, I did not do it. A young man by the name of Conrad Cox was the very one that did this. I had fought him a few days before all this happened down at my uncle Ellis Johnson's still. I had been belittled as long as I was going to. I whooped that yellow belly and went up to my Pap's a couple days to get myself together. I was going to go home to my wife and seven children. A couple days later, Ellis and Conrad came to deliver my Pap his hooch. After that, they had several deliveries to make down in the mountain. Lots of the menfolk bought a little moonshine off of Ellis. Some kept it on hand to take for coughs and colds and have some for a nip or two around Christmas. Apparently, some took a nip or two too many and died from alcohol poisoning. My Pap didn't quite drink enough, although I can't understand why, because he had a taste for liquor and so did my Ma. Next morning, I found him out in the barn. He had been passed out all night and when he awoke he was blind. Me and my Ma finally got him in the house and I knew I would get the blame for this since I had been down there helping Ellis. So all I could think of was run, and that I did." Joe never said a word. He got up and took his coffee cup and placed it in the dish pan. He turned to Caleb and said, "Boy, you can sleep in the barn tonight. There is some hay and an old blanket we keep out there when we have a new calf or colt. It's clean. You can cover up with that. Breakfast is at the crack of dawn, so you might want to draw you some water and bathe as best you can." Caleb's voice began to tremble, "Joe, you turning me in tomorrow?" Joe's heart melted when he heard Caleb's voice crack. He had been young once himself and didn't always do like he was supposed to do. He had even been in some trouble with the law for stealing at one point. But he met Mabel and she turned his life around. She introduced him to Jesus and he took the walk. He had tried to live a Christian life from then on. Sure he had made mistakes, but he would always feel that tug on his heart from the Holy Spirit and he'd ask to be forgiven right then and there. He kept a short account with the Lord and that's the way he liked it. Something inside him was tugging on his heartstrings now. Joe knew it was the Lord. He just felt this boy was telling him the truth. He just had to follow the Lord's lead on this one.

"Not for now. I'm not going to utter a word to nobody, James. That is what you said your name was, wasn't it?" Caleb held out his hand and Joe grasped it, "Yes, sir. That is what I said and I sure do thank you. I'll be ready for church and breakfast in the morning." Joe showed him to the door and pointed to where his old barn was located. "Now don't let that bossy heifer scare you. She just thinks she owns the barn." Caleb gave Joe one last glance before he pulled that old barn door open. He had never met anybody quite like Joe and Mabel Lambert. He had instantly took a liking to Mrs. Mabel and Joe. There was something speaking to his heart tonight as well. "Lord, is that you?" Caleb said. Then he remembered a Bible verse he had heard Martha Rae quote many times. "Yea though I walk through the valley of the shadow of death, I will fear no evil: for though art with me; thy rod and thy staff they comfort me." Was the Lord really with him tonight? Had he guided him to Joe and Mabel's. *Is sure did seem like he might have had something to do in all this,* Caleb thought. He wrapped up in the blanket he found and curled up in the hay. *Lord, you know I'm not guilty of what I am accused of. I am not blameless in all this, when I should have been with my wife and children.*

*Please, clear my name.* The hay was the best bed he had slept on in ages. *Tomorrow would be a better day*, he thought, and his eyes went together in the most restful sleep he had in a long time.

# CHAPTER 19

It was getting closer to Thanksgiving. It was hard to think another year was coming to a close. Martha Rae had been down to her prayer rock this morning, and talked with the Lord for a long time. Many verses of the Bible had come into her mind, but the 23$^{rd}$ Psalm of David flooded her heart, and it had begun to spill out her eyes. "Lord," she said. "It has been a pretty rough year. Well, in fact, a really awful year," she said. "But I want to take time today to praise you in this storm. Although I don't understand why, I trust you and know what Satan means, for bad you will turn it to good. You have kept us from the poorhouse. We have been fed from the bounty of your table. Some look at this old mountain as a curse. But Lord, I see it as my blessing. For without it, I may not have seen your goodness and sustaining power had I been raised somewhere else. I pray when this fiery trial is over, Lord, you will receive glory and honor for it all." She sat quietly for a long time, thinking the Lord would speak to her heart. She watched as the leaves had turned and most were fallen off by now.

The squirrels were busy gathering nuts for the upcoming winter. She had often heard a hard winter was coming if the animals "squirreled away" food. She laughed at the thought. That's probably where that phrase had come from. Someone else had witnessed squirrels gathering food. *Well,* she thought. *I'd better get back up the hill. It's getting on up in the evening and I may have to get a fire going to knock off the chill tonight.* Just as she rounded the bend to start up the hill toward her house, she recognized a little chubby lady making her way up the mountain. It was Edna Sue. She was carrying all that her arms could hold. "Hey, Edna!" Martha Rae called. "Wait up and let me help you." Edna Sue instantly threw down her belongings and ran to meet Martha Rae. By the time she got to her sister, she was crying a flood. Martha Rae had tried to hold her emotions back, but when she saw Edna Sue crying, there was no more holding back. Edna grabbed her sister, and they both danced around crying and laughing at the same time. "Oh my goodness," Edna said. "Step back and let me look at you." Martha Rae timidly stepped back and bowed her head. Edna reached over and lifted her chin, and their eyes met with nothing short of sisterly love for each other. "My, my," Edna Sue said. "If I took you to that college, you would have the boys swooning all over you. You are more beautiful as the years go by." "Oh hush up, Edna! You are just saying that," said Martha Rae. "But say it again. I kinda like to hear it." And with that, they fell over laughing. "Come on, you crazy woman. Let me help you get your belongings up the mountain. What did you bring with you?" said Martha Rae. "You sure never left with more than a sackful, and here you come back with both arms loaded." "You'll see," said Edna Sue. "Now come on. I am anxious to see Mama and Daddy."

Martha Rae and Edna Sue trudged on up the mountain. It was like they picked up where they left off. Martha Rae reminded Edna of the time that she had sat down in a yellow jackets' nest and almost got stung to death. "Yea," said Edna. "But at least I got to get into the creek. You know how much I love water." They chattered all the way up the mountain. Edna Sue had brought with her a calming spirit to the mountain today. Of course, she always could be calm even in turmoil. Martha always said it was a gift of God, and she was so glad to open this gift back up today.

Sal was sweeping leaves that had gathered on her front porch. She had to do it every day and sometimes twice. It was something that she loved to do. Most would call her crazy sweeping leaves, but Sal found it to be relaxing and it often helped her sweep her troubles away. Just as she bent to pick up a stick that had blown in, she saw her children coming up on Big Oak Lane. She commenced to dance and holler for John. John was out back with CJ and Laymon. They were stacking wood. They had been stacking wood for what seemed like a week. John had a special knack for predicting what the winter would be which was well-known throughout the mountain, and he had predicted a harsh winter this year. CJ perked up when he heard his grandma hollering. It just wasn't a holler like "Come here and carry this. It's too heavy for me to lift," it was more like "Come quick, hurry up, and come here." CJ recognized the urgency in her voice and relayed the same in his voice to his brother and his Papa. He dropped the stick of wood he was fixing to stack and took off toward his grandparents' house, "come on, y'all. Grandma is in trouble." They all three took off. CJ rounded the house first, with Laymon fast on his heels. Papa John was out of breath when he finally got there. "Sal," he said between breaths. "This better be good. I am pert near dead from running." Sal had quit dancing, but was jumping up and down and pointing down the mountain. She could not get two words together. She finally said, "Look!" John cupped both hands and put them above his eyes. His eyesight wasn't what it used to be, but it was no mistake. Here come his two girls together up the mountain. He had not seen Edna Sue for six months or more. He had missed her so much, it had actually had made him sick at first but he knew he couldn't hold her back for his sake. Her heart was in nursing, and she wouldn't be satisfied with no less. He took off down toward them, his arms held open to receive the precious children his Lord had entrusted him with. Martha Rae stepped back and let Edna Sue embrace her daddy. Here they were all crying again, including her daddy. It was a time of rejoicing. John had a touch of what the father felt when his prodigal son came home. But in this case, his wasn't prodigal. "Here, girls, let me carry your belongings the rest of the way. Or better yet, let me get those two strapping grandsons of mine to do it." John waved his big, long arms for CJ and Laymon to come down. They immediately knew what he wanted, and without even being told, they loaded up Edna Sue's things and went ahead. "My," said Edna Sue. "You making men out of those boys." "That's the way we do it up here in this mountain, girl. Looks like you are doing pretty good yourself," said her daddy. Edna gigged her daddy in the ribs and said, "You got that right, Pa."

When they finally reached the porch, Sal wrapped those big arms around Edna so tight, she did not want to let go. "Oh girl," said Sal. "You will never know how much we have missed you. How long are you getting to stay?" "Two weeks, Mama," said Edna. "I get to stay until after Thanksgiving. But I am sorry to say I won't get to come back for Christmas. I signed up to help out at the hospital during Christmas because they will be so shorthanded during the holidays." Sal felt her heart break, but she knew she couldn't let Edna see her disappointment. "Well then," she said. "We will have to make the best of what we got. Come on in and let's stir up some supper for all of us. Martha Rae, you go get all your children and be down here for supper at six o'clock on the dot. John, you go cut me some tenderloin from off that hog you killed the other day. We are going to have us a big country supper tonight in honor of my two girls." Martha Rae was taken aback when her mama said two girls. Sal knew she had to be very sensitive in this case. Here was Edna going off to learn to be a nurse, and Martha Rae struggling just to raise her brood. But she knew Martha Rae was also a shining light for the Lord in this mountain. People even commented on her strength. They didn't see how she could have any joy in her heart for all she was going through, but she did. She could make you laugh and always seemed to see the better side of things than most folk. When they complimented her, she would just point up to heaven and tell them "He gives me peace and strength. Don't know what I'd do without him." Sal looked through the eyes of a doting mother. "I love both my girls, and to me they are my gifts from God. Anytime I can get all my family under one roof, I am going to see they get fed and fed good." Martha Rae had never had more pride in her heart for her parents than right now. She was so thankful God had placed her in this particular family. *One day,* she thought. *I am going to repay them for all they have instilled in my life and my children.* "OK, then. Come on, CJ and Laymon, let's go down and fetch Violet, Susie, and Little John from Ella and Sid." Edna Sue frowned up her face and asked, "You didn't give three of your children away to the Pattersons, did you?" Martha hollered and laughed, "Well, I didn't officially give them away, but Ella has been keeping them until this mess with Caleb calms down." Sal piped up and said, "Tell Ella and Sid to come, too. We will prepare enough for everyone." With that, she locked arms with Edna and said, "Now let's get to cooking."

About the time Martha Rae reached her own front porch, Angela and Lilly had put their wraps on to see what all the commotion was down at their grandma's. "Hey girls, where do you two think you are going?" Martha Rae asked. "Well, we heard a lot of hollering and such down at Grandma's, and we thought we go see what was going on." "Well," said Martha Rae, "I'll tell you. Your Aunt Edna Sue is home." You could see the twinkle in Angela's eyes at the mention of Edna Sue. She loved her aunt and had missed her tremendously since she had went off to school. "Can we go down to see her?" asked Lilly.

"Yes you may," said Martha Rae, "your grandma is going to need some help preparing supper as she is feeding quite a number of people. Now you all hurry down there and do as she says." Martha Rae watched as her two oldest daughters walked down towards their grandparents home. Where had the time went, Angela was going on thirteen and Lilly was twelve. Martha thought, I was just a few years older than them when I got married, I can't imagine one of my girls getting married off at fifteen. Her mind drifted back to the day her and Caleb said their vows, for better or worse, richer or poorer, til death us do part. Had it been so hard for Caleb to love her and these children, she thought. They never asked for much, just that he would be there for them, but he couldn't bring himself to settle down to being her husband and their children father. She was a million miles away in her thoughts when CJ came running up the hill and told her to come on, Laymon had the mules hitched up and they would proceed down to get the rest of the clan. "Hold on boys," said Martha Rae, "let me get my hair combed and I'll be right there." She had worn her hair up for a long time but today she thought, I believe I'll wear it down. She combed her long mane down and put on her shawl that she was so proud of. "Here CJ, give me your hand and help me up," Martha Rae said. Laymon looked at CJ and bushed up his eyes, "Boy you sure do look pretty today mama," said Laymon. "Oh hush and lets get going," said Martha, "I don't want to be late for supper tonight, mama is fixing a special meal." That was all CJ needed to hear was the word "food", he was that much like his daddy.

When Martha Rae and her boys got to the Patterson's, Little John was the first to run out to meet them. "Mama, mama I'm here" said Little John. Martha Rae couldn't keep from laughing, her precious baby boy could bring a smile when no one else could. Martha Rae picked him up and swung him around and said "I do declare, Ella must be feeding you good, you feel like you weigh as much as one of papa's pigs." Little John thought that was so funny "Do you really think that he said?" "You better believe it son," said Martha. "Now where is your sisters, we are going home today?" "Really?" said Little John. He quickly ran to find his sisters and when he did he announced for them to get their clothes they were going home. Martha Rae stepped into the mercantile and there was Violet running the store. "Honey where may I ask is Ella and Sid?" said Martha Rae. Violet held up her hand to let her mama know to wait until the customer had left. Martha nodded and began to walk around the store admiring all the dry goods that Ella had stocked. Her cotton fabric had the prettiest print she had ever seen. Wouldn't my girls be pretty in a dress made out of that, she thought. Just as she looked up Violet motioned for her to come on over. She was marking down some credit this family had used. "Oh yea Sid and Ella had a Dr. appointment," said Violet. "Who is sick and what is wrong?" asked her mama. Violet chewed on her no.2 pencil and finally said, "Oh its Ella, she has some kind of stomach trouble. Seems to stay sick a lot here lately." "Really?" said Martha Rae. "Hmmm," she thought out loud. "Well anyway we will leave them a note, you all get your belongings together and Violet you lock up. Edna Sue is home and grandma is wanting all her children and grandchildren together tonight for special supper." Violet gave her mama "the look." Martha Rae had seen "the look" more and more since Violet had been staying with the Patterson's. It was a look that said "Do I have to?" "Can't I wait until Sid and Ella come home and come up with them?" asked Violet. "They should be home any minute." Martha Rae studied for a minute and replied "I really don't want you here by yourself with no adults, you can never tell who might come by, now hurry and get your stuff." Martha Rae couldn't take any chances leaving her children alone. Ole Conrad Cox might venture through and no telling what he'd try on a girl by herself. Violet made a face, but she knew there was no arguing with her mama. "Get me some paper and pen and I will leave Sid and Ella a note." Martha wrote Ella and told her she had come for her children for a special supper tonight for Edna Sue who had come home with some exciting news. She also invited Sid and Ella to join them. "Now come on children we have a lot to get ready for supper tonight" said Martha Rae. Little John was dancing, he was so excited to get to go home and so was Susie, she was talking a mile a minute. Only Violet didn't seem to be so happy. "What's wrong Vi"? Asked her mama. "Oh nothing much, I'll just miss Ella and Sid and all the customers I help" said Violet. "Don't fret so much, you can come back down here in a few days, I need you home with me too" said Martha Rae. Violet tried to act excited but she had gotten used to staying with Sid and Ella and it seemed more like home down here with them than it did with her family. Violet laid her head over on her mama's shoulder and whispered something in her ear that made the expression on Martha Rae's face to exclaim. All she could repeat was "you have got to be kidding, well do tell". "Come on Laymon get these animals moving we have a lot to do"

# CHAPTER 20

It had begun to get late. Ella was getting worried about Violet being at the store alone for so long. She had not anticipated her doctor's visit would be so long, but indeed it had. The test was conclusive. She was expecting a child sometime around June. Maybe a little earlier or later, said Dr. Kane. But they would know more as time went on. Ella knew most folks would be asking why she didn't go with the mountain midwife. Sure she had birthed nearly every child up in that mountain with no problems at all, but since she had such a hard time getting pregnant, she thought an M.D. would be best suited for her. She could hardly wait to tell Violet. She had become just like a daughter to her and had filled that emotional gap in her heart for a long time. That would never change. Violet would always be taken care of for whatever she would need, regardless if she was with her and Sid or at her mama's house. She loved her more than she had words to speak.

Just as they rounded the bend, she noticed all the lights off in the mercantile. "Wonder what has happened Sid?" asked Ella. "Honey," Sid said. "I cannot imagine. I hope nothing bad." They hurried their wagon up a little and finally arrived at the mercantile. Ella quickly ran up the steps of her front porch and stuck the key into the lock. Sid yelled, "Hold on, Ella. You let me go in first. No telling what had happened." Ella agreed. She didn't want anything to risk her losing her baby. She had tried for so long and it had finally happened. Her only explanation—God had answered her prayers just like he did Hannah in the Bible.

Sid slowly cracked the door to the mercantile and yelled, "Violet, you in here?" When he got no answer, he then became frightened.

He told Ella, "You go get in the buggy in case something has happened. You can go for help." In all reality, he had provided her a way to escape had anything happened. Sid pulled the long string that was attached to the light and saw a note. It said "Sid and Ella, I have came for my children. Edna Sue has returned home from school and mama is cooking us a family supper tonight. They ask me to invite you all to join us tonight as well. Hope to see you soon. Love, Martha Rae." "Well," said Sid. "That was a relief." He proceeded to go out and tell Ella not to be alarmed. "Violet and her brother and sister had gone home for a family supper." Ella was slightly disappointed. She could hardly wait to tell Violet her good news and here she would have to wait a little longer. But it was fine that way. She could break her good news to her best friends, too. "Sid, you tend to the horses. Give them extra feed and water. They may need extra to make it up the mountain." She snickered under her breath, "They are just a tad soft."

Ella ran into the mercantile and grabbed her basket to fill with goodies to take up with her. She would not arrive empty-handed. *Let me see what would go well with the supper Sal was preparing.* Her eyes followed all the canned goods she had on her shelf. Nothing appealed to her that much until she spotted some canned peaches she had just gotten in. Matter of fact, she had never eaten any out of a store-bought can before, and this would give her a chance to try them out. *Perfect,* she thought. She reached up and gathered four big cans. Surely this many would suffice this hungry crowd. *Now,* she thought. *Something extra special for the children.* A big bag of penny candy. She already knew John and Susie loved it and was sure the rest would, too. She filled her bag with BB bats, Mary Janes, peppermints, and best of all, orange slices. *Wow,* she thought. *They will be really riled up when they see all this.* Sid came in to help her with all she had to take with her. He knew she would not go empty-handed. It was in her nature to be generous. She had freely helped most of the families in the mountain who had lost members of their family to the terrible moonshine tragedy, and she had also sent food up to Pap and Corry to acknowledge her love to their daughter-in-law Martha Rae. They seemed truly thankful, and had come to the mercantile after that to thank her for her generosity.

Sid jumped down to help his now pregnant wife up into the wagon. He had been thinking for some time into investing into one of those buggies with a motor in it. He knew Henry Ford had halted making civilian autos to produce military equipment, but he really liked the 1928 model A and knew a fellow that could give him a good deal on it. Now that the baby was coming, they needed something that she could go to her doctor's appointments in during the winter and not get cold. It was also a perfect excuse for Sid to get something he always had wanted with no fuss with Ella over if they could afford it or not. Sid was not one to stay behind. He knew they needed to go with progress if they were to stay in business. Next week, he would go into the city and talk to his friend about purchasing a car. But for now, they needed to get up that mountain to John and Sal's place for supper. Even though Sal and John would never submit to moving on into the future with new advanced gadgets, he admired their commitment to the old ways. Really, that's all they knew but he also knew all the old ways were not bad. The younger generation could learn a lot from their elders. "Come on Tom and Betty," Sid called out to his team of horses. "Let's go up in that mountain for some supper." Tom and Betty were about the most sure-footed pair anyone had ever seen. Many mountain folk had tried to barter Sid for them, with no such luck. Sid would tell them, "They are my legs when the going gets rough. These horses would be here no matter how many Fords lined his driveway."

Ella was already getting excited. She could see the smoke coming out of John and Sal's home. She had counted her cans of peaches over and over and would always say after each count, "I hope I have brought enough." Sid would reassure her that she had enough. Finally, they pulled their wagon into the back of John Jenkins's house. He had a place where you could tie up your rig until you were ready to leave. Laymon had heard Sid and Ella coming, and darted out the door to help Sid tie up his rig. "Come on, Mrs. Patterson. Let me help you down." Ella extended her basket of goodies first and told Laymon, "You take those in to your grandma and no peeping in the bag." Laymon agreed with curiosity in his heart as to reckon what Ella had brought them. Sid gently helped his sweet wife down from the rig. By that time, Violet had rushed out to meet them, along with Martha Rae and Edna Sue. Sal was standing in the back door, smiling like a mule eating briars. "Get on in here, children," said Sal. To her anyone a whole lot younger than her, she called "children." Some looked at her strange, but most just felt honored.

Edna Sue embraced Ella in the same fashion as she had her sister. She was a crier. She just couldn't help herself. She wore her emotions on her sleeves and could cry at the drop of a hat. "Come on, Sid," she grabbed him as well, and gave him a big bear hug. "I have missed you two like money," she laughed. "As if I ever had any." Ella entered the Jenkins home to the aroma of fried tenderloin, gravy, cooked apples, cat head biscuits, half runner green beans from her garden this year, black raspberry jelly that Angela had made, and a big pot of coffee and a pitcher of sweet milk for the children. Ella felt like she had died and gone to heaven. She had experienced some morning sickness at first, but that had passed and now she was ravenously hungry all the time. "I'll say," said Ella. "You all have outdone your selves. Look in the basket, Sal. I brought us something for dessert." "Law, let me look!" said Sal. They hardly ever had anything for dessert, and this would hit the spot. "Oh my goodness!" said Sal. "Look, Martha, store-bought peaches! I don't believe I have ever seen them put up like this. Let's make a cobbler." Although she thought to herself, *how do you get into this can?* Ella knew exactly what was going through Sal's mind. "I just happen to have a gadget to open this can," said Ella. Out of her purse, she pulled the strangest looking thing Sal had ever seen. "Now come here and let me show you how it works," said Ella. Sal stepped over to watch Ella open up the can of peaches and exclaimed, "Well, bust my britches! I guess you're never too old to learn." Ella just laughed and said, "I don't know nothing about no cobbler." "Well, you need to pay attention. I'm fixing to teach you something. It's easy as pie," said Sal. "I guess easy as peach pie."

The mood was so good, everyone was chitchatting away. Sal had Ella backed up in her kitchen, teaching her a thing or two. Martha and Angela were in the front room playing games with all the children, and John was kicked back in his old rocker in front of his roaring fireplace. All of a sudden, Sal began to shout, "Really!

Good gracious! Really, Ella!" All the women ran to the kitchen. Sid knew exactly what had happened. Ella had just announced her pregnancy. Martha Rae was the first to enter the kitchen. "What's wrong, Mama?" said Martha Rae. "Wrong? Nothing's wrong! For once, everything is right," said Sal. "Ella and Sid are expecting a baby next summer." Martha Rae had to put on, because Violet had already told her she went to the doctor today to see if she was really pregnant or not. She jumped up and down with Ella and the rest of her girls. Little John was jumping, too. He loved Ella and Sid and was just as happy as the girls were. Laymon and CJ sat with a silly grin on their faces. They surely couldn't act like everyone else. It just wasn't manly, or so they thought. It sure didn't stop John, though. He just sat there in his rocker and cried. "Surely, the Lord had visited Sid and Ella. And if two people deserved this, they did," he said.

Sal called the family to the supper table. "John, you bless this bounty for us tonight. We have so much to be thankful for. Good food, friends, and family have graced our home tonight." She raised her hands to the Lord and cried out. "Lord, we lift up our hearts in our hands tonight to bless you." John's grace was so humble. He told his family and friends, "Let's take hands and call out to a merciful God who has privileged us to be together under one roof tonight. We have so much to celebrate. Edna Sue being home with us and Martha Rae and all her children gathered together. We have missed having all of us in one spot. Lord, we see the results of much prayer. Thank you for blessing Sid and Ella with a soon-to-be new baby in their home." And with that, John instructed them to dig in.

After they had all ate their fill, Ella and Sid hugged and kissed everyone good-bye. When Ella got to Violet, she hugged her extra hard. "I love you, Missy." That was what Ella often called Violet. Violet looked like she was going to burst out crying at any minute. "Well," Ella looked at Violet. "What you waiting on?" "What do you mean?" said Violet. "Get your clothes. Your mama said you could go back down the mountain with us and help me since I was in the motherly way." The expression on Violet's face said it all. She was hoping her mama would let her return with the Pattersons. She somehow doubted she would ever return up here in this mountain to live. Violet quickly gathered her some clothes. Her grandma had made her a new blouse for Christmas, but under the circumstances, she knew she might need it now. "Here, Vi," said Sal. "This is an early Christmas present. Now, you take care of Mrs. Ella and don't forget where we live." Violet admired the fine handiwork of her new blouse. Angela and Lilly admired it as well, and knew they would probably be getting one similar for Christmas, too. Martha Rae walked her daughter out to the Patterson's wagon. She stroked her hair back and kissed her on her forehead. "I love you so much, Violet. You will never know or understand until you have children of your own one day. It is very hard to let you return with the Pattersons, but I know there is a world out there calling you and I will not hold you back. So go, my dear, with my blessing." Violet did not know what to say back to her mother. She had never talked to her this way. She knew in her heart that her mama loved her dearly, but she had never spoken to her in this manner before. Now she felt guilty for wanting to leave her family and didn't know if she could do it or not. Martha Rae picked up on what her daughter was feeling. You could read it on her face. "Now listen, little girl," said Martha Rae. "Don't you go getting all emotional now. We are not that far away and you know the way home, so you get in that wagon and help Ella get through this pregnancy." Violet smiled a sheepish smile and jumped onto the back of Sid's wagon with her clothes tied up in a rag. She waved good-bye and off she went. Martha Rae turned away from her daughter. She didn't want her to see her cry. She felt her heart just about to burst, but she was tough and knew Violet would stand a better chance down there with the Pattersons than up here in the mountain. Martha Rae knew life was different outside this mountain. To her, she couldn't imagine living anywhere else. All her hopes and dreams of life had been snuffed out in one day of bad choices. She hoped her children learned from their daddy's poor choices. The decisions you make today may turn around and bite you.

Edna Sue was calling for her to come on in the house. Martha wanted another bowl of that peach cobbler before she went to bed tonight. Susie and Little John were busy catching crickets. CJ and Laymon had challenged Angela and Lilly to a checker championship, and her daddy was right there making sure no one cheated. He secretly wished one of them would back out because this was his favorite game of choice. Sal and Edna Sue were washing dishes, and Martha was sopping the peach cobbler pan. Right now at this very instant, life was good. If Martha could freeze time, she thought she would. But she knew that was foolish thinking. *One day,* she thought. *One day, things will be better.* And with that, she put the last spoon of peach cobbler in her mouth and smacked her lips. *Gosh, that was good.*

# CHAPTER 21

Sal was beaming with pride when she looked out and saw John coming up the mountain with a turkey in each hand. To her, this is what a real man did. He provided for his family in every way. John Jenkins had never let her down. She had loved him since the first time she saw him, and she knew she loved him even more as their years rolled on. "Get on in here with those fine looking birds, honey," said Sal. John was in his glory. She knew he would talk about killing two turkeys in one day for weeks on end. But she thought, *That's OK. I won't steal his thunder.*

Laymon and CJ just happened to be down at their grandparents' house this morning when John brought the turkeys in. They were in utter disbelief. Laymon had wanted to get up and go with his Papa this morning, but John had slipped off early. He didn't want any distractions and knew if Laymon went, that was exactly what it would be. John had told Laymon he would have to be very quiet. But he also knew his oldest grandson. He'd get bored and go to talking, or worse, throwing rocks down the mountain. If they were going to have turkey for Thanksgiving, he'd have to go by himself. He would take him another time when it didn't matter if they killed anything or not. Sal began calling for Laymon and CJ to get down to the spring and bring up some water to scald these birds with. She was an expert at dressing anything John killed. She could help gut a hog and work up all the meat and pluck a chicken, or in this case turkey and have it for supper the same night.

"Here, boys," said Sal. "Take these big buckets. You won't have to make but a couple trips." They had been in a big game of checkers and didn't want to go get water but knew if they wanted some turkey for tomorrow's Thanksgiving meal, they'd better get going. They grabbed up the buckets and took off down through the woods to Marley Knott's Cliff to catch some water. This was the coldest and most refreshing water they had ever drank. Today, it ran swift and cold out of the old pipe. CJ couldn't resist bending over and drinking from the pipe. He cupped his hand to catch some and drank his fill. "Keep on drinking and we will never get our buckets filled up," said Laymon. CJ just looked at him and kept right on drinking if nothing else to aggravate Laymon. Finally, Laymon stuck is hand under the stream of water and sprayed CJ good. "You idiot! Why did you do that for?" said CJ. Laymon was laughing so hard, he didn't see CJ do the very exact same thing to him. He just turned his hand slightly and it sprayed Laymon. "You just wait. I'll get you back. I am soaked to the gills," said Laymon. CJ said, "It's not so funny when it comes back on you, is it, my brother?" These two could fight each other. But if anybody else messed with either one, they knew they would have to fight both these boys. They kicked rocks and each tried to make the other spill some of the water so he would have to go back down to fill up his bucket. Sal Jenkins would not take nothing less than full. "Hey, Laymon," said CJ. "You ever think about our daddy?" "What do you mean?" said Laymon. "Oh, I just wonder sometimes if he has gotten him another family and forgotten about us. You would think he'd sneak around here once in a while to see us if he loved us, don't you think?" said CJ. "Yea," said Laymon. "I don't understand why he did what he did. If I ever get the chance, I'll give him a piece of my mind." "Oh, you would not," said CJ. "You watch and see. One of these days, I'll run into him. He can't hide forever. I hope I am around when that happens. He has made it so hard on Mama," said CJ. "He'll get his just reward one day. You just wait and see," said Laymon. "The tables will turn against him. Come on, bro," said Laymon. "Let's get this water up to Grandma so she can boil it up and pluck those turkeys." CJ said, "I am going home when she does. I can't hardly stand to smell that stink when she goes to plucking them."

Sal already had a big fire going when Laymon and CJ arrived with the water. "Here, boys," she said. "Pour it into this tub, and go get me two more buckets" said Sal. Angela had tied a big rag around her like an apron to help her grandma pluck those turkeys. Of all the grandchildren, Angela stuck to Sal like glue. Sal had taught her how to make her famous jelly and can all sorts of vegetables. Angela could hold her own with a hog, too. She looked like a pro when she began to work up that hog. She had also taught her some arithmetic and spelling. "They need to know something besides mountain school," said Martha Rae. Hopefully, when Ella had her new baby, she was going to teach the rest of Martha Rae's children some of the more advanced learning that she knew. But for right now, they needed to talk turkey. They had a big crowd coming to their house tomorrow for Thanksgiving dinner.

Edna Sue was making what she called a casserole. She had gone on and on about eating it at school, and wanted her family to get a taste of what she had grown to love at school. "I don't know about no casserole, but I expect we will have some half runner green beans, mashed potatoes and sweet potatoes, corn pudding, icicle pickles and chow chow, pumpkin pie, apple pie, and a big surprise cake that Ella and Sid were bringing," said Sal. Martha Rae had invited Corry and Pap down, too. She knew they would most likely eat alone. And to be honest, she didn't know if Corry could cook or not. So Sal and John's house would be running over tomorrow. Martha Rae hoped for fair weather, so some could eat on the porch.

Martha Rae had stayed up most of the night helping her mama roast the turkeys. She thought, *this is such a good time of the year. We have so much to be thankful for.* Sal had worked herself almost to exhaustion. John had fussed for her to take a nap or two, so she would be ready when her company arrived. "I'll be alright if everything is not perfect," said John. You are putting too much emphasis on this Thanksgiving dinner and you are missing the real reason why we celebrate it. He knew he was fighting a losing battle, but he tried.

Sal arose early on Thanksgiving morning. There was a big frost on the ground and the air had that winter chill to it today. "Goodness, I sure hope it doesn't decide to snow," said Sal. "Now wouldn't that be something?" Martha Rae heard her mama talking and stepped into the kitchen to see who she was talking to. "Do we already have some company, Mama?" said Martha. Sal had not expected anyone to be up this early in the morning. "Oh child, no. I'm just talking to myself. You know you get the answers you want when you do that. Don't you think so?" Martha Rae laughed and hugged her Mama. "I guess you are right, Mama. Sometimes for lack of conversation, you just have to create some yourself." Sal opened up her oven, and there laid before her was two of the most beautiful roasted turkeys Martha had ever seen. Martha Rae gasped when she saw her mama start to pull them out. "Here, Mama, let me help you. We don't want you to get burned." "Law, honey! After all the years of roasting turkeys, I know exactly how to handle these birds." She had her several dish-cloths she had made put together. She laid each bird upon the shelf of the warming closet. "There," she said. "That will keep them warm until we eat. Now, let's get those sweet potatoes peeled and ready to roast," said Sal. "I am going to need my oven for the pies later on." Martha Rae hurried and began to peel sweet potatoes. Angela had heard them talking in the kitchen and had come in to join them. John soon arose. He just could not escape the aroma these ladies were stirring up in the kitchen this morning. He stuck his head through the kitchen door and said, "You all laid any eggs? I thought I heard some hens cackling." With that, he grabbed his hat and jacket, and told the hens he was going up to see how the rest were faring this morning.

Little John had heard his grandpa step up on the porch and before his grandpa could knock, Little John jerked open the door. "Come on in, Papa," said Little John. "We got us some breakfast cooking." "You do?" said John. "Who in the world is doing the cook-ing?" CJ peeped his head around and said, "Yours truly. Come get you a seat, we have some of that bacon off of Squealers hind end and I am about to fry some eggs to go with it." "Yea," said their Papa. "Old Squealer was a fine hog. He dressed out to be the biggest hog I've ever raised. What are we going to do for bread?" said John. "If we don't have any, I'll send Lilly down to the house to get us some biscuits." "Oh no," said CJ. "We have bread Angela left us some from last night so we wouldn't starve." "Well," said John. "I'm right proud of you boys for taking care of your brother and sisters. You boys will make some girls fine husbands one of these days. But we won't be in any hurry." John ate a bite with his grandchildren. It was good to have them all home. He had missed them terribly. If only ole Caleb could have straightened up. It was sad, he missed that boy, too. He was still part of this family and he prayed each night he was OK. *Lord, if you see fit, please guide Caleb back to his family.*

Long about noon, everyone began to arrive at Sal and John's house for Thanksgiving dinner. Laymon had taken the wagon up to haul Pap and Corry down. They were very excited to have been asked. Since Pap had lost his vision, Martha Rae and her family had taken to make sure they had enough food. Laymon and John had cut and hauled several loads of wood up to them to make sure they make it through the winter. Corry looked like she had cleaned up a bit when they arrived. It didn't matter to Martha Rae if she did or not, she would show them a Christian welcome and treat them as if they were kings. "Come on in," said Martha Rae. "Here, Pap. We have fixed you a special place beside the warm morning stove." CJ had carved his Pap a special cane to walk with. It resembled a snake going up a tree limb. Martha had complained that she didn't like the snake, but CJ reminded her of the rod that turned to a serpent in the Bible story about Moses. God let Moses use that rod to do many miraculous things. I believe God will do a miracle in Pap's life as well. She could not believe she heard these words coming out of CJ's mouth. She thought, *he pays more attention to me than what I thought. God has some big plans for that boy, I believe.*

Edna Sue had prepared her casserole. She was talking a mile a minute, telling everyone exactly what she had put in it. Ella and Sid had just arrived. Ella was instructing Sid, "Now you hold that box straight. I don't want my cake to slide sideways." When Sid finally got to the table with the mystery box, Ella unveiled her masterpiece. It was a big three-layer chocolate cake. She had icing that looked to be at least an inch thick all over. Of course, Little John had to run his finger through, "just to get a taste," he said. The whole gang was here, all the food was prepared, and the table was set. Sal instructed all to gather around the table and hold hands. Even if they couldn't eat at the table together today, at least they would join hands for the blessing.

"John," Sal said. "Bless this food." John raised his hands to heaven, "Our dear, kind and gracious heavenly Father, today we thank thee for this bounty of food you have given us this Thanksgiving day. Not only for the food, but for good neighbors as well. I pray you will bless each family down through this mountain. I know some have family members who have gone on, give them the peace and comfort to put one foot before the other and go on with life. We pray a special prayer for Caleb today, Father. Give him a good Thanksgiving and guide him home. In the name of Jesus, we pray. Amen." Martha Rae had to leave the circle when her father began to pray for her husband. Her heart just couldn't stand the hurt that his name often brought up. Edna Sue saw her leave and go to the front porch and followed her. "Sis," She said. "Please come on in. Daddy never meant nothing with his prayer." "I know," said Martha. "It just hurts my heart. Oh Edna, I miss him so much. Do you understand that?" said Martha. "Yes," said Edna. "Most people think you ought to hate him for doing you the way he has, but I know you, Sis. Your heart loves forever." "Yes, it does, Edna. Thank you for being here for me today." Edna reached up and wiped the tears from Martha's eyes. "Now let's get in here and eat. Hopefully, there will be some leftovers. I want to take Aunt Mae and Roy a plate of food. You heard Roy had taken polio and was crippled in one of his legs. I want to talk to them and see if he will come over to the hospital where I will be working through Christmas and see if there is anything they can do to help him." "Edna, you are always thinking of others," said Martha. "Look who's talking," said Edna Sue. They both went into the house. It was abuzz with talk. Pap had his grandsons laughing. Martha Rae thought, *Goodness knows what he's telling them.* Corry was talking to Ella about how good her cake was. The kids were playing some games, and Sal had fallen into the rocker and was snoring so loudly that the whole gang got a big laugh out of her. John asked Susie to go fetch a quilt and lay across her grandma. This had turned out to be a bittersweet day for all. Angela and Lilly cleaned up the dishes, and Edna had carried a couple of plates of food down to Mae and Roy.

Martha Rae and the rest of her children had gone home. Laymon and CJ took Pap and Corry home, and just as they turned around to head home, a soft gentle snow began to fall. "Yippee!" said CJ. "A snowball fight tomorrow, big brother."

# CHAPTER 22

By the time Caleb arose the day after Thanksgiving, the ground was already covered with about four inches of snow. It was hung on every branch. It reminded him of some pictures he had seen on some calendars for the month of December, but it was still November. Where had time gone? He had been staying with Mabel and Joe ever since he arrived at their farm, having gotten caught for trying to steal one of Joe's hens. They had truly shown him a Christian spirit and extended a hand of fellowship in return for help to Joe on the everyday operation of the farm. Mabel had cooked up everything in sight for Thanksgiving, you would think she was expecting a large crowd, but it was only for her Joe and Caleb. Mabel had grown quite fond of Caleb. She had never had any children of her own. Although she and Joe had taken in several wayward girls and boys, she had never felt this close to any of the others as she did with Caleb. Joe warned her several times, "Mabel, you are going to get hurt. He will leave here one of these days, most likely return to the family he left up on that mountain." Mabel would just look at Joe. He could already see that frightened look in her eyes. She never offered any answer other than, "You never know, Joe."

Indeed, Caleb had been thinking of his wife and children lately, especially since the holidays were coming. Joe had been giving him a small wage for his help, plus a room in their home and food. He had kept every penny that Joe had given him. This day, he emptied the old sock. He just sat there on the edge of his bed and stared at his money. He separated the copper from the silver. He still had not a clue as to how much he actually had. He had been saving to buy his family a small Christmas present. He had sat and thought about what he would try to get each child, and something special for his dark-haired Raven. Then, reality would set in. He would have to sneak up the mountain early in the morning and leave their gifts on the porch. He would not get to see the look of surprise on each face when they find the bounty. No doubt, the smaller kids would think Santa had left them this. He would have to come up with something so Martha Rae would know he had been by and dropped this off. He heard Mrs. Mabel coming up the step, and he hurried and gathered his money and put it back in the old sock until the day comes when he would spend it. Mabel stuck her head around the door of his room and said, "Caleb, are you ready for breakfast? I have been hollering for the last few minutes and didn't get no response. I was afraid you might have taken ill." "No, Mrs. Mabel," Caleb said. "I was just lost in my thoughts." Mabel came on in his room and started gathering his dirty clothes. Finally, she sat down on the bed beside him and looked him square in the eye and said, "Caleb, I see a faraway look in your eyes here lately. What, pray tell, are you thinking about?" Caleb just hung his head. He did not know how to start to tell this precious lady that he had grown to love her like a mother. Joe and Mabel had been as good as he had been low down and sorry. Finally, Mabel reached over and got Caleb by his hand and said, "Listen, son. We all have made mistakes we wish we could take back, but you can't un-ring the bell. The only thing we can do to go forward in life is to confess our faults. That's what the word says, Caleb." Caleb just sat there and finally said, "Mrs. Mabel, one of these days, I will tell you, but I just can't today." Mabel knew to leave him alone. In his own time, he would open up about all that she already knew anyway. She had read the papers. She knew what had taken place upon Marley Knott's Mountain, but she could not believe that her precious Caleb had anything to do with it. "Come on, sweetheart. I have fixed you and Joe a big country breakfast. I do declare, I believe you are putting on a little weight. And by the way, Joe has a proposition to lay out before you this morning." "What do you mean, Mrs. Mabel?" said Caleb. "You come on down. He'll speak to you over breakfast."

Caleb hurried and got dressed. He could not imagine what Joe had on his brain. Surely, after all this time, they would not turn him in, or would they? The only way he would find out was to go down and face Joe man-to-man. Joe had already been sipping on his piping hot coffee. Mabel had Caleb a big cup, ready to pour him some when he arrived for breakfast. "Come on, son. Mabel has really outdone herself this morning. Ham and sawmill gravy with cat head biscuits, scrambled eggs, and grits." Caleb always gave Mabel a big hug every time he graced her table. She had been the mother his mother failed to be. He scooted up his chair to the table and Mabel began serving up their plates. Caleb looked at Joe and said, "Mabel tells me you have a proposition for me?" "Yes, son, I do, but it comes with conditions." "Oh, I figured as much," said Caleb. "OK, spit it out, Joe." "Listen," said Joe. "I am getting on up in years, and quite frankly, I cannot run this small farm like I used to. Your help has been tremendous, and I am very appreciative for all you have done to help me." "Say it, Joe," said Caleb. "You are going to sell out and I must move on. Is that what you are trying to tell me?" Joe cleared his throat. He wanted Caleb to hear him well for what he was about to say. Caleb had his head hung down, looking at his plate. Somehow, he had lost his appetite. "OK, here goes," said Joe. "I want to give you a few acres of this farm. You know, to give you a start in life. We know what went on with you and how it happened to bring you into our lives. Mabel and I have discussed it and we would like to deed you ten acres of land." Caleb just sat there stunned. "Ten acres, Joe?" "Just turn yourself in to the law. We will help you with the legal expense, but you must own up to the authorities." "I just don't know what to say, Joe," said Caleb. "Nobody has ever given me anything before, much less land." "Well, all you have to say is yes. We will go with you into town and be with you when you turn yourself in," said Joe. Mabel looked as if she would burst if she didn't get the chance to speak. "Go on, Mabel," said Joe. "I know you have something you want to add." Mabel was already getting teary-eyed. Her voice began to quiver when she began to speak. "Caleb, as you know, me and Joe have never had any children. Although we have kept children, none means as much to us as you do. I don't know why. You are a grown man with your own children, but I feel a bond deep in my soul for you. If you were to accept our offer, Joe has a stand of timber over in the next county. We would have it cut and hauled over to the saw mill close to where you were raised, and use that lumber to start building a home for you. If your family wants to join you, that would be even better." Caleb could not believe his ears. He looked at Mabel and Joe. They had been the best thing besides marrying Martha Rae that had happened to him. Caleb tried to talk, but he himself began to tear up. "I don't know why you all helped me when I came to rob your chicken house. I truly deserved to be run off. I don't deserve your kindness, Joe." Mabel started embracing him like any good mother would. "You see, Caleb, none of us deserve mercy. But our kind, gracious, heavenly Father renews our mercies every day. He even died for us so that we could inherit eternal life with him when we die. Don't you see, Caleb? Joe and I love you. Can you see that?" said Mabel. "Yes, ma'am, I sure can," said Caleb. "OK then, it's settled," said Mabel.

"Hold up a minute," said Caleb. "How is all this going to take place if I'm locked up?" "We have been much in prayer about all this, Caleb, and the Lord told us to just have faith and that's what we are going to do—have faith." Caleb let out a sigh of questioning. *They might have faith but mine is might near gone*, he thought to himself. "Would you all be willing to wait until after Christmas? I have my money saved that Joe has been giving me to help him on the farm. I would like to take my wife and children something special for Christmas." Joe and Mabel just sat there for a few minutes and looked at each other. "What you thinking, Joe?" said Mabel. "Well," Joe hesitantly said. "I don't guess it would hurt much. I hate to deny him Christmas. Yes, it's settled then. We can wait until after Christmas, but not later." A big smile came across Caleb's face. "Oh, one more question," said Caleb. "What if I can't make a go of it with the land you are giving me? What then?" Joe looked him hard in the eye. "You think the law is hard on you? You ain't seen nothing if you renege on my offer." Caleb knew Joe meant what he said. "Oh I won't, sir. I will make you and Mrs. Mabel proud." "See that you do," said Joe. "Now that we've gotten that discussion over with, let's get out to the barn. I bet those old heifers are just about to bust this morning. We liable to get three or four gallons of milk this morning." Caleb jumped up and threw on the old coat that Joe had given him. He turned around and looked at Joe and said, "Well, what you waiting on?"

# CHAPTER 23

Sal started singing "Christmas time's a coming" the very first week of December. The snow that had fallen over Thanksgiving had put her in the Christmas spirit. John had joined her. He would intermittingly sing a while and then whistle a while. Little John was fascinated by the fact that his grandpa could pucker his lips together and make music. "Papa, help me do that," Little John would say. John would pucker up and show him how to hold his tongue, but the poor little fellow just could barely get a sound out. If anybody could whistle, it was Susie. She could pucker those lips and whistle dixie. Her Papa often remarked that a whistling woman and a crowing hen are neither fit for God nor men. "What you mean by that, Papa?" she would say. "Aw, nothing sweetheart. Nothing to worry your pretty little head with. You just keep right on whistling. I sure get a kick out of hearing you."

The whole family was getting excited for the coming for Christmas. The snow has just heightened their excitement. Martha Rae could hear them late at night after they had gone to bed, discussing what they would like to get for Christmas. Little John always said he wanted one of those trucks like he had seen down at Ella's mercantile. It had to be one of the red ones, though. He always ended his wish with "if it ain't red, I'll take a green one." Susie had her heart set on a baby doll. She already had named it "Betsy" and would often pretend that her baby was down at Sal's, waiting on her to come get her. The little ones were the most excited. The others knew most likely it would be a hard Christmas for presents. Martha Rae had been trying to take in extra ironing and chores to make sure each child got a little something. But most of her mountain neighbors were just like her, they also had children to try to make a Christmas for and they could not afford to hire someone to do the work they could do themselves.

Laymon and CJ had worked tirelessly over the last few months, trying to get enough wood cut to sustain both their home and both sets of grandparents. Every evening, they would come in from cutting wood and sit for hours pulling out the splinters from their hands. Their hands were rough and calloused. It looked hard to see how a splinter no bigger than a sewing needle could penetrate those callouses. But somehow, they did and these were often the worse to get out and made their hand sore. So sore that Martha Rae often soaked a rag in lamp oil and wrapped their hands at night to relieve the pain. She had seen some gloves down at the mercantile, and worked out enough with Ella to purchase two pair. She was tempted to give them to her sons now, but they would have to wait a little longer. She wanted all to have a gift to open on Christmas morning. All the rest of her girls were going to receive one of those lovely shawls that she and her mama were making down at her house. Every time they needed to go out, they would grab her shawl just to wrap up in to go a short distance. Most of the time, just to gather eggs or visit their Grandma Sal. Martha Rae and Sal had been working on these shawls since early September. The biggest problem was getting the cloth. All the shawls were made out of feed sacks that John bought his animal feed in. They couldn't afford to buy enough feed at one time to make all the shawls, so they patiently would wait until every dab of feed was taken out of a sack before they would wash and iron the prettiest material they had ever seen. Most was colored up with all sorts of flowers and crazy print. Sal estimated it would take at least two sacks apiece to make the shawls. She and Martha Rae had to work a lot at night, so the girls would not see what they were making. Every shawl that was finished always made Sal say "I do believe this is the prettiest one yet," until the next one was made, and she would then say the same thing again. Now, they were working on the last shawl. She laid all four across her bed and asked Martha, "Which one do you like best?" I love them all mama said Martha Rae, each and every one of them. We have stitched every one with love. I think the girls will go crazy over them, probably trading depending on what color dress they would be wearing. So really, they will all have four to choose from." Sal picked them up and hugged each shawl, "I think this is our best work yet. Maybe after Christmas, we can make some and see if Ella could sell them in her store. What do you think, girl?" Martha Rae had not said anything, but that very thought had crossed her mind many days ago. "Yes, Mama," she said. "You have got an idea going there."

It was getting on about a week to Christmas. Martha Rae had gotten up early to go down to Ella and Sid's mercantile to pay on Little John's red truck and Susie's baby doll. Ella had been so good to let her iron out the money to pay for these two store-bought gifts. She had even offered to just give her these presents, but Martha Rae would not hear of it. "No, ma'am," said Martha Rae. "If I can't pay or work it out with you, I'll just think of something else to give them." Ella always admired the pride that Martha Rae showed even in trying to provide for her family. She also knew that all the mountain folk had a great respect for Martha Rae, too. She could have easily given up after what had taken place this year, but she hadn't. She never wavered in her faith in God either. She had reached out to each family on the mountain with condolences and offering to help if she could. Her witness for the Lord carried a lot of weight to all her mountain neighbors. None lashed out at her or made her feel ashamed. Most never believed Caleb had anything to do with it, either. "If only we could prove it," said Martha Rae. But as far as she knew, she couldn't find any evidence to help clear his name. "In time," she said. "In time, the Lord will clear it for him."

Martha Rae had gotten to the mercantile early this morning. There was just enough snow left from Thanksgiving that had made traveling by any means treacherous. But she had walked this path so many times in sunshine rain and snow that she felt like she had it etched in her mind. She could see Violet and Ella talking through the frosty window. In some ways, it made her a little jealous of the relationship Violet and Ella shared, the little bit of gossip that each customer shared, or the latest fashion, or discussing the new baby's name. Martha Rae stepped up on the steps to the mercantile and began to stomp the frozen snow off her shoes. She was not about to carry a mess like that into this store. Violet looked up and saw her mama. She gave her a big smile that reminded Martha Rae of Caleb when he smiled. Violet quickly ran and opened the door and handed Martha Rae a broom. "Sweep it off your shoes, Mama, and come in out of the cold." She did just as her daughter instructed and entered into the warmth of the mercantile. "My goodness," she told Ella. "You have really got it toasty in here this morning. But I must admit, it sure feels good." Ella stood to come around from behind the counter, and Martha Rae could see her little baby was growing. She had already started wearing maternity clothes. "How's the new mama-to-be doing this morning?" as she hugged Ella. "Well, I have been a little nauseous but it's not as bad as it has been," said Ella. "I'll be alright in a few months." "For sure, you will be," said Martha Rae. "What can we do for you this fine day?" said Ella. "Oh," said Martha. "I am coming to make the last payment on Little John's red truck and Susie's baby doll. Can you hold it down here until Christmas Eve?" said Martha Rae. "Of course, I can," said Ella. "Tell me, what are you getting the other children?" Martha Rae looked at Violet and said, "A pretty piece of … coal." "Mama," said Violet. "You are telling me a fib." Martha Rae only laughed and said, "Do you think?" "Come," said Ella. "Let me show you what Sid has gone and bought." Martha Rae couldn't imagine. Maybe something for the baby? Ella grabbed her sweater and said, "It's outside." Martha Rae gave her one of those looks that said "Outside?"

Ella and Martha Rae walked around to the back of the mercantile to the barn. "Oh, did you get some new horses?" said Martha Rae. "Well, sort of," said Ella. She opened the barn door and there sat a buggy like Martha Rae had seen in one of the newspapers her daddy had brought home one day. "Wow! What exactly do you call this?" said Martha Rae. "Well, I call it a horseless carriage. But the real name is a 1928 Model A car made by Mr. Henry Ford. Is it really horseless?" said Martha Rae. "Well, they claim the horse power is in the motor. Do you want to take a ride?" said Ella. "Can we?" said Martha Rae. "Do you know how to operate this contraption?" "Yes, Sid has been giving me some driving lessons. Violet rides with me and helps keep me out of the ditches. It really is quite fun." "Well," said Martha Rae hesitantly. "Where do you want me to ride?" Ella began to show her how to get into the newfangled buggy. "Here," she said. "Open this door." "A door," said Martha. "You mean to tell me, this thing has a door?" Martha Rae gently opened the door to the horseless carriage and slid across the very comfortable seat. Never had she seen something so extravagant in her life. *Sid had gone all out for this,* she thought. Ella slid behind the big wheel that she referred to as the steering wheel. Martha Rae watched as Ella went through what looked like a complicated process just to get the car started. Ella finally pulled the left lever all the way down and the car began to move. Violet let out a cheer, and Martha Rae was holding on for dear life. Never had she ridden in one of these buggies before. She had seen them in newspapers, but never thought in a million years she would ever get to take a ride in one. "Let go," said Ella to Martha Rae. "And enjoy the ride. It took me several times before I ever got the hang of it. Violet just watched Sid a few times and she's a pro." "What?" said Martha Rae, as she looked at Violet. "You are too young to be trying to drive." About that time, Ella ran right through a big mudhole and splashed mud everywhere. The windshield was covered, and all of a sudden, here comes two sticks from the top of the window swishing back and forth and cleaned off all the mud. "I can't believe my eyes," said Martha Rae. "No, sir. I can't believe my eyes. I can't wait to get back home and tell everyone I have been riding in a real horseless carriage." Ella rode her over to the county line and they began to turn around. Just as she was fixing to pull out and go home, Martha Rae caught a glimpse of a man that looked like Caleb. "Stop," said Martha Rae, as she held up her hand. When she looked in the direction of where she seen the man that resembled Caleb, he was gone. "What's the matter?" said Violet. "You look as if you've seen someone you knew." "Well," said Martha. "I thought I did, but it must have been a mistake. Let's go, Ella," said Martha Rae. "Tell me some more about this wonderful buggy." Ella laughed and said, "Do you want to drive?" Martha Rae quickly replied, "You did want to get home in one piece today, didn't you? You don't want me driving and I will end this sentence with yet." She finally relaxed and sat back in the seat. "Drive my troubles away, Ella," said Martha Rae. "I really believe I could ride all day long in one of these."

Martha Rae let her mind wander back to the man she spotted today. It had looked just like Caleb Moses. But on second thought, it couldn't have been him. That man was not hiding. He was openly walking through the small town. *Oh well,* she thought. *I have heard everyone has a double.*

Caleb peeped out from behind the old abandoned building's half-opened door. *What was Martha Rae doing riding around in a car?* he thought. He thought that the young girl was Violet. It sure did favor her. And if he was right, Ella Patterson was driving. He had spotted her about the same time she had spotted him. The very image of her made his heart pound. He did not realize how much he had missed his sweet wife and children, and seeing them today just made him that much more homesick. *Just a few more days,* he thought. *A week or two at best and I'll get to make me a trip up in that mountain. I may not get to speak or embrace my family right now, but after Christmas, I'll turn myself in to the proper authorities. Only two ways it can go, they will either send me to the pen or I'll go free. And if I cannot win back my beloved Martha Rae, it doesn't really matter anyway,* thought Caleb.

Ella, Martha, and Violet pulled in front of the old barn. "We can just leave it here. I think Sid has some errands to run later and he can put it up when he gets back." Martha Rae followed Ella back into the mercantile and finished paying her for the little red truck and Susie's baby doll. Ella stopped her before she started back up the mountain. "Here, Martha, take this basket of canned goods with you. I have put some of those delicious peaches and some more canned goods in there. Send Corry and Pap a few of those apples. She can make all sorts of things with them." Martha started to shake her finger at Ella, "You are spoiling us, Ella. What on earth would all of us up in that mountain do without you extending a bit of charity every time I come down? Ella said, "You take that home. The good Lord blesses me every day. Seems like the more I give away the more I have. So don't even try to rob me of my blessings." Martha hugged her good friend Ella and her daughter Violet. "Now don't either one of you forget where I live." Violet kissed her mama on the cheek and said, "How could anyone forget the best place on earth? And where would that be little girl?" said Martha Rae. "Why, right up on the top of Marley Knott's Mountain," said Violet. "Let me get out of here before you make me cry," said Martha Rae. And with that, she took her basket of goodies and headed home. *What a good day it has been,* thought Martha. *I can hardly wait to tell Daddy and the boys I rode in a real car today. Won't they be jealous! I hope so.* She laughed and up through the mountain she went.

# CHAPTER 24

Caleb had memorized nearly every coin he owned. He had never in his life had any money that he could honestly say was his. But every coin that fell out of the old odd sock that he kept them in was his. It made him feel more of a man to know he had a little money. Today, he and Mrs. Mabel were going to count and see how much exactly he had. He had a figure in his head but felt like it was probably wrong. So just to be sure, he had asked Mrs. Mabel to help him. "After I get my kitchen cleaned up this morning, Caleb, we will count out your money," said Mrs. Mabel.

He was just about to put his money back into his old sock when he heard her coming up the steps. Those little heels she wore would make a very distinct sound. He could always tell when she was coming by the little tippy tip sound her shoes made. "Today is the big day. I see you have your money laid out on your bed." She slowly sat down and separated the quarters, dimes, and nickels, and what few pennies he had. "OK, Caleb," said Mabel. "I am going to teach you how to count for yourself. That way, you can keep up with how much you earn. That way, when you start to run your own farm, you won't get cheated. How does that sound?" said Mabel. Caleb just sat there with his head hung down. "How do you know I will get to run a farm, Mrs. Mabel? What if I get locked up?" "Now, Caleb," said Mabel. "Joe and I would have never entrusted you with this much responsibility had we not sought the Lord for the direction we needed to take. We feel the Lord had given us a go on this, and we are trusting him to guide us and exonerate you when we go to court. He has never failed us and ain't about to start now." "I sure hope you are right," said Caleb. "Hope," said Mabel. "It's not a hope so. It's a know so. OK, now pay attention," said Mabel. The big round one is a quarter and it is worth twenty-five cents. We don't see many of those, so it might be best if you hang on to it for a while." Caleb was listening and studying everything Mabel was telling him. "Now, the next silver coin is a nickel and it is worth five cents, and the smallest is the dime worth ten cents." She jumbled up the coins and looked at Caleb and said, "Now you tell me how much each coin is worth." Caleb looked at the small pile of money and picked up the one and only quarter he had. "This one is worth twenty-five cents," said Caleb. "Right, my boy. You are catching on. Now what is this small silver one worth?" said Mabel. "Hmm, let me think," said Caleb. "Is it ten cents?" "Why yes, it is. You are a very smart young man." Caleb had a sheepish grin on his face. He already knew the value of each coin, but he didn't want to hurt Mrs. Mabel's feelings, so he just went along with her. "This next size coin is a nickel. Is that right, Mrs. Mabel?" "You are a fast learner, Caleb. You are going to make a fine and shrewd businessman. I can feel it in my bones. Now, let's count." She pulled a number 2 pencil and began to scribble out how much money Caleb had accumulated. She would bite her bottom lip and erase some of her adding until she was finally confident she was right herself. "I do believe you have one dollar and fifty-eight cents." Caleb had added the same amount, but could not believe he had earned that much money. He had never had so much money in his entire life. "OK," said Mabel. "What are you going to do with all your riches? New shoes or a fancy new hat, maybe?" "Oh no," said Caleb. "I am going to get Christmas presents with every dime of this. Since I cannot go to town to shop, will you do my shopping for me?" Mabel began to tear up. "I would be honored, my precious boy. Do you have anything special in mind?" Caleb instructed her to buy each of his children a gift. He gave her their ages and told her to use her own judgment. "Now, I have a very special gift I need for you to make for my wife, if possible." "Me, make?" said Mabel. "What on earth could I make for a special lady like your wife?" "Do you think you could get your hands on some corn husks?" "Corn husk, Caleb? Are you crazy? But yes, I can get some corn husk," said Mabel. Caleb began to tell her of the perfect present for Martha Rae. "I love it," said Mabel. "I just love it. It will be beautiful. I guarantee it," said Mabel. "If there is any money left, please get you and Joe something you would like from me. Is that OK?" said Caleb. Mabel had the look of a proud mama. But in this case, he was not her son by blood. But he sure was in her heart. She envied his real mother and hoped to meet her one day and tell her what a fine young son she had. But until then, she had some shopping to do. She knew exactly where she would shop. The prices were reasonable and she really liked the lady they called Ella who ran the place. Her work was done and there was nothing stopping her from going there today.

"Caleb, hitch up the carriage for me. I think I will get this task done today." Caleb shot out of his bedroom and ran out to the barn. "Come on, Ruthie," said Caleb to the old broodmare. "You have some Christmas to go get." The old mare just snickered and stood as still as could be for Caleb to hitch her up to the buggy. Caleb had seen Mabel coming and walked Ruthie out to meet her. Mabel grabbed Caleb's hand and he lifted her up into the buggy. She clicked her tongue and off she went. Caleb watched her go completely out of sight. He had never had the feeling that giving gives. He thought to himself, *I believe giving makes me happier than getting. I really don't quite understand why that is, but that's the way my heart feels today.*

Martha Rae had rambled the mountain over to get some ivy to hang across her fireplace. She had been down around Sutphin's Bottom and had Laymon and CJ to climb a tree or two for some mistletoe. "Now you two boys be careful. I don't want any broken limbs for Christmas." CJ just laughed. He climbed trees a lot and was about the best sure-footed young lad around. But on the other hand, Laymon had many mountain talents but skinning a tree was not one of them. CJ finally told him to stand under the tree and he would drop him some mistletoe down. Martha Rae agreed that would be the best thing to do. So before long, CJ had enough mistletoe for the whole mountain to hang over their sweethearts. "Mama, what on earth are you going to do with all this mistletoe?" asked Laymon. "Well, I haven't no money so I thought I would give every family on Marley Knott's Mountain some for Christmas. You know, to get a little Christmas spirit going." CJ just had to ask, "Well, Mama, who are you going to kiss?" "Oh hush up, CJ. You know I haven't anyone other than all my dear precious children, and I think I need to get started now." She was close enough to Laymon to grab him and give him a big smack on his cheek. "Aw, Mama. I am too big to be kissed by my mama." "Oh you think so?" said Martha Rae. "Well, here's an extra one just in case that little brown-headed girl by the name of Jewel won't kiss you." "Now then you hush Mama! Who told you anything about Jewel?" "None of your business. Maybe a little bird," said Martha Rae. "Yea, I bet a little bird named Ella told you," said Laymon. "You never know," said Martha Rae. "You never know. Come on, boys, let's get on up the mountain so we can do some decorating ourselves for Christmas."

By the time all her gang got home, it was a regular brawl. Lilly was the tallest girl, so she thought she should be the one to place the star on top of the tree that their papa John had cut for them. The rest of the children were so excited, they had what few decorations Martha had managed to make. And of course, they all wanted to put them on the tree at the same time. Finally, Martha Rae started clapping her hands. All the children looked around with a stunned look on their faces. "Hey," said Martha. "Before we get all giddy in the Christmas spirit, let's stop and reflect on why we celebrate this joyous season to begin with. OK, Lilly, you go first. Tell me why you think we celebrate, and when you are through, place your star on the tree." Lilly was without words. "Uh. Let's see," said Lilly. "OK, I have it. It's Jesus's birthday and that's the reason. Right, Mama?" "OK, very good," said Martha Rae. Lilly was very proud that she was the one who would get to place the Christmas star on their tree this year. In years past, one of the boys would get the honor of hanging it. But Martha Rae had decided since Lilly had grown so much over the past year, she thought she was tall enough now to do the honors. "Now, y'all step back," said Lilly. "And let me see exactly which angle this star needs to be hung." "Come on, Lilly," said CJ. "You are taking up too much time. We want our turn." "Hush your mouth, CJ. I see the perfect spot." Lilly hung the little paper ornament as if she were hanging the most expensive ornament in the world. "Oh Mama," said Lilly. "Isn't that beautiful?" "Now, Laymon. You are next. Tell us what you think is the reason we celebrate this joyous holiday." "Because we are family," said Laymon. "Yes, son. That's a reason, too. Now where are you going to place your ornament?" "Well," said Laymon. "I found a deer antler in the woods this spring and I have saved it all year to hang on our tree. Is it OK, Mama?" "I think it would just make our tree even prettier," said Martha Rae. Just like any boy, Laymon just reached up and hung the antler, never even thinking where he should hang it. "I think that is a good spot for it. What y'all think?" said Laymon. Little John piped up and said, "Looks real pretty to me, Laymon." "Angela, now you tell me what you think we celebrate for." Martha Rae knew Angela would give her a very deep answer. She loved the Lord and studied her Bible every day. "Well, Mama," said Angela. "God knew we were in need of a savior, so he gave us the best gift he had and it was his son Jesus. Jesus was born poor just like us. But he loved the whole world and even died for us so we wouldn't have to go to Hell." Martha Rae had tears streaming down her face. "Yes, my sweet girl. You are exactly right. Alright then," said Martha Rae. "Since Angela gave us such a spiritual answer, let's the rest of us think on this as we finish decorating the Christmas tree."

The children quit fussing and arguing over who was going to be first, and actually were very gracious to each other the rest of the evening. After the tree was complete, Martha stood back and looked at the wonderfully decorated tree. It was perfect. Every little ornament had been placed by the loving hands of her children. *Oh my,* she thought to herself. *This fills my heart to the running over point.* She lifted her heart in her hands up to God and began to give him thanks for the sweet children he had given her to raise. Angela followed after her mother. Her small hands were lifted up to heaven and praising God for a godly mother who stood by her family, never faltering. Sometimes stumbling under the heavy load she carried, but always putting her children first and herself last. Martha Rae felt the hands of all her children hugging her. "What a blessing! What a blessing!" she shouted. She opened her arms and embraced every one of her babies. "Thank you, Lord, for these precious children."

# CHAPTER 25

Christmas Eve had finally arrived. There was a chill in the air, as Martha Rae was getting a fire going in her old wood cook stove. It was especially hard to get the fire going this morning for some reason. It just seemed like it wanted to go out. *I'll get Laymon up there to see if our chimney needs a little cleaning,* thought Martha Rae. Her daddy had cleaned everything out good just a few weeks ago, and she hadn't had any trouble until this morning. *Lord,* she thought. *Seems like trouble follows me. Hide me, Lord, hide me good.* "Get up, young 'uns," said Martha Rae. "We will go down to Grandma Sal's for breakfast. I can't seem to get my fire going this morning. After breakfast, you boys get up on the house and see if there is anything stopping up our chimney."

Sal looked out her kitchen window and saw Martha Rae and her brood coming down the hill. "John" said Sal, "better go cut a little more ham." I see we are going to have company for breakfast." John just smiled. He loved for his daughter and grandkids to come see him for whatever reason. He left the comfort of his own rocking chair and fire, and swung open the door. "Come on in, young 'uns," said Papa John. "Merry Christmas." Little John twisted his little mouth and said, "Papa, it ain't Christmas yet, is it?" Papa John got a big laugh out of that, "Well no it's not but we call this day Christmas Eve, the day before Christmas." "So you mean tomorrow is Christmas?" said Little John. "Yep, it sure is. Ole Santa comes tonight." "Really?" said Little John. "Yes, really," said Papa John. "Get in here before you freeze to death." John could see the aggravation on Martha Rae. It stood out like a sore thumb. "What's the matter, Sis?" said her daddy. "Oh, not much. Just our chimney is not drawing like it's supposed to. I wanted everything to be perfect today for my children." "Oh, honey," said John. "Don't let the little stuff fret you. Me and the boys will check things out for you after breakfast. Now help your mama get the rest of breakfast going and I'll step out and cut some more ham." John gently hugged his oldest daughter. He loved both his girls, but Martha Rae had a special spot in his heart. He didn't know if it was because of all the hardships she had faced so early in her life or what, but his heart always went out to her. "Come on, Susie," said her Papa. "Let me and you go cut us some ham for breakfast. I'd like to hear you whistle me a Christmas tune or two." "Oh, for sure," said Susie. "I have been practicing a lot here lately, and I'll bet you will be surprised at what all I can whistle." She placed her hand in her Papa's big hand and said, "Well, let's go."

Christmas was looking good this year in spite of all that this family had endured. God had been more than gracious to them. John felt the closeness of the Lord as he stepped out on his front porch. He stopped and took a big deep breath of that good old mountain air. "You smell that, Susie?" Susie sniffed and said, "All I smell is an oven full of biscuits." "Naw," said John. "I smell snow. And if my snout is correct, we will have snow before noon. Let's hurry and get back. We don't want to miss that good breakfast Sal is cooking up for us this morning."

Caleb had all his presents wrapped for his children and his wife. He had looked over all the gifts that Mabel had purchased for him. *Wow*, he thought. "Never thought I'd be able to give such fine of gifts as these," said Caleb. She had purchased Laymon and CJ pocket knives. Caleb knew every boy needed a pocket knife, especially those who lived in the woods. Angela and Lilly got some really fragrant toilet water. Caleb had taken the tops off to smell and thought it smells good to be toilet water. He never thought toilet water would smell this good. *Wonder what toilet this came out of,* he thought. Violet had a drawing pad and pencils, and Susie and Little John had some small toys. There had been enough money left to purchase an orange and small bag of candy for each child. Mabel had helped Caleb work on Martha Rae's gift. "I do declare, boy," said Mabel. "I think we did a pretty good job. It has turned out better than I thought it would. At first, I thought you were crazy but I am beginning to see something take shape here." They had worked diligently, and now everything was wrapped and ready to be taken to Marley Knott's Mountain.

Caleb pushed his hair under his cap and let out a blow of "it's now or never." He did not know how this would go over with Martha Rae, but he had to start somewhere. Sometime after the first of the year, he, Joe and Mabel would take a trip to the Sherriff's office and he would turn himself in. What would happen after that, he did not have a clue. Joe and Mabel had more faith than he ever even thought about. All he could do is tell the truth and let God handle the rest. It would take a couple of hours' journey for him to get up to Martha Rae's, so he figured he had better get started if he was to get there before morning. Caleb gathered all gifts, and ever so gently placed them in the burlap sack Mabel had given him to use. She had made him a scarf for Christmas, and Joe had gotten him gloves. "Here, Caleb," said Joe. "You will need these this winter." Caleb had ever been given little to nothing for Christmas from his folks. He did not know how to accept these good gifts. Caleb said, "Y'all giving me way too much. You already have given me a place to come out of the weather and food. I couldn't ask for no more." "Now listen here. Mabel has worked for months on that scarf and those gloves were some that I hadn't used. Now don't hurt our feelings by not accepting our gifts. It's Christmas, Caleb. God gave us his son. If we don't accept this free gift he has given us, it's like we are rejecting God. Do you see what I mean?" Caleb nodded yes, he hugged these two fine people who had stood by him and was going to help him get on his feet. "I love you, Joe and Mabel. Don't ever forget that." Joe patted him across his back and said, "Now you be careful, boy, you hear." Caleb assured him he would. And with his burlap sack full of Christmas, he started off.

Papa John and CJ had found what was stopping up their chimney after breakfast that morning, and Laymon had a good hot fire going by the evening. "Son," said Martha Rae. "You are almost as good as your mama at building a fire." "Sit down, Mama. You have been going since daylight," said Laymon. "I know," said Martha Rae. "It's just, I have been thinking about your daddy all day long. Just wondering how his Christmas was going to be. Listen, Angela, you get everyone in bed I think I might walk down the mountain to my prayer rock and talk to my Jesus." Angela quickly ran and got her mama her shawl and an extra blanket to wrap around her shoulders. "Please, Mama," said Angela. "Don't stay too long. It's getting cold and I worry about you when you are down there at night." "Don't be silly, girl. And besides, I'm not afraid. Do you not know Jesus sends a big angel with me everywhere I go?" Angela started to say something else, but Martha Rae interrupted her and said, "Y'all better get ready for bed." She wrapped up in her cloaks, and down through Marley Knott's Mountain she went.

She immediately spotted her prayer rock. *Law,* she thought. *My high tower of refuge.* She stepped over several fallen trees and finally reached that spot that she loved so dearly. She let out a big sigh and began to speak to her Lord. She folded her small hands and began to pray. "Lord, you have been so good to me and my family this past year. I'll admit, though, it's been tough. But we have come through with your help. Tonight, Lord, I am standing in the gap for my husband who I still love as good as the first day I met him. Take care of Caleb. Lead him to truth, Lord, please. I want him to be with his family soon. Merry Christmas, my sweet Jesus. I could never have made it without you." She sat there and began to hum a Christmas hymn. *Silent Night* came flooding through her soul. *Holy night, yes,* she thought. *It is most definitely holy.* All is calm, all is bright. The moon was still shining a little bit, but the clouds had started moving in. *I'd better think about getting home and putting Christmas under my tree.*

Caleb had walked for two hours, he guessed. The familiar path up the mountain made him more homesick. He turned and started climbing up Marley Knott's Mountain. He got as far as Marley Knott's Cliff and stopped to get him a good drink of that mountain water. *Gosh,* he thought. *This tastes so good.* He cupped his hands again and drank some more. *I guess I had better drink my fill. I may not get another drink for a long time.* At last, he saw his little house that he had shared with Martha Rae. He could see through the window that Martha Rae had fixed a beautiful tree for the children this year. *Wonder where she's at,* he thought. He stepped up on the porch and left the burlap sack right in the doorway, so that they for sure would not miss it. *I'd better get out of here before I am found out.* Caleb turned and darted down through the mountain. *Wonder how Ole Pap and my mama are doing. I would love to sneak up there but I had better not,* he thought. The tears had filled his eyes. What a split second bad decision had cost him! He should have never run. It made him look guilty even though he wasn't. Finally, he had gotten about halfway down when he heard someone speak his name. "Hold it right there, Caleb Moses." Caleb turned around to face a whole load of law. He immediately lifted his hands in the air and told them, "Hey, I am not armed. I will go peacefully." "We figured you might come up in this mountain to see your family for Christmas. I guess our theory was correct. Now let's go and don't try to run or we will shoot you dead," said the High Sheriff.

Martha Rae could not believe what she just saw. She had just witnessed the arrest of her estranged husband. *I must get home,* thought Martha Rae. *Daddy. Yes, Daddy is the one I need to talk to.* She was running as hard as her feet would carry her. The recent snow had brought down a lot of tree limbs that blocked her from running as fast. She bounced up on her parents' porch and began to pound the door with her fist. "Daddy, get up! I need you." John jumped from his bed, with Sal right on his heels. "What's the matter, baby?" said her daddy. By that time, she had fallen to knees, crying. "Daddy, oh Daddy! They have just caught Caleb coming out of the mountain."

John Jenkins knew that this would probably happen. What he didn't know was his dear daughter would be a witness to it. "Now calm down, Martha," said her daddy. "Martha Rae, you knew this would happen one day. I just hate it happened on Christmas. And by the way, what in tarnation were you doing down in the middle of this mountain on Christmas Eve?" John could see the anguish in his daughter's face and didn't want to push her right now. "It don't make no never matter now. you can't un-ring the bell. Now listen," said John. "You get yourself up to your house for the time being. You still have Christmas to celebrate for your young 'uns. After the holidays, we will go to the magistrate's office and talk to them." That's all Martha Rae needed—the consoling voice of her daddy. He could fix anything, but she wasn't sure he could fix this. "Sal, get me my coat and I will walk Martha Rae up the hill to her home." Sal ran as quickly as she could. His old work coat was the closest. He kept it hung on a nail in the wood room. She grabbed it and ran back to John. "Here, honey. Are you coming back down here tonight?" "I don't know. I may stay the night up there in case anybody from the sheriff's office drops by," said John. Sal gave him one of those looks that meant "you ain't going nowhere without me." He knew that look well. "OK," he said. "Come on. We will all stay the night together." Sal grabbed her shawl, and all three headed up the hill to Martha Rae's little house.

"Look, Daddy," said Martha Rae. "What's that on my front porch?" John squinted up his eyes to get a more clear view. "Looks like an old burlap sack to me. But wonder what's inside? Sal, you and Martha Rae get on inside. I'll check this out." John sat down on the side of the porch and reached into the sack, not knowing what he might pull out. The thing was full of a lot of different shapes. He poured it out on the porch and there was all sorts of Christmas gifts. "So that's what that rascal was doing up here." He couldn't help but chuckle at the very sight. He couldn't imagine ole Caleb doing anything such as this. *But reckon where he got the money? I sure hope these are not stolen goods,* thought John. Martha and Sal were watching out the window and saw all the surprises laying out on the porch. Martha Rae knew exactly where these had come from and it wasn't Santa Claus. It was Santa Caleb. "Martha Rae, come out here," said her daddy. "You take these and place them under your tree. They have all their names on their packages. Caleb tried to do good for once and we ain't going to ruin it for his children." "If he stole these, I'll pay for them myself." said her daddy. "My goodness daddy you ain't got no money" exclaimed Martha Rae. John Jenkins always had something on hand he could barter in the case of an emergency. He looked at Sal and Martha and said" I may not have much money, but I do have something better than money, country ham. I'll just sell a couple and pay for these. Now hush, I don't want to hear any more about this."

Martha Rae carried the ole burlap sack into her house and pulled each present out. He had each one wrapped up with each child's name on it. "I'll say this, he did a fine job wrapping his gifts," said Martha Rae. She placed them toward the back of the tree so each child would have to dig to find it. "I wonder what that man of mine bought me," said Martha Rae under her breath. At last, she pulled out her package. "No peeking, sweetheart," said her mama, "It's still not officially Christmas for a few more hours. You need to get in your bed. We all have a big day tomorrow. We still are doing a big Christmas meal and I will need your help doing that. Come on, John. There ain't no law going to come back out in the dead of night on Christmas Eve. They probably have children to make Christmas for, too. Let's head back down to our shanty and sleep, because we will all need a good night's rest for tomorrow." Martha Rae hugged and kissed her mama and her daddy. "I could never make it without you two. You just don't know how much I love you." John repeated the words back to his daughter, and off down the pig path home, he and Sal went, locked arm in arm with a love that could not be shaken.

CHAPTER *26*

"Christmas Day on Marley Knott's Mountain turned out to be one that will be talked about for a long time," proclaimed John Jenkins. Well, at least for him and his family anyway. Just a couple of pieces to the puzzle was missing—that being Edna Sue and Caleb. He understood that Edna could not get up here for this Christmas and he had resolved that in his heart, but Caleb, he would sit in jail this Christmas. John had pondered over Caleb most of the night. He prayed earnestly for his son-in-law. Even though he had caused him and his family hardship, he couldn't help but have compassion for him. Pap and Corry were coming down for Christmas dinner today, and he dreaded telling them the news that Caleb had been caught in the mountain last night and was in jail for no telling how long if he was found guilty of this horrendous crime. But he had to shake all this bad news off him and make a merry Christmas for his family. Sal, as usual, was cooking up a storm. John had been trying to tell her for days on end, "Now, Sal, you can't invite the whole mountain up here to eat. I can't feed but so many." She would just smile and flirt a little and in her little girl voice say, "Now, John, you know better than that." "Yes, Sally, I do know you and that's what I'm afraid of." But he knew in his heart this was what made Sal the most happy on Christmas, cooking and feeding those neighbors who had not fared as well as they had in last year. They always seemed to have enough. The good Lord just seemed to stretch what they had, so he knew he might as well hush because she won this battle years ago.

Martha Rae and her children had been up for hours. The children had opened all their gifts, except the ones Caleb had brought.

They didn't even know he'd been up in the mountain, much less in jail now. The girls were so excited when they saw the shawls that she and Sal had made for them. Sal had also made each girl a new blouse. Angela and Lilly were trying on each other's outfits, trying to decide what to wear today. Sid and Ella had brought Violet home up in the night with a buggy full of presents for Martha Rae and her family. Ella had given each child a book. "Come springtime, we are going to learn to read." "Come on, Ella," said Martha Rae. "You shouldn't have done all this." Ella just smiled and said, "Hey, it's Christmas. I am in the giving spirit." The boys were oh so proud of their gloves that their mama had bought for them. "I'll bet there ain't another man in this mountain with gloves as fine as these," said Laymon. CJ just sat there, rubbing his hands over his new gloves. "Yep, mighty fine indeed." Susie was rocking her new baby doll. She had gotten one of Martha Rae's sugar sacks and wrapped her baby in it. Martha Rae watched her love and cuddle her little doll just as if it were a real baby. *Yes,* she thought. *She'll be the one to bring me a load of grandchildren,* thought Martha Rae. Little John had his little red truck driving over the mountain along the back of Martha Rae's settee.

"Hey, kids," said Martha Rae. "Is that all the presents? Dig toward the back of the tree. I think there is a few more packages for you all." Little John was just like a squirrel. He dove under the tree and began to pull out some more packages. "I can't read these names," said Little John. Violet piped up, "Hand them to me, Little John. I can read and pass them out." Violet read each child's name and handed them their package. "Who sent us these?" said Laymon. Martha Rae knew these children needed to hear the truth, and she was not going to lie to them now. "Your daddy brought these and left them on our porch last night." "I don't want nothing from him, he ain't my daddy. He had caused us a lot of shame," said Laymon. Martha Rae could feel her heart pounding. She slowly stood to her feet and looked at each child. "Now, you listen here," said Martha Rae. "He is always going to be your daddy, like it or not. Maybe we haven't given him a chance to explain his side of the story." "We already know his side of the story," said Lilly. "He helped poison and kill a lot of good people up here in this mountain." "Well," said

Martha Rae. "How do you know?" She looked at each child, and tried to read the answer that was written in their mind. Laymon spoke first, "That's what all the mountain folk are saying." "Really?" said Martha Rae. "When did you speak to all these folks on this mountain, Laymon?" Laymon stuttered and tried to come up with a good answer, but Martha Rae knew he hadn't spoken to anyone because the people up here did not think he was guilty. "Next," said Martha Rae. Violet took the floor, "Well, why did he run if he wasn't guilty? Tell me that, Mama." Martha Rae knew she was cornered and did not have a reasonable explanation to give back to Violet. "Violet, you have a very good question that I do not have an answer for. The time will come very soon, I expect, when your daddy will be tried in a court of law among his peers and we shall find out why he ran. But until then, we must believe that the good Lord will bring to light the real perpetrator. If you all don't want your gifts, just lay them back under the tree and I will see that he gets them back." Martha Rae looked at each child and not a one was willing to part with this small token of love that they had received from their daddy. "OK then," she said. "I don't want to hear no more bad talk from any of you. Understand?" Each child nodded in agreement. "Now gather some of your gifts, we have a big day down at Grandma Sal's home today. I must help her cook, so you all can show your family what all you got for Christmas."

The girls, of course, wrapped up in their new shawls and blouses, and Laymon and CJ put their new gloves on to get in a little wood for their grandparents. Susie and Little John took their toys, of which they were so proud of. The last present that was left unopened was Martha Rae's. She waited until everyone was gone and sat down at her kitchen table and opened it. Inside was a hair bow exactly like the one she wore when she met Caleb. Her heart could not stand anymore. The water began to run out of her eyes faster than she could wipe them away. *He remembered*, she thought. *He remembered*. She picked up the bow to put it in her hair and found a note. *My dearest Martha Rae, I hope you can reed my rightin', My hart is heave because i miss all of u. Just know I am not guilte, I am fine and goin to turn miself in after Chirstmas. I love u Martha Rae and hope u can fergive me for all mi failures. Love Caleb.*

Martha Rae was numb. Never did she expect to receive a letter from Caleb. All she could think to do was hug his letter. It was all she had of him at the time. All of a sudden, she heard Little John calling her, "Come on, Granny Sal said she needed you." Martha Rae got up and took the letter and placed it inside her Bible for safekeeping. She pinned the blue corn husk bow in her hair, just like she wore it the day she met Caleb. From now on, I will wear this to show this mountain that I believe my husband is innocent. "I'm coming, Little John!" shouted Martha back to her baby boy. "I'll be there in a minute."

Caleb had been arraigned and was already sitting in a jail cell. All he could think of was, how on earth could he ever prove his innocence? He did not have one sprig of information. All he had was one name he could offer that was most likely the real killer, and that name was Conrad Cox. But he knew a name meant nothing if you didn't have any proof. *I am doomed,* he thought. *I must get word to Joe and Mabel and tell them where I am. No doubt they are wondering where I am.* Caleb looked up and immediately saw one of the guards coming toward him. "Hey, you," he said. "Get up! You have someone here to see you." Caleb reached down and laced his old boots up and stood up as fast as he could. *Wonder who in the world is here to see me?* he thought. *I haven't had time to let anyone know I am here.* "Hold out your hands, boy," said the guard. Caleb held out his hands and the guard placed cuffs on his wrist. "Not too tight, please," said Caleb. "Where you are going, this will seem like a picnic." Caleb gave him a foul look, but never answered him in any way. "This way. You in the front." Caleb walked down past all the other prisoners. He had never been in jail, so he just hung his head so he wouldn't have to look them in the face. One old guy taunted him, "You the one that killed all those men up on the mountain?" Caleb never acknowledged him one way or another. The old man said, "You are, ain't you? You need hanging." "Hush up, Toby," said the guard. "I am tired of hearing your mouth today anyway." Caleb pushed open the door, and there stood Joe and Mabel. Caleb could see that Mabel looked like she had been crying. *I have caused a lot of people a lot of grief,* he thought. He stood in front of Joe and said, "I would hug you two, but as you can see, my hands are tied." "Sit down, Caleb," said the guard. "You two sit on the other side of this table. You have exactly fifteen minutes to talk, no more no less." Caleb sat down and asked Joe, "How did you know I was in here?" "Everybody knows, Caleb. This news has spread like wildfire. We got word of it yesterday, Christmas Day. We didn't know you were going to turn yourself in after you took the gifts up to your family. I thought you were going to go with us after New Year's and turn yourself in." "Well, Joe, they caught me just as I was going down the mountain to come to your house. They told me they thought I might try to see my family for Christmas. Looks like they were right. I think Martha Rae might have seen the whole thing take place. I glanced up the mountain just as they were escorting me out and saw what looked like her to me. I have made a mess of things, haven't I, Joe?" Joe just sat there and looked at Caleb, "Well, say something Joe. Anything. I deserve everything you hand me." Finally, Joe began to speak, "Caleb, I have never doubted your innocence, not one time. And I still stand on what I believe. The Lord has spoken to me and Mabel and showed us you will not go to jail. And no matter how bleak it may look now, we still stand on what God has shown us. Hang in there, son. We will see if we can come up with some bail and get you out until the trial. I will stand good for you." Caleb was without words, but he held his heart on his sleeve. Now he was crying. "Joe, Mabel, if this don't go like you think, I just want you two to know I love you with all my heart." "What we want you to do is stop talking defeat, Caleb. Don't want to hear no more of that, you hear?" Caleb shook his head yes, but his heart was not sure. "Time's up," said the guard. Caleb reached for Joe and Mabel the best he could, but the guard pushed him to go ahead of him. "We will be back," said Joe.

# CHAPTER 27

The jail cell that Caleb had been in for about two weeks was getting pretty boring. He had counted every brick for what seemed like a million times. *I will never forget that number: 777. It will be ingrained in my mind forever,* he thought. He could hear some of the other prisoners moving about in their cell. He had made friends with a guy named Moe. He had no idea what he looked like, only the sound of his voice was familiar. "Caleb, you up?" said Moe. "Yes," said Caleb. "I don't hardly sleep little to none. By the way, what you doing up?" said Caleb to Moe. "Well, I just wanted to fill you in on a little news." "Yea," said Caleb. "What kind of news, good or bad?" "Well, I'll let you decide. Seems like they are getting a bit overcrowded here, and they are going to ship a bunch of prisoners off to Richmond in a few. I heard your name come up." "Really?" said Caleb. "I was hoping to get this trial over and done with so I could get my spring planting in." Caleb could hear Moe laughing. "What's so funny, Moe?" said Caleb. "Oh, do you think you are going to get off scot-free?" "Well, yes. I guess I do. I ain't done nothing, anyway." "Well," said Moe, "You better get your testimony down 'cause if you don't, you ain't got a leg to stand on." Caleb felt like someone had just poured hot water on him. "Yea, I guess I see what you are saying. You heard any dates when they might start moving us?" said Caleb. "No," said Moe. "But if I do, I'll let you know. Hush up, now," said Moe. "Here comes old Big Nose. He must have heard us talking." Big Nose came walking up the row of prison cells with his little stick in his hand. He always thought he was a big man when he held that stick. "Who's talking?" said Big Nose. He stopped in front of Moe's cell. "You got something to say, Moe?" Moe just sat there with his head hung down, and never acknowledged Big Nose as even being there. "Speak to me, boy, when I am talking to you." Moe raised his head and looked at Big Nose with a glare that would kill most people. "No, sir," said Moe. "I haven't got anything to say." "That's better," said Big Nose. "Now get quiet. Lights out in five minutes." Moe said nothing more, and Caleb sure wasn't going to say a word but that did not make him stop thinking about what Moe had just told him. *What on earth am I going to do?* thought Caleb. *I can't go to Richmond. I need to stay here. Surely they will try me before too long.* Caleb laid down on his cot but he couldn't sleep anyway, and he began to think. *My sweet Martha Rae and all my young 'uns. If I could do all this over, I would sure do my life different.* All of a sudden, a thought ran through his mind. *Caleb, you can do different. With me, there is always a starting over point.* Caleb sat right up in the middle of that old hard cot. *Where on earth did that thought come from?* "Lord, are you speaking to me? If you are, please tell me what to do and don't allow them to move me from here. Forgive me Lord and help me out of this mess if you will. I promise I will serve you the rest of my days." Peace seemed to come over Caleb like he had never felt before. He lay down on that old hard stinky cot and slept like a baby that night.

The next morning, Big Nose came and ordered Moe to get up and get ready to travel. "Travel?" said Moe. "What are you talking about?" Big Nose gave him a big old grin, showing his front tooth missing and said, "You going down the road, is where you going." Moe spoke up with panic in his voice, "Down the road? What do you mean down the road?" "Just what I said, or should I say Richmond? You ever heard of that place?" He poked Moe in his side and ordered him to move forward. Moe stopped and turned to look at Big Nose, "Anyone else going besides me?" he asked. "Nope. From what I gathered, they had a change of plans at the last minute for some reason. Now hush up and get going." Caleb lay still as a mouse. He didn't want to draw any attention to him. When Moe walked past his cell. He got a little glimpse of his friend. His red head stood out like a sore thumb. He was a short and stocky fellow that reminded Caleb of his Uncle Ellis. He had been accused of robbing a local store a few days before Christmas. *I guess everybody wanted to get a little Christmas for their families,* thought Caleb. *I hope he gets his life straightened out. I must pray for him,* thought Caleb.

Martha Rae had been sitting on her front porch all evening, thinking about Caleb. "Lord," she prayed. "Please let the truth come out. There must be someone that knows the truth and proof of it." Martha Rae knew, if he got sent off to prison it was likely he would be there for life. Her life would not go on without him, because she knew she could never love another man. She had prayed the new year would bring better, but so far it didn't look like that was going to happen. She saw her dear daddy coming up the hill to her house. He sometimes just came and sat and they talked the blues away. "Come on up, Daddy," said Martha Rae. She hollered at Lilly to bring her daddy a chair to sit on. "Which one" said Lilly. Papa John hollered back, "That big old one with the fluffy cushion in it," he answered. "Oh, Papa. You know I can't move that thing. Now be real. Which one?" "Oh, honey," he said. "It doesn't matter. Any one will do." She pulled one of the chairs from the kitchen and he looked at her and said, "Until you are better paid, little girl." "Aw, Papa. You say that all the time." "Well, it's the truth, child." Lilly turned and went back in the house.

Martha Rae was wrapped up in her shawl and an extra quilt for good measure. "Daddy," she said. "You reckon when this winter is going to break?" John Jenkins rubbed his hand through his hair and made a humming sound from his throat. "If I am guessing correctly, I'll wager that we will have an early spring. Watch the animals, Martha. When you see them venturing out, you know springtime is coming soon." "Shhhh," said Martha Rae. "Do you hear what I hear, Daddy?" John Jenkins stood up and pulled his hat down just a little to knock off the glare from the sun. "Well, I'll be," said her daddy. "Who is it?" said Martha Rae. "Two of my favorite people," said John. "Your sister and Sid Patterson. What on earth are those two doing together?" As they got closer, he could see Edna Sue waving a handkerchief at them as if to say "Look, I'm home." Her daddy couldn't stand it any longer. He jumped down off the porch with Martha Rae on his heels and ran to Sid Patterson's wagon. Edna Sue jumped off the wagon like she had been shot. She fell into the arms of her daddy and began to weep. "What's wrong, honey? Tell me." "Nothing's wrong, Daddy. Everything is right," said Edna Sue. "Well, pray, tell me, why are you crying?" said her daddy. "I am getting married," said Edna Sue. John looked at Sid then to Martha Rae, and they all three began to laugh. "That's just like our Edna. Come on, honey. Let's head down and tell Mama," said Martha Rae. "By the way, how many days are you going to get to stay?" "A whole week," said Edna Sue. "I didn't have any more classes for a week and Robert … That is, Robert Meadows, my fiancé, told me to go home and announce to my family that we are wanting to wed. He is coming by the week-end to meet everybody and ask my daddy for my hand in marriage." Martha Rae and Edna Sue took off arm in arm down the hill to tell Sal all the news. It seemed like it had been forever since they had any good news to tell. *This was so refreshing*, thought Martha Rae. "We must plan a wedding," she told Edna Sue. "Mama will want to make your dress, I'm sure of it," said Martha Rae.

John asked Sid, "Won't you get down and come on in? I'm sure Martha Rae had a little coffee brewed. If we go down to my house, we won't get a word in edge-wise for Sal and those girls of mine." With that, Sid gave a chuckle and said, "I understand, John, and if Ella were able to have ridden up here with me, she would have been right down there with them." "By the way," said John. "How is Ella doing?" You could see the pride in Sid's face when he said, "For a lady that is going to birth a baby soon, I think she is doing great." John poured him and Sid piping hot cups of coffee. Sid cleared his throat and spoke, "John, what I really came up here for was to discuss the building of our new church this spring. I just ran into Edna Sue down near Sutphin's Bottom and gave her a ride. John, you know I am not a builder. I said that I would foot the bill for the cost of all the materials that would go into the building of the church, but I couldn't build an outhouse if I had to. I know you are a builder by nature, and I was wanting you to oversee the construction of our church. Do you think you could do that?" John looked Sid square in the eye, "I thought you'd never ask. I would be proud and honored to help construct the Lord's house. I'll get the men from this mountain that I know are gifted in building to help me. When do you want me to get started?" said John. "Well," said Sid. "Is next week to soon? I know the weather is warming and I have been seeing a few buds on the trees, so spring is coming soon I believe." "No, it's not early. Besides, this winter is wearing me out this year. I am itching to get my hands into something." "Then it's settled," said Sid. "I will open an account over at the lumberyard, and whatever you need, just put it on the account and I make good on it." "It's a deal," said John. "I can hardly wait to get started."

You could hear Sal Jenkins shouting all the way up to Martha Rae's house. She had already pulled out some cloth she had saved for Edna Sue's wedding dress should she ever marry.

"Oh, Mama! This is so pretty, where on earth did you get this. Sal had a distant look come across her face, child this is what if left of my wedding dress. My parents house caught fire and this is the first thing I grabbed. I salvaged this much out of it. It had a lot of blacken from the smoke. I trimmed what was good and decided to save it for something. Looks like something came along. I will be proud to wear this said Edna Sue, now don't get me crying, y'all know I can cry on a dime. They sounded like chattering squirrels that had just found a ground covered in nuts. Maybe things were turning around, one thing for sure there is a stopping place somewhere. Sal had heard her grandma say this so many times, especially when they were facing hard times. To everything there is a season, and a time to every purpose under the heaven. Ecclesiastes 3:1."

# CHAPTER 28

John Jenkins was over-the-top excited about being put in charge of the building of the new church. He would plan and then tear it up. He would plan some more and then tear it up. Finally, Sal couldn't take anymore. "John," she said. "You are going to have to settle on something! Everything you have put down on paper has been good. I don't know what you are envisioning." John turned to look at his dear little opinionated wife. "You know, Sal, you are right. This time, I am going to let you be the one to decide which plan we need to go with." He knew he would open up a can of worms, but he took the lid off anyway. "Well, John," said Sal. "Let me take a look at all those drawings you threw away." John reached down on the floor and picked up all the wadded up papers he had discarded. Sal ironed each paper out flat as she could with her hand and studied each plan. "Well, after much deliberation, John, I think I see the perfect plan." "Really?" said John. He couldn't believe she came up with a solution so fast when she usually couldn't decide on what dessert to fix on most Sundays. She would ponder on chocolate cake and go to chocolate pie, and then out of the clear blue sky settle on something entirely different like blackberry cobbler. *Oh well,* he thought. *I better grab her answer and go with it before she changes her mind.* "OK, my darling wife. Let me see what you have picked." Sal slowly handed him the very first design he had come up with. A small foyer that led into a sanctuary. A couple of Sunday school rooms off to the side. "Very simple," said Sal. "What led you to decide on this design?" said John. Sal was very careful with her words. "John, I have faith that our church will fill up fast. This design allows for us to add on or take out a wall for a larger sanctuary." John was just as surprised as Sal was, "Yes, this was the perfect plan. By George, Sal! This is what we will go with." Sal slapped her knee and exclaimed, "Well, I knew it all along." John knew he had really better brag on her good judgment. After all, it was his Sal who decided the actual plan. "I will get in touch with Tucker Bean tomorrow and we can start digging some footers. I kinda hate to tear down our brush arbor until we complete the church. That way, we can still have services until the church is built. I feeling better and better each day about this church. Did you ever hear of the prophecy that was given out a long time ago about this mountain, Sal?" "What kind of prophecy are you talking about, John?" "Well, my daddy was the one who told me and mama. He was just a small lad when my grandpa took him to a tent revival down around Sutphin's Bottom. The old circuit rider preacher gave out a prophecy that this mountain would one day bring forth a multitude of souls. At the time, no one lived up here until Marley Knott hewed out a rugged road and built his home up here. I think right above Caleb's people's house. Him and his wife lived up here until they died, and no one was brave enough to venture up here until my Mame and Pappy decided to give it a try. By that time, several families were moving up here as well, including yours." "Really," said Sal. "I had never heard this spoken before as long as I have lived up here. Are you sure you know this to be the truth, John Jenkins?" "I am just going on what my Pappy used to tell me. That's all I know," said John. Sal gave him one of her looks and he knew what was coming next. "I ain't never seen anything come out of this mountain but hurt and heartache," said Sal. "I just thought I'd pass this little bit of information along to you, is all. I didn't know it was going to start a war," said John. "Oh, hush up. I ain't got time to argue with you, John. I need to get some supper started. What do you think we should have? Some greens and cornbread would be good, or better yet, some hoe cake and gravy would be good, too." John just smiled and kissed her on her cheek, "I have confidence you will make the best choice, honey."

John thought he would walk down to Sutphin's Bottom and look around for the best possible site to build the church on. He kissed Sal on her forehead and told her he wouldn't be gone long and would try to be back in time to fill up her wood box. "But if not, get Laymon and CJ to come and do it." Sal nodded in agreement. She was busy talking to herself about supper. She threw up her hand to shoo him off. He knew he'd better go now before she thought of something to tell him or he'd never get down there.

John trudged on down the mountain. His mind and heart was so full, he felt like letting out a big holiness holler. "Woohooo!" he shouted. *Man, that felt good. I think I'll shout again.* "Yes, Jesus!" He could hardly wait to get started on the new church. Maybe, just maybe, this would really unite this mountain. As of lately and ever since the moonshine tragedy, the people on Marley Knott's Mountain were distant to each other. John could remember a time when someone got sick, all the mountain came together to make sure their work was done, whether it be milking the cows or gathering up the garden, and the womenfolk even would join together with the canning. He chuckled a little when the memory of the gathering just a few years past had brought all his mountain neighbors together to have a day of fun and food. Poor little Edna Sue had gotten all those bee stings, and Sal had lit out like a mad bull when Caleb came to retrieve her to come help Edna. Yes, this mountain was once united, but not so anymore. People were suspicious of each other. It was a very unsettling time for everybody. John knew it would take more than a building to fix all that had happened on the mountain. It would take the power of an Almighty God to mend the hearts of the people of Marley Knott's Mountain.

As he neared the bottom of the mountain, he could see someone down where he had thought about building the church. The closer he got, he saw it was none other than Reverend Avery. The instant he saw John, he started running toward him. Finally, after being out of breath, he reached John and with much gratitude, he grabbed John's hand and gave him a handshake that let John know this man loved him. "Good to see you, my friend. What brings you down the mountain this fine day?" said Rev. Avery. John smiled and said, "Well, Reverend, I came down to scout out a place for our new church. As you know, Sid Patterson is paying for all the lumber we will need to erect a church. I have several good carpenters from out of this mountain that have agreed to help with the construction. We are so excited about the prospect of having a real church. What brings you to these parts, Reverend?" "Well, sir, I have come to see how things are progressing and to see if it will be built in time for myself and Miss Bess to be the first to be married in our new church." "Hmmm," said John. "Just what is the date that you want to get married?" Rev. Avery began rubbing his chin and said, "Well, it depends on when you tell us you will have this church ready. I have a church from down east that had agreed to give us their old pews if we can come and get them." "Well," said John. "Let me think. Spring will be officially here in a week or so. If I can get all these men together ... Of course you know we all have spring obligations such as getting our gardens ready for planting and all the other springtime jobs." "Yes. Yes, I understand," said Rev. Avery. "I haven't been among you all and learned nothing for all these years." Rev. Avery could see John figuring in his head. He would roll his eyes up and count on his hands. Finally, he said, "I'll tell you what, we should be ready for a wedding about first part of June. What do you think, Reverend?" "Well, John, let me run that past Bess and I will get back to you. By the way, where you all going to build?" John thought for a minute and said, "Well, I think right here is as good a place as any. This is where we figured out this plan, so I will plant a marker right here." John grabbed a limb that had fallen out during the winter snow and took a rock and beat it into the ground. "This is like what they've done in the Bible. They would mark a place with rocks for a remembrance. We have marked ours with wood." Rev. Avery suggested they have a prayer unto the Lord and John readily agreed. "You go ahead, Reverend. Speak unto God on behalf of this mountain." The Reverend Avery began his prayer just like he always did, "Our dear, kind, and gracious heavenly Father, today, John and I have forged out a plan for this mountain a church. We pray in your name, Jesus, that you will bring to us every craftsman and tool that we will need to build this place of worship. Bless the hearts of the people of this mountain, Lord. Let souls be won for you, Father. Bless this ground that we have decided on and let no weapon that should be formed come against us building this for you. In Jesus's name, we pray. Amen." John reached over and gave the Reverend a hug. "Thank you, sir, for all you have done in the past and what's in store for the future. You will never know until eternity what a difference you made to the people of this mountain." Reverend Avery just stood there. He was for once speechless, but he mustered out a hearty, "Thank you, sir. I, too, am honored to serve you people." They parted ways and John headed back up the mountain. He had so much to think about, pray about, and do. "Lord, help me and give me your strength. Bless that good woman you gave me, and I hope she finally got me some supper on the table." John Jenkins felt the power of the Lord every step he took back up that ragged path that Marley Knott had hewed out many, many years before. *Yes, God is still here on this mountain. I feel him walking right beside me.*

# CHAPTER 29

Ella Patterson felt her time drawing nearer and nearer. "Sid," she would say. "This baby has got no more room to grow. I feel the little feet up in my throat." Sid would just look at her and say, "Honey, in God's time, he will make room if necessary." Ella would roll her bottom lip out as if to say "Oh pooie, Sid!"

The roof was already under construction on the new church. John had estimated about another three weeks or so, and they would be done. Everything had gone as smooth as silk, other than a few springtime storms that hindered their work. But the hearts of the people on this mountain was eager to see the completion of the new church. Mrs. Bright had ventured down one day to give it a look. "John," she said. "What you going to name the new church?" "Well," said John. "Hadn't given it much thought. Maybe the folks on this mountain need to be the one to give this church a name. Mrs. Bright, why don't you talk to all your neighbors around the mountain and see what is everyone's thoughts about the naming of the new church?" John could see the pride in her face. She had never had so much responsibility in her life, and it was something she would put her heart and soul into. "I'll do it, John Jenkins. When we all come up with a fitting name, I'll let you know." John agreed and patted Mrs. Bright on her back, "I have every bit of confidence in you and know we all can come up with the best name ever. Maybe this will inspire people to come if they can take part in naming the church, but God will do the saving part." "Come here, John," he heard Tucker Bean yell. "I need your help here." John bid Mrs. Bright good-bye, and proceeded in helping Tucker Bean.

Caleb Moses had been in jail nearly five months and had heard nothing about a court date. He was tired of just sitting there and counting bricks. Big Nose, or Jed, as Caleb had learned his real name to be, had brought the newspaper a few times. Although Caleb thanked him, he could hardly read enough to get an understanding of what the article was about. This day, Jed had brought him the newspaper and told Caleb, "You are from over near Marley Knott's mountain, aren't you?" Caleb immediately perked up and replied, "Why, yes, I am. Why?" "Well, I see an article and picture of the new church they are erecting over around the bottom of that mountain. Would you like to see?" Caleb never even responded. He just grabbed the paper out of Jed's hand and thanked him under his breath, as he looked at the picture. Jed turned to go away when Caleb called out to him, "Jed, could you please come here?" He didn't want the other prisoners hearing what he was about to tell him. He was ashamed that he couldn't read. But if the truth be known, most in there didn't know either. Jed came close to the bars and Caleb told him, "Jed, I can't read or write very well. Do you think you could somehow read this to me without anyone finding out?" Jed just stood there a minute and said, "Yes, I think I can. Hand me back the paper." Caleb stuck the newspaper back through the bars and Jed aggressively grabbed it. "Yes, sir," said Jed. This is what all you boys need, some churchin'." That got the whole cell block's attention. "Yea," said one of the guys. "Who made you judge and jury anyway?" "Some little church wanting to come and sing to us, boys." "Aye," said another. "Well, let me just read this to you and you will know for yourselves." Jed began to read the article that the newspaper had written about the construction of the new church up around Marley Knott's Mountain. It told of John Jenkins being lead man over the project. Caleb soaked up every word. He couldn't believe the very mountain that he was from was erecting a church. "It says here, they are expected to have their first service sometime around the first part of June. You boys need to go on up there. That is, those of you that are out of here and hear some word of the Lord." Several offered up sneers, but a few including Caleb hung their heads in shame. Thoughts of his doom came into his mind like a flood. *I have made a mess of my life. I deserve everything that is thrown at me, but dear, Lord, please give me one more chance.* He was very quiet the rest of the day. Jed came by several times, trying to chat a little with him. Still, others tried taunting him. But he just mostly kept quiet and didn't give any of them any response. "Oh," said Jed, just as he was fixing to leave for the day. "I saw Joe Lambert here a while ago. Just thought I'd let you know. You may have some company before long." "Thanks," said Caleb. "Good to know."

It wasn't long until the evening security guard came and informed Caleb of a visit. Maynard was not as friendly to the jail-birds as Jed was. He was truly business all the way. Caleb arose and Maynard placed cuffs on his hands and opened the jail cell door. "In front," he told him. Caleb knew the routine. After all, he had been here for nearly five months. As he opened the door, he saw Joe greet him with a big smile. He was already seated at a table where they let prisoners and their guest sit and talk for only fifteen minutes. "Good afternoon, son," said Joe. Caleb returned his smile and let him know he was doing fine. "I got some news I have to share to you. I was notified by the court system that they have set a court date for you. Looks like you will be heard under Judge Gardner. From what I hear, he is a tough judge but fair." "When?" said Caleb. "June first, at ten o'clock a.m. Would you like me to notify your next of kin for you if they want to attend?" Joe looked down at Caleb, sitting before him with handcuffs on. He had gripped his hands so tight, his fingers looked as if there was no blood present in his hands. He wanted more than anything to reach over and embrace Caleb's hands, but even he knew that was forbidden here at the jail. They had signs posted everywhere. No physical contact of any kind permitted in the room. Joe just looked at Caleb and said, "I know you are worried, but I have faith in the good Lord. You will be exonerated. Been doing some powerful praying for you, son." Caleb tried as hard as he could to give Joe an authentic smile, but he knew Joe saw right through him. "I'll be alright, either way. But keep on praying, Joe. How is Mrs. Mabel doing?" Joe nodded his head. "She's working me to death. You know, springtime and all." "Yes, I do," said Caleb. "And if I get out,

I intend to get to know more. Right, Joe?" "Right you are, my boy, right you are."

Joe left, and Caleb was ushered back to his cell. He had a lot to think on. If no one from that mountain had any credible evidence, he couldn't see how he would get off. His mind was racing in a million different directions. He knew the lights would be turned off before long. He just laid down and let his mind think on all he had found out today. He thought of the little church that was being built. *Boy, I sure would love to be able to attend that church, but most likely won't.* He thought of Martha Rae and all his children. *If I could start over, things would definitely be different.* His oldest children had been without a father almost all their lives. If he was not convicted, how on earth would he be able to make up all those years to them? Finally, he drifted off to sleep. His mind was tired, although his body was not.

*Daddy, daddy where are you?* Caleb could see his little Laymon when he was a small boy. He was almost grown now, by most people's standards. *I'm here, boy, can't you see me?* Caleb answered him in his dream. *No, daddy, I can't. Come home, we need you. Mama needs you.* I'm *Coming, boy. I'm coming.* Now you just hold up. Why was this scoundrel up here? Conrad Cox was a lowdown dirty somebody who had pinned this whole mess on him. Caleb began running, and all of a sudden, a big angel stepped out in front of him and declared, "Stop, Caleb! Fight for what belongs to you." At that moment, Caleb sat straight up in the bed.

*Wow, what a dream.* His heart was pounding, and he could hardly stand for fear his knees would buckle. *Was that a visitation from God?* There was no other way to explain it. It had to be. The words of the angel rang over and over in his head. Fight. He didn't have anything to fight with, except on his knees. He had seen Martha Rae kneel and pray many times and tell him "I'm fighting a battle Caleb, but I fight on my knees." Yes, God was telling him to pray. His mind was so overwhelmed at this moment, he hardly could speak. He bowed beside his shabby cot and prayed like he had never prayed before. The whole cell block got very quiet. No one heckled him. No slurs were spoken. He arose from his prayer and felt what Martha

Rae often told him. I feel like I have prayed through. Caleb had never understood what she was saying, but he did now. He felt like he had been right in the room with God himself. He lay back down and slept like a baby the rest of the night. He had a newfound confidence in the Lord. His faith was as high as Marley Knott's Mountain. *Yes, Lord, I have heard from heaven.*

# CHAPTER 30

Joe knew the court date was drawing ever so near for Caleb. He had ventured up into Marley Knott's Mountain and found the little cabin where Caleb and Martha Rae called home. He gently knocked on the humble door. Inside, he heard the scrambling of feet that he felt like were trying to be the first to answer the door. He decided that they hardly ever had any company, so if anyone knocked it had to be someone they didn't know. Finally, he raised his hand to knock again when the door flung open and there stood six of the prettiest children he had ever seen. Martha Rae pushed her way to the front and asked Joe if he would excuse her children's rude actions. "We don't have much company up here in these part, mister. I am sorry, you are who?" Joe introduced himself and told them whereabouts he lived. "What kind of business do you want with me, or are you just seeking directions?" asked Martha Rae. "Well, no. I have come to speak to you. Could I talk in private on your porch?" said Joe. "Well yes, sir," said Martha Rae. She turned to Angela, "Honey, can you get everyone to sit down for some lunch? I just had finished preparing a bite to eat. Would you care to join us?" she asked Joe. "No, no. I'm fine."

Martha Rae closed the front door and looked Joe square in the eye. "Mrs. Moses, your husband Caleb has been living with my wife Mabel and me for several months. We took him in after he tried to steal a chicken. I knew he bound to be hungry, so I made him go in my home where my wife sat him a plate of food and milk before him. I don't believe I have ever seen anyone eat as hard and fast as he did that day. We let him stay in our barn, and soon he won our hearts and we fixed him a room upstairs to winter over in. You can most

175

likely tell we have no children of our own, but we have taken in several only to have them return home. Caleb is our first adult, although my wife automatically took to him as being her child. He had been helping me on my farm with chores and I paid him a small wage. He finally confessed the whole story of why he was running." Martha Rae extended her hand to Joe and said, "Thank you, Mr. Lambert. I appreciate all you have done for my husband. I guess he also told you about the moonshine poisoning that also took place up here last year. That is why he was running. I do not for an instant believe he done this. Matter of fact, I know who the responsible party is but have no proof." Joe was nodding yes and told Martha Rae, "Let me finish. My wife and I are Christian people. We have been praying and seeking God for Caleb, and I believe Caleb has accepted the Lord as his Savior. We have offered Caleb a little piece of ground to make a fresh start on. The Lord has shown us he will be proven innocent. How, I do not know. But we trust God with this whole situation. The main reason I have come to your house is to tell you Caleb has a court date of June 1. If you could get the people from this mountain to come, somebody might know the answer to this mess." Martha Rae's countenance immediately changed. "Do you mean Caleb wants me to come?" "Yes, indeed he does," said Joe. "That's all he talks about when I visit him is his dark-haired Raven, and I can clearly see why now. So can I count on you and those involved in this tragedy to come to the trial?" "I can only speak for myself. I will be there with my parents. I will get the word out around this mountain, and it's up to each individual to decide if they will come. Is that fair enough?" "Yes, ma'am, it is," said Joe. "It has been a pleasure to meet you. I will try to get word to Caleb you are coming. I know he will be glad to see you. Take care, until we meet again," said Joe.

Martha Rae was just bewildered. What should she do? Yes, she would attend the trial with her parents. Should she get word out amongst the mountain folk, or just keep all this information to herself? Caleb would need all the help he could get. Maybe he had left a good impression on some of his neighbors, and if they were lucky somebody might know the truth. She would have to personally go up and tell Pap and Corry. *I am sure they will want to attend,* she thought. "Children, come here," said Martha Rae. "I have some errands to run today and it is very important that you all listen to Laymon and Angela." She wasn't too worried about most her children, but she knew Little John would have to be really looked after as he had a tendency to wander off sometimes, chasing butterflies, rabbits, or sometimes an imaginary friend. "Angela, you know who to keep both eyes on today, don't you?" Angela winked at her mama and smiled, "Yes, Mama, I know. Don't worry, we will be fine. Is anything wrong that we need to know about?" asked Angela. Martha Rae was taken aback. "Well, I don't really think so, but ask me again sometime." Angela knew that meant it wasn't for all ears to hear. "Get me my shawl, sweetheart. I have a long day ahead of me." "You need the wagon?" asked Laymon. "No, the weather is warming. I think I'll just walk. You know it clears one's mind."

She decided to go tell her parents first. Sal was washing out some of her winter blankets this morning. "Hey, girl. You coming to help? Getting a little early start on my cleaning." "I wish, Mama," said Martha Rae. "But I have come to tell you and Daddy that I had a visit from a man named Joe Lambert this morning. He and his wife Mabel had taken Caleb in before he got caught. He came to tell me that Caleb's trial will be June 1. He asked me to come." "Well, what did you tell him?" asked Sal. "I told him yes I would be there with my parents, is that OK?" "You know it's alright," said Sal. "No daughter of mine is going to her husband's trial by herself. Yes indeed, me and your daddy will be going." "Boy, that's a relief to know. He asked me to tell all the people around the mountain to come. I told him I would, but I couldn't answer for them. I am heading up to Pap and Corry's first. I know they will want to come. I hope, anyway." Martha Rae wrapped the shawl around her shoulders tight, and off through the mountain she went. Her heart felt light today. Almost like she didn't have a care in the world. She was almost scared to feel this way today, but she was going to take advantage of it. Most days she felt the heaviness of life itself.

Corry was sweeping off her front porch when she looked up and saw Martha Rae coming up the path. "Get on up here, girl. I ain't seen you in a month of Sundays. What in tarnation you been doing this winter?" Martha Rae was almost out of breath. She could tell she had been cooped up all winter and hadn't been out much. "Just staying around home with all my young 'uns, trying to keep warm. How are you and Pap?" Corry snarled up her nose. "Pap's had a pretty hard winter. What the alcohol didn't get, the flu did. He pert near died. I finally had to go down to Mrs. Bright's and get her to mix me up one of her concoctions to ever get him rid of that stuff. Go on in the house. He's in there sitting by the fire."

Martha Rae entered their little humble abode. Pap heard her walking and asked, "Who's coming?" "It's me Pap. Martha Rae." When she got to where he was, she bent over and kissed him on his forehead. "I have heard you have been quite under the weather this winter? You feeling better?" Pap coughed and spit in the fire and got Martha Rae by the hand. "Sit down. I know you didn't come all the way up here to chitchat. Spit it out, Martha. What have you come to say? Is our boy alright?" "I'll declare, you can read my mind. Yes, as far as I know, Caleb is fine. His trial date is June 1. A man that befriended him came to see me this morning and tell me of the impending trial date and asked me to come and see if I could get any of the other mountain folk to come. That's why I've come. Will you and Corry go to the trial?" Pap sat there for a while and said, "I don't see little to none, but I will go to show my support for my boy." "Good," said Martha Rae. "I'll send Laymon and CJ the morning of the trial to come up in the wagon and get you and Corry. You can ride with me and my parents." "Sounds good to me," said Pap. "I know Corry will be glad to see someone besides me for a change. Maybe on the way back, we can visit with you all and see our grand young 'uns a while." "For sure," said Martha Rae. "I'd love to stay longer but I have a lot of people to visit today. I hope this mountain will come out and show support for Caleb. I don't know of many that think he is guilty, anyway. But thinking and evidence to prove it are two different matters. Maybe someone will have something that will clear Caleb." Martha Rae left Caleb's parents' home and headed down to talk to the other folks. By day's end, some said they wouldn't miss it for the world, and others just grunted and made no promises. By evening, Martha Rae was beat. She had talked her head off today and felt like she had gotten nowhere. That feeling she had when she started out had faded fast. Now, the weariness of all this made her feel like she was weighted down to the point of exasperation. All she had on her mind was getting to her home and hoping Angela had fixed something for supper.

When she arrived home, she heard no sound coming from her home. Usually when her children heard someone step up on their porch, they already had the door open. She had tried to no avail to teach them to allow company to knock first, then open the door, and be very courteous. Not her bunch. You would think they were raised in a barn. Martha Rae could hardly wait until the church was built, and Ella could teach some proper schooling in the Sunday school rooms. There was only one other place they could be—down at their Grandma Sal's. She never even took off her shawl. She just turned and headed to her mama's, She knew her mama probably went up there and got them. Yes, she heard the chatter of Little John telling Lilly a thing or two, and Susie backing him up all the way. CJ was trying to beat Laymon in a game of checkers and was fussing with the little ones to be quiet. All was normal, or it sounded to be. She opened up the door and all the children started talking at once. She couldn't make sense of anything they said. "Hey, hey," said Martha Rae. "One at a time. Laymon, where on earth are Mama and Angela?" Little John spoke right up, "They down with Mrs. Ella. She's getting herself a baby today." "What?" said Martha Rae. "Is that right, Laymon?" "Best I know," answered Laymon, and never even raised his head when he jumped one of CJ's checkers. "You all stay here until I get back. I have got to get down there. I thought she was going to a hospital to deliver anyway."

Martha Rae shot down through the woods as fast as she could. She could see Sid's horseless buggy pulled up in the front. *I hope nothing has gone wrong for Ella and Sid.* She hurried her footsteps and burst through the front door of the mercantile. Violet met her with a big hug. She was white as a ghost. "Tell me!" screamed Martha Rae. "Is Ella and the baby OK?" Violet's face soon had the biggest smile Martha Rae had ever seen. "Yes, Mama. Her and her daughter Emma are doing fine. It's Sid I am worried about." Martha Rae rushed to her dear friend's side, "Ella, honey. It's Martha Rae. Can I get you anything?" "No, sweetheart. I am doing fine. Have you seen my little girl yet?" "No, honey, I haven't. I just wanted to check on you and Sid first." "Poor Sid. He has near about fainted a dozen times before I had her, and finally did just as I gave birth. He's fine now, though. He sure did give Violet a scare." Martha Rae tiptoed over to where Sid was holding his new daughter Emma. "She's a doll. Can I hold her, Sid?" He nodded a yes and she took the little baby from Sid's arms. "My goodness! Look here, Mama. It's been a long time since I held one this little." Sal couldn't help but grin. In fact, she was one big grin. "I delivered her, you know." "No," said Martha Rae. "You didn't, did you?" "Yes, I did. Ella didn't have a choice. No problems at all."

They all heard someone enter the front of the mercantile, and soon John Jenkins came and stood looking over the newborn little girl. "Ain't she something?" he said. "Nothing like new life." *What a happy ending to a long dreary day,* thought Martha Rae. She stayed a while and talked to Sid. Of course, Violet would stay until Ella could get on her feet. In fact, Martha Rae knew Violet would never make the mountain her home again. But that was alright, she knew where she was. It had been good for Violet to be down here with Sid and Ella. She was different than her other children. Maybe being off this mountain wasn't so bad after all. It sure had made a big difference in Violet, thanks to Sid and Ella, two good and precious souls. She couldn't help but think on the day Ella had come to her house asking for one of her children. Little did she know that her Violet would have the best of two worlds. *God works in mysterious ways,* thought Martha Rae. "Come on, Angela. We have some talking to do before we get home."

# CHAPTER 31

Martha Rae got up the morning of the trial in a nervous tizzy. June the first had come so quickly. *What on earth should I wear?* she thought. *My Sunday best or an everyday dress? Let me see.* She had laid out several dresses she thought would be appropriate. Most every dress was pretty close the same color. Feed sacks just didn't vary that much. *Oh well,* she thought. *It's the best I can do.* Finally, she picked up a pretty print one. *Well, at least this one will match my hair bow that I want to wear.* She had her water warming on the cook stove to bathe in. She dipped her finger into the water to test the temperature and thought, *yes, perfect for a good bath. This good warm water sure felt good,* she thought. Most of the time, she had to take the cold water and let her children have the warm, but not today. She would get the warm and was going to take advantage of every minute of it. Lilly had knocked at her bedroom door. "Mama, Grandma Sal said was you about ready?" *Oh my goodness,* she thought. *I have taken longer than I had planned.* She quickly got out of her galvanized bathtub and told Lilly to tell her mama she'd be ready in about fifteen minutes. She dried off and put a little of Angela's toilet water perfume on. This is a funny name for something to wear to make you smell good. But nonetheless, she dabbed a little on around her neck. She had made up her hair a little different today. She was going to let it hang down her back just like it used to when she and Caleb first met. She combed and combed and pulled the sides up on top of her head and placed the hair bow Caleb had gotten her for Christmas right smack dab in the middle. *There,* she thought. *I don't look too bad for a mountain girl,* she thought.

Sal and John Jenkins hitched up the wagon and John was whistling for Martha Rae to come on. "We are late as it is." Pap and Corry had decided at the last minute to stay home the day of the trial. The journey would be enough in itself without having to deal with them. Martha Rae had given Angela and Laymon instructions for the day and told them, "You watch your brothers and sisters today, especially Little John." She kissed them all and told them she would be home by dark. As she bounced up into the wagon, Sal looked her daughter up and down, "My, my. Who might you be trying to impress?" "Oh Mama, hush up. I just want to look my best today. You know it might help Caleb someway." "I know, honey, just trying to jab you a little this morning. You are beautiful no matter what." "Aw Mama, I love you." John quickly interrupted, "Have you told the young 'uns where you are going today?" "Well, only the older ones, Angela, Laymon, and Lilly. The younger ones might not understand." "Yes. Yes, I agree," said John. "Get up. Come on, get up, I said," John's two old mules were not as vibrant as they used to be. "Just like me," said John, slowing down a bit.

They arrived at the bottom of the mountain and pulled their team of mules around behind the mercantile. Sid had agreed to drive them to the trial, and he already had his horseless buggy warming up. Martha Rae shot off the wagon, with John hollering as she did it. "Now Martha Rae, don't get in there messing with that baby and cause us to be late." She never even looked back at her daddy. She knew he'd never leave her. Violet had little Emma in her arms, talking and cooing all over her. "You want to hold her, Mama?" she said. "No, child. I am in a hurry. Sid is driving me and your Papa and your grandma into town today." "Really?" said Violet. "Where you going?" "Just some business to take care of. We shouldn't be long. You take care of Ella and Emma, and I'll hold her when I get back." Martha kissed baby Emma on top of her head and said a word or two to Ella, then climbed into the back of Sid's buggy and told him, "Well, what's the hold up now?" Sid put the car into "go" and Sal grabbed the sides like she thought she was going to be thrown out. "Mama," said Martha Rae. "Relax and enjoy some easy riding. This is the wave of the future." "Well," said Sal. "It might be for you, but not for me. I'll take the old way any day." John and Sid were sitting up front, listening to every word. "Yea," said John. "I really like your new buggy. I might have to get one myself." Sal never said a word out loud, but under her breath, she said, "Over my dead body. That is, if I get back alive today."

As they arrived at the courthouse, they were astonished. The place looked to be packed. John recognized some of his neighbors' wagons, and matter of fact, all these wagons were from off Marley Knott's Mountain. He helped Sal and Martha Rae get out from the seat behind him. "Easy there, Sal. This is easier than jumping down off a wagon, don't you think?" She just gave him one of those red-headed looks and locked her arm into Martha Rae's and said, "Come on, child. Which way do we go to get in?" Sid and John were following close behind. John saw Bean Tucker waving his hat at him. "Come this way, girls. I think Bean is showing us the way to get in." "Come on in here," said Bean. "The place is crowded today. If I ain't wrong, just about every soul on that mountain is here except for Pap and Corry. And seeing their situation, I can understand that. Here," said Bean. "Let me hold the door for you all." They all entered the foyer of the courthouse. An officer of the court was there, ready to show them where to sit. "Do you all know the defendant?" he asked. Martha Rae piped up and said, "Yes. Matter of fact, I am his wife and these are my parents." "Oh okay," he said. "Then I have a special place for you all to sit. Follow me." She saw Joe and Mabel and whispered to her daddy that this was the family Caleb had been living with before he was apprehended by the law. "You can sit beside Mr. and Mrs. Lambert," said the officer. They all scooted over toward Joe and Mabel.

They spoke only briefly to neighbors, thanking them for coming out to show their support for Caleb. They had not been there long when the judge entered his bench and they escorted Caleb in with shackles on his hands and feet. His eyes immediately went to Martha Rae and hers to him. She looked more beautiful than he could remember. It seemed like a lifetime since he had seen her. He gave her a little wink and she immediately blushed, just like she did when they had begun courting. The judge called his lawyer to his bench and the proceedings began. To Caleb, the judge looked pretty tough. He hammered his gavel on his desk and said, "Today, we are trying the case against Caleb Moses and the blind and deceased folks up on Marley Knott's Mountain. As you all know, eight men died and six were blinded from drinking tainted moonshine. It was a well-known fact that Caleb Moses had been helping his uncle, Ellis Johnson, brew with what was to be his last batch of the year because of cold weather setting in. No one seen anyone actually taint the moonshine, but Caleb Moses quickly left the mountain running and became a wanted fugitive. Do we have any witnesses to testify on behalf of Caleb Moses?" the Judge asked. "Yes, we do, Your Honor," Caleb's lawyer stood up. Martha Rae thought he was very well dressed and knew exactly what he was doing. But after all she heard, lawyers made very good money. How could Caleb afford such a spit shined lawyer? She guessed Joe and Mabel had hired him for Caleb. "We'd like to call Mr. Manny Horton." Manny's wife Elisabeth led him to the chair beside the judge. Caleb's lawyer, Bob Jackson, quickly went to asking him questions concerning Caleb's part in the poisoning. "Mr. Horton, will you tell the judge what left you in this condition?" Manny was a soft-spoken man who was a law-abiding citizen. He only drank a little when the weather cooled because it seem to help keep him warm while he would cut wood or hunt for food for his family. He began to speak. The judge quickly told him, "You must speak up, sir. We all need to hear you." Manny cleared his throat. "Well, Your Honor. The day I bought my shine from Ellis, he came to my house early that morning, said he was going to try to deliver all he had that day and get it over with. I bought a mason jar full off of him. I never seen Caleb with him, just some other guy that I didn't recognize as being from the mountain. I just bought my shine and they left." "So you did not see Caleb with Ellis that day? Did you ever visit Ellis at his still? asked the judge. Manny dropped his head and said, "Yes, I did. Sometimes while out trying to shoot some game for my family to have supper at night, I'd drop by and see Caleb there. We'd talk about nothing in particular and I'd go on my way." "I see," said the judge. "So in fact, you did see Caleb at the moonshine still, is that right?" "Yes, sir. I guess it is," said Horton. "Let it be noted that

Caleb Moses was in fact a regular at the site where the moonshine was made." The clerk nodded her head and one by one all those that had been blinded tried to testify but ended up doing more harm than good. Only one of the deceased family members agreed to take the stand. The others felt like it was asking too much and the emotional toll was enough in itself.

Martha Rae could feel knots tying up her stomach. Caleb did not have one ounce of evidence that could clear his name. It looked like he would for sure go to jail. *What would she tell her children? That their daddy was in prison for killing their neighbors?* It was more than she could bear. She suddenly felt lightheaded, and the next thing she remembered was slumping over in her chair. Her Mama immediately called for some help. She knew this would be hard on Martha Rae, but she never dreamed it would come to this. They carried her out on a stretcher and she was given smelling salts under her nose. Sal told John, "I'll just stay here with her. It might be best she's not in the courtroom when the judge renders judgment." John agreed, and he and Sid reentered the courtroom just as Mrs. Bell stepped off the stand. Her husband had been one of the men to die, and she wasn't in much better shape than Martha Rae. "Do we have anyone else to testify today?" asked the judge. "No, Your Honor," said Caleb's lawyer. "Does Mr. Moses have anything to add to this hearing?" the judge asked. His lawyer looked at Caleb and asked, "Mr. Moses, would you like to take the stand?" "I don't guess. I have no evidence to present other than my word, and right now that's not much." Joe and Mabel looked at each other with puzzling looks. *How could this be?* they thought. The Lord assured them Caleb would be exonerated. But it sure didn't look that way now. They were sure of what the Lord had spoken to their hearts. Had they heard something that they wanted to hear, or had the Lord really spoken? The judge told the rowdy crowd they would return at 2:00 p.m. for the verdict. Slowly, the folks began to make their way outside. Most knew this would be a long day and had packed a small lunch to tide them over. Most congregated under some large oak trees in the courthouse yard, while others walked down beside the creek to cool off a bit before this evening. Martha Rae had got her bearings back, and Sid had offered to buy their lunch at the little café down the street. Martha Rae declined, "I don't want to eat any better than these folks that are eating biscuits and tomatoes or jelly for their lunch today." Sal readily agreed. She had brought them some biscuits and jelly today and had fried out some country ham if the menfolk wanted that. Sid was so very proud of his friends. When all this was over, he would take all of them out one day for a fancy hamburger and coke. He knew Ella could talk Martha Rae into it. But for now, he'd eat a ham biscuit and cup of coffee the courts offered for his lunch. Two o'clock would arrive soon anyway, and he didn't want to be pushed to hurry up and eat.

Sid looked at his watch. It was one thirty, time to get back in. Martha Rae was feeling better from her recent attack of nerves and very embarrassed of having to be carried out on a stretcher. She wondered how Caleb was feeling. Now she wished she had visited him while he was in jail. They all had gotten back into the courthouse. All had their own opinion as to what happened, but Martha Rae knew what happened. It was that Conrad Cox. She was sure of it. But there was no evidence to convict him. After all, he wasn't the one who ran. Caleb made himself look guilty, even though he wasn't.

The court officer asked everyone to rise for the judge as he entered the courtroom. "Mr. Caleb Moses, would you please stand for the verdict." Caleb slowly stood. He had to hold on to the table to keep from collapsing himself. "Mr. Caleb Moses, you have been tried today for the deaths of eight men and the blinding of six men, one being your daddy. I find it hard to believe that a man would poison his own daddy, but I have no evidence to prove otherwise. Your verdict will be, you will spend the rest of your life in prison with no parole. Do you understand?" Caleb shook his head and said, "Yes, sir, I do." The judge hammered his gavel on his desk and said, "This is the sentence of this court."

Martha Rae could not believe her ears. She began to wail and cry. "No. No, this can't be so." John got over to where his daughter was to help her in case she collapsed again. "Sit down, honey," her daddy said. He embraced his daughter, just like he did when she was a little girl. "It will be okay," he said. "Here, lean on me and let me help you out." They got up, and Sal and John each embraced Martha Rae around the waist and walked her toward the back doors of the courtroom. They were sure themselves this would turn out different. But it hadn't and they would have to just accept the verdict and try to help Martha Rae finish raising her children. "Come on, honey," her daddy said. "Sid has the buggy pulled around here to the door. Let's get in and leave. You don't need to talk to anyone right now." Martha Rae felt like her feet weighed a hundred pounds. *How on earth would she make it?* she thought. Just then, she remembered the Lord telling her before she married Caleb the hard road she would travel, but to trust in him only. Right now, all she had was the Lord. Although she felt a little let down, she knew God was on her side. All she could do now was trust him, and that she would do.

# CHAPTER 32

M artha Rae was just about to leave the courtroom when she heard the sound of a woman crying, and loudly, too. "Your Honor! Your Honor, please, I must talk to you. Please speak with me." The old judge just sat there and looked at this wailing woman, and thought, *I will be late for my supper. I can taste those chicken and dumplings now. But if it's something that will help this boy, I will listen.* "Order! Order! Who are you, lady?" "Your Honor, my name is Mrs. Wilma Bright and I think I have some information for you. Will you take time to listen to me?" *What else could he do?*

He asked her and Caleb and his lawyer to step in his chambers. Everyone else needs to wait outside. They all four gathered in the old judge's chambers and he asked her, "Mrs. Bright, did you mean to imply you had some information?" Mrs. Bright was crying and the judge told her to gain some composure and talk to him. She finally did calm down and looked at Caleb and said, "Caleb, I am so sorry. I have had all the information needed to clear your name all along. I was so ashamed to let anyone know I was up in the mountain to buy moonshine. I had bought moonshine off of Ellis Johnson for many years in the winter. People far and wide came to me for cough medicine for the flu and such, and they always said I had a cure for what ails them. That particular day, I had walked up in the mountain and bought my usual amount off of Ellis. I had started back down through the woods when I remembered I had left my basket sitting up there. I knew it was a very familiar basket that I often carried to collect my herbs in. Most people would recognize it in an instant." "What does your basket have to do with this court case?" "Well, Your Honor, I turned to go back up to retrieve it. I am a God-fearing woman and knew if anyone seen my basket, they would know I had been up at Ellis Johnson's still and I was concerned about my reputation more than anything. Just as I topped the little hill, I seen someone pouring something into the moonshine. It scared me and I took off walking as fast as I could because I was afraid he had seen me." I hid in the woods until Ellis and that boy filled up the mason jars with shine. They loaded up the wagon and left, so I ran back up and grabbed my basket and high tailed it out of there. "Well, Mrs. Bright, who do you think you saw?" "Well, sir," she said. "I saw the real culprit that is responsible for this dastardly deed in this courtroom today." "You did?" said the judge. "Could you point him out?" "Yes, sir, I can. I am so sorry, Caleb, for putting you through all this when you could have been out months ago." Caleb looked at Mrs. Bright, "Lady, you may never know this but you did me more good by not coming forward until now than you will ever know. But thank you, Jesus, you came forth right now." "Okay," said Judge Garder. He looked at Caleb's lawyer. "We must find a way not to scare off the real culprit until we have our hands on him. By the way, what was his name, Mrs. Bright?" "I really don't know," she said. "Bailiff, you go out there and announce for all the people to come back in, that we have some more information that will likely add to this case," Said Judge Gardner. "Yes, sir," said the bailiff.

The young bailiff entered the courtroom and raised his hands. "Listen, here," he said. "We would like everyone to please come back in for just a little while. The judge is not quite done." You could hear the whispers going through the courtroom. Martha Rae looked at her daddy, "What do you think has happened, Daddy?" "I don't know, dear. I can't imagine why Mrs. Bright went back with them, but we need to get back in there and find out." It didn't take long for all the mountain folk to sit down. They were anxious to find out what was going on. This was the most excitement they had witnessed since the poisoning. And besides, they spotted the newspaper outside and was standing where they could be seen in hopes of getting their pictures in the paper.

Judge Gardner reentered the courtroom and the people proceeded to stand. He raised his hand to let them know just to stay seated. He had his mind on that big pot of chicken and dumplings, and if he didn't hurry, they would be cold by the time he got home. Caleb and his lawyer were right behind the judge, with Mrs. Bright behind them. Judge Gardner told the courtroom officer to shut the back doors and stand until the hearing was over. He then began to speak. "It seems we do have a witness to what actually did take place. Mrs. Bright, would you please take the stand? Would you please tell the courts what you've seen?" He would have liked to add "and quickly," too, but he was a professional man and had to conduct this courtroom with respect for everyone. Mrs. Bright had started crying, "Yes, sir, judge," she said. After she got seated, the judge looked at her and said, "Now Mrs. Bright, try your best to compose yourself and tell the courts exactly what you told me in my chambers." Everyone in the courtroom was still as a mouse and took in every word she said. "Yes," she said. "I went back to retrieve my basket and seen the fellow emptying a bottle of something into the moonshine." "What do you think was in the bottle?" he asked. "Well, I don't rightly know, but I figure it was something to do with all the men dying on the mountain. I had done took a sip of mine and Ellis had to when I bought it. He told me it was a good batch, but I'm still here and have been doctoring with it all winter." The old judge was scratching his chin, "Mrs. Bright, was it Caleb you seen who poured the unknown substance into the moonshine?" Conrad was getting squirmy. He immediately rose and told the court officer he needed to go to the bathroom. "You will have to wait a few more minutes. The judge said no one was to leave this courtroom." Conrad looked like a scared rat, hunting a hole of escape." "No, sir. It wasn't Caleb. Matter of fact it, was that fellow at the back of the door talking to the officer." Conrad knew he had been exposed. *What could he do now?* he thought. He yelled, "Caleb told me to do it!"

Caleb stood up and spoke for the first time since the trial. "As God is my witness, I would have never told you to do anything as mean as that. My daddy is blind from the shine and my Uncle Ellis died. I may be guilty of a lot of things, but not this Conrad. This was done all by yourself." Judge Gardner hammered the gavel. "Order! Order!" he said. "Apprehend this man at once." The courtroom officer he had been talking to reached behind his back and got his cuffs. He ordered Conrad to put his hands behind his back and he cuffed him. "I guess you was about to use the bathroom. Where you're going, you can use it anytime you want." He gave Conrad a little snicker and took him out the door. "Upon hearing of this evidence, I guess I have no other choice but to release the prisoner. Caleb, I pronounce upon you … not guilty." The whole courtroom cheered. "However, you are not altogether free. I am placing you on one year of probation. You must not be up in that mountain and reside with Mr. and Mrs. Lambert until that full year is up." Caleb was relieved. Now he could get on with his life. He had crops to plant and a house to build, with Joe's help of course. "Your Honor, may I ask one request? May I attend the new church over at the foot of Marley Knott's Mountain? My wife and children will be going there and I would like to attend with my family." "Hmmmm," said Judge Gardner, "a very unusual request, but I think church will do you a world of good. It is granted only if you go with Mr. and Mrs. Lambert, understood?" "Yes, sir," Caleb said. "Thank you, sir. Thank you. God bless you, too."

The people were shaking Caleb's hand, and telling them they knew he wasn't guilty. Caleb was scanning the courtroom for Martha Rae, *where did she go so fast?* He darted out the front doors of the court-house and spotted her with her mama and daddy and Sid Patterson down under one of the big oak trees. "Martha Rae! Hey, wait up!" he yelled. Martha Rae looked up and saw Caleb running toward them. It was almost like the first time meeting him. She could feel her cheeks glowing. But in her heart, she was happy for the first time in a long time. He was out of breath when he caught up with her. "Hello, Mr. and Mrs. Jenkins. Sid, you doing okay?" They exchanged greetings and he asked Martha Rae, "Could we talk?" "Well, I'm not sure. Sid drove us over here and I am not sure he'd want to wait since he's got a new baby daughter." Sid overheard them talking, "Sure, go ahead. I'll treat John and Sal to supper over at that little café. They need to eat a hamburger and those fancy fried potatoes." "A what?" said Sal. "A hamburger and fried potatoes. Come on. You need to get a taste of something different." She was trying to put up a protest, but John got her by the arm and said, "Come on, Sal. Let's try this hamburger out. Give them a chance to talk." Sal didn't really want to leave Martha Rae alone with Caleb. She still didn't trust him, but she knew she didn't have a leg to stand on, so she complied. "Well, it might be pretty good. Let's go."

Caleb looked at his beautiful dark-haired Raven. "You are still the prettiest girl on that mountain. You know, that don't you?" he asked. "Oh hush, Caleb." She tried to hold up some defense, but her heart was already melted. "What now, Caleb?" she asked. Caleb reached for her hand. "I have so much to try to make up to you and my children. Are they doing good?" he asked. "Yes, they are doing fine. Growing like weeds, though. You might not even recognize Laymon. He's as tall as his Papa." "How is my Little John?" "Sweetest child you have got. He loves everybody and everything. He's such a blessing to our family." "Is my Pap and Corry still up in the mountain? I thought maybe the mountain folk might try to run them off after all this happened." "No, we have taken your mama and daddy under our wing and welcomed them into our family. Laymon and CJ kept them in wood for the winter, and Mama feeds them." "How about you, Martha Rae? Anybody been trying to take my place?" Caleb was so full of questions. He had had a lot of time to think about things while counting bricks in jail, and one question that always plagued him was reckon Martha Rae had found her another man. "Caleb," she said. "I took our vows very seriously when I married you. Times have been hard for us, very hard at times, but my heart is and will always be toward you. I love you just as much, if not more than I ever had. What I want to know is what's going to happen to us since you can't come back up in the mountain for a year." "Well, honey, Joe and Mabel Lambert have offered me a tract of land. They assured me I would be exonerated. That God had confirmed this in their hearts. That's them standing over by the fountain." "Yes," said Martha Rae. "He came up in the mountain and asked me to come to the trial today." "Martha Rae, I want you and my children to come and live with me when I get us a house built. Joe is going to help me get a fresh start and I want you all with me." Martha Rae was blown away. Could she ever leave the mountain? "Caleb, I will have to think this over. A lot. Violet has been back and forth with Ella and Sid, and I know she won't come. But I will need to talk to my other children, especially the bigger ones. And then there is Mama and Daddy. I have a lot to pray about and ponder. Will you give me time?" "You bet I will, and I am going to be praying for you to come live with me. You do know I accepted the Lord as my Savior, didn't you?" "Why, no" she said. Nothing he could have told her could have made her any more happy. "I'll tell you what," said Caleb. "When are y'all meeting for the first time in the new church?" Martha Rae said, "I heard Daddy say probably in about two weeks." "I will be at that meeting," said Caleb. "Do you think you will have an answer by then?" "Yes, I think so," she said. "I love you, Martha Rae. I never quit loving you. Just didn't know how to be a man and take care of my family. Joe and Mabel have taught me so much, and I owe them a lot. Can I kiss you?" he asked. "You know you can," said Martha Rae. Caleb embraced Martha Rae, and kissed her ever so sweetly. "Well, that was nice. But I see Mama giving us the eyes, so I better go before I end up walking." "I'll see you in two weeks, okay?" said Caleb. "Yes, my dear. I'll have your answer by then."

Caleb had walked free today, just like Joe and Mabel had told him the Lord had spoken. His faith was as high as any mountain and he intended to honor God the rest of his days. But first, he would need help with getting a house built for his family. That will be the easy part he thought.

# CHAPTER 33

Caleb had never worked so hard in all his days. Joe was a slave driver, he thought one day and spoke up and told Joe, "I'll say this for you, Joe. I believe you could outwork a team of mules." "You think so, do you, Mr. Caleb?" "Yes, sir, I do," said Caleb. "Well, I'll have to say I have several—no, lots of years on you. When you get my age, you will say the same thing. Now get busy." They had worked hard for a week and already had the framing up on the newly-constructed house. Even some of the young men Caleb knew from the mountain dropped by some and helped. "How long do you think it will take us to get this built, Joe?" asked Caleb. Joe took off his old hat and scratched his head. He always did that when he was thinking. He saw him figuring in his head and counting on his hands. "I would speculate, it will be done in about a month. Does that suit you?" he asked. Caleb replied, "Yes, sir. Sounds good to me. I just hope Martha Rae will come and live here." "She will," said Joe. "How can you be so sure?" said Caleb. "Well, I ain't never seen a woman in all my days run from something as nice as what this house will be." "You don't know my, Martha," said Caleb. "You are right, Caleb. But I know women. Wait and see what I told you."

Caleb prayed every night that Martha Rae and his children would make the right decision and come live here with him. Martha Rae was praying, too, that God would show her what she needed to do. Live in the new house with Caleb or stay put on this mountain. She loved this place more than anyone knew. After all, it's where she met her Savior Jesus. She was free to roam down to Marley Knott's Cliff and get a bucket of the best water coming forth out of that mountain she had ever drank. It seemed everywhere she looked she could see God. The trees, animals, the food they could grub, and especially her mama and her daddy. *I don't know if I can ever leave here, Lord,* she thought one day while praying at her prayer rock. The Lord began to speak to her, "You will never leave here, Martha Rae, because part of this mountain is embedded in your very soul. But you must consider what Caleb has offered you. Whether you think so or not, there is life beyond this mountain, and I have work for you to do. You will not be far, but far enough." Martha Rae bowed over on her lap and the tears fell like rain that day. She knew all along she would leave. She just felt like she needed the Lord's confirmation. And today, she received her walking papers. Now, to tell her children and Mama and Daddy. That would be the hard part.

John and Bean Tucker had gotten the church close enough to being finished to have service next Sunday. The benches had not arrived that the other church had given them. But Sid assured John the truck would probably be here in a day or two. John had asked CJ if he would build the preacher's podium and put one of his beautiful carvings in the front of it. CJ was so proud his Papa had asked him to do this special part for the new church. He had been looking through the Bible to find exactly what he was looking for to carve in the front of the podium. "What have you settled on, son?" asked his papa John. "It's going to be a surprise, but I think you will like it," said CJ.

The next two weeks had been especially hard for everybody, but it was also the most exciting time this mountain had ever seen. The truck that had brought the used pews over to the new church arrived at the first part of the week. They had sent word by Sid's latest innovation, the telephone, to tell them to have enough help to unload the benches because they were quite heavy. John had summoned every able-bodied man on that mountain to come and take part. They labored and carried ten oak pews into the little church. They were so proud of what the Lord had accomplished here at the foot of Marley Knott's Mountain. Who would have ever guessed they would ever have their own place to worship.

Everybody was buzzing to come see the little brown church that the menfolk under the guidance of John Jenkins and Bean Tucker had erected. Martha Rae had been looking for the right time to talk to her daddy, and she just watched him walk always alone down toward the creek and knew this would be her opportunity. "Daddy," she called. "Wait up." John Jenkins turned around and smiled at his daughter Martha Rae. He already knew in his heart what was coming and had told Sal just as much. "She's going to leave us, Sal." Sal had tried to hide her hurt, but she, too, knew this day was coming since Caleb was set free. They both knew her and those kids' place were with Caleb. She would have to accept it, and know that's what God said in his word to do. "Leave father and mother and cleave to your mate." She had been praying hard for Caleb to be the man, husband, and father that God wanted him to be. She actually felt good about all this. She and John were waiting for Martha Rae to come and tell them, and today John knew that was what Martha Rae had on her heart. "Daddy, the church looks really good," said Martha Rae. "Yes, honey. The good Lord has provided us a nice place to worship. Don't you think the benches are nice that the other church down east sent us?" "Oh indeed, I do," said Martha Rae. Martha Rae was finding it hard to bring up what she really wanted to talk about and her daddy knew that. Finally, John looked at his sweet daughter and said, "Martha Rae, I know you have got something on your mind and have a pretty good idea what it is. Let's go down by the creek and sit on that big old rock that shoots out over the water and talk." "Okay, Daddy," said Martha Rae. "I do have something to say."

The water was running brisk today, sitting there on that big rock. The sunshine made this a most pleasant place to spill her guts. "Daddy," she said. "I don't know exactly how to say this, but—" John interrupted her and said, "You are leaving this mountain, aren't you, sweetheart?" Martha Rae bowed her head, and the tears begin to slip down her face. "Yes, Daddy, I guess I am. I have prayed and I do love Caleb. Our place is with him, and he has assured me he is a changed man. Did you know he accepted the Lord as his Savior?" Martha Rae felt like she had blurted out her life story in a couple of sentences. But this was her daddy, and she knew he understood her more than anybody. John reached over and hugged his eldest daughter. "Honey, me and your mama have known this for several weeks. Matter of fact, I knew it the day at the trial when you and Caleb were talking.

I could see that you two really loved each other. Me and your mama have been praying for you all, and will always pray for our girls. Sure, we will miss you, but we will be fine. Give me and your mama somewhere to go. Maybe get another one of those hamburgers and fried taters. Your mama ain't quit talking about how good it was since she sank her teeth into one that day." Martha Rae laid back on the rock and laughed. "My mama. They will never be another one like her." John picked up his daughter's hand. "One thing we want you to know is, you and your family are always welcome to come home anytime you want to. Our home is your home." "I know, Daddy. I love you both more than you will ever know. What is that saying I used to tell you?" Her and her daddy both said it at the same time. "I love you. A bushel and a peck and a hug around the neck. Things are going to be alright, Martha Rae. I can feel it in my soul. Thank you, Daddy. Will you tell Mama what I just told you?" "Honey, she already knows. We both knew weeks ago." They heard a loud hollering and John said, "Let's go see what that rowdy bunch is up to."

# CHAPTER 34

Reverend Avery Banks and his soon-to-be bride Bess were the first to arrive at the little church. "Can you believe this? No more wet, hot, or cold meetings in a brush arbor, honey. We actually have a church. I hope we have a full house today." "Yes, honey," said Bess. "I am so happy to have a church for us to worship in." The first to arrive was Sid and Ella with Violet and baby Emma. They were so proud of their new addition to their family. Emma was just a tad fussy this morning, but soon settled into her mama's arms and drifted off to sleep. Soon, the folks up on Marley Knott's Mountain begin trickling in. John and Sal were among some of the first. They had gone up and carried Pap and Corry down this morning, too. Martha Rae and her brood walked down. She knew she was leaving this mountain, so she wanted to get her senses filled up every chance she got. Mrs. Bright was coming with her little basket on her arm for any herbs she might run across. She had carved herself a walking stick this past winter to aid her in her tracks across the mountain. It looked like every single family from off this big mountain was coming to the little brown church this morning. Martha Rae began singing "Oh come, come, come, come to the church in the wildwood. Oh come to the church in the vale. No place is so dear to my childhood as the little brown church in the vale."

The spirit that flowed out of that mountain this morning was one of peace and harmony and worship unto God. Caleb, Joe, and Mabel had been there about thirty minutes. Caleb stood outside in the church yard waiting on his wife and children. He caught a glimpse of them and took off in a run. His children had not seen him since he left their home. They were not as forgiving as their mama. But after Martha Rae talked to them, they all agreed to give him one more chance. He would talk to them, too, but they needed to gather in the church. They could talk later. Caleb and Martha Rae sat with Pap and Corry. The children were scattered here and there amongst the congregation. Joe and Mabel were cozying up with Little John. Mabel was hoping this whole family would come live close to her. *She would finally get her family,* she thought. But in the form of grandkids, she didn't care whose kids they were she would love them as if they were hers. Last but not least, Edna Sue and her fiancé Robert Meadows arrived. They walked hand in hand into the sanctuary and found them a seat beside Sal Jenkins.

Finally, Reverend Avery stood up. "Good morning, you fine folks. I am so happy, and am sure you all are, to get to gather in our new church. The Lord had seen fit to give us a building to gather in. So this morning. The first order of service is to thank CJ Moses for this fine podium he has built and carved a picture of Jesus in the garden praying. You do some fine work, young man. Mrs. Bright has been undertaking to find a name for our little church and I was wondering if she had come up with anything." Mrs. Bright so humbly stood up and walked to the front of the church. "I would like to thank John Jenkins for giving me this assignment to find us a name for this church. I have come up with something and thought we all should take a part and vote. What I came up with was Marley Knott's Mountain Church of God of Prophecy." A huge clap went up, and Rev. Avery confirmed that this would be the name of the new church. They sang several hymns, and finally, he took his text out of Psalm 127, "Unless the Lord builds the house. He showed there was many houses the Lord builds some are physical houses such as churches and others are spiritual houses, God is always building." The Sutphin boys had brought their instruments and Rev. Avery asked them to play something appropriate for an altar call. Pap Moses was the first to stand. After him, Corry got him by the hand and led him to the altar. "We both need saving," she said. Soon, another person came and then another, until the little altar was running over with souls crying out to God to save them. Martha Rae was right up there, too, praying and lifting her hands to God for this miraculous day. Some of the old-timers were shouting and praising God. It was truly a time for rejoicing. Reverend Avery was just taken aback, he felt someone might be saved this morning but not the whole mountain. "Folks," he stood and said. "This has been quite a day. Mr. Banks, may I have the floor to say something?" They all turned around and there stood Joe Lambert. "I have to say this or I will burst. Many years ago, my daddy told me, well, when I was a little boy, that he had attended a tent revival over in these parts. His grandpa and my great-grandpa were circuit-riding preachers that went about doing tent revivals. He said his grandpa had had a red-hot revival. A few souls were saved. Others delivered from affliction. The last day of the revival, he said the Lord had shown him that the mountain behind him would bring forth multitude of souls. No one lived up there at the time until Marley Knott hewed out a road. Old man Knott and his wife lived up there until their deaths and no one else lived up there. He was called a false prophet. Little by little, families began going up that crude road building houses. All of you are offspring of those first families that came up in Marley Knott's Mountain. Today, we can honestly say that this prophecy has come to pass. A tragedy such as what happened here in the fall has stirred the hearts of you people to know you need the Lord. I thought I was just coming to be with Caleb, but was reading in my Bible the other night and saw where my daddy had recorded this prophecy many years ago. The Lord is always faithful to his word."

John looked at Sal and said, "I told you about this, but you acted like you didn't believe me. Here's proof that what I heard was true." "I never doubted you for one minute, John," said Sal. John just winked at Edna Sue who was grinning. She knew her mama and had no doubt she brushed her daddy off when he told her of this prophecy. But that was all behind them now, all that counted was that this mountain had come to know Jesus Christ as their Lord and Savior. The service ended that day with everyone chatting and the ladies hugging each other like they used to when they had service at the old brush arbor. You could see where the brush arbor had been. The winter snows had caved it in. But to these folks, it was a reminder of days gone by. Both good and bad.

Caleb had a red, hot question on his heart and he needed an answer today. "Martha Rae, will you and my children come with me over next to the clearing so we can talk? Make sure you bring Violet, too." Martha Rae knew what Caleb wanted, and he would not leave until he had an answer. Violet was standing with her Grandma Sal and Ella when Martha Rae approached them all and made a little small talk. "Violet, your daddy would like you to meet him along with the rest of us over in the clearing." Violet looked like she was going to faint. She did not want to leave Ella and Sid. Violet loved her mama and guessed she loved her daddy, too. Although maybe not as much. "Mama," she cried. The tears had already began to flow. "Are you going to make me come and live with you all?" She asked. "Now, Violet, I know where your heart is and I wouldn't make you come if you didn't want to. And besides, I know where you are at if I need you. Instead of coming to stay all night with Ella, you can come and stay all night with me. Now won't that be fun?" Asked Martha Rae. Violet hung her head. "I love you, Mama. You do know that, don't you?" "You bet, I do," said Martha Rae. "Now let's get over here and talk with your daddy."

Little John was already sitting up in his daddy's lap, talking a mile a minute. Laymon and CJ were trying to play hard to get, but she knew with a little cozying up from Caleb, they would warm up, too. Angela and Lilly were quiet, but that was not very unusual. Susan was hiding behind her mama's skirt tail, and finally, Violet arrived to listen to see what their daddy said. "Well," said Caleb. "I see all of my bunch is here. What I want to start off by saying is, I am still your daddy, but a different daddy, too. The Lord Jesus saved my soul when I ran out of this mountain the day I left. I was scared and running because I knew everyone knew I had been up at Ellis's still near about all summer. When I found Ellis dead, my first instinct was to run. By the grace of God, I ran to Joe and Mabel Lambert's farm and they took me in. By pure piety, I would guess. I worked there until Christmas and had every intention of turning myself in to the authorities after Christmas. But as you all know, I was caught coming out of this mountain after bringing Christmas presents to you all. I love all of you and realize I made it very hard on all of you and your mama. What I would like to say, will or can you all ever forgive me?" He looked each child over and then settled his gaze upon his dark-haired Raven. Little John piped up first, "You bet I will, Daddy." All the other children began to laugh a little, and finally, much to Martha Rae's surprise, Laymon reached out his hand to his daddy. But Caleb grabbed him and embraced him instead of the handshake. One by one, every child followed suit. Violet was the last to step up to her daddy. "Well," he said. "From what I hear, you have been helping Ella and Sid for a long time." Violet could not bear to look him in the eyes. "Yes, that right," she said ever so sadly. "Are you going to stay with them? I hear you might. But before you answer, I must say something. I cannot ask you to leave those fine folks after the way I abandoned you all. All I can hope for is you will always consider me and your mama your official parents. I would hope you will come. But if I had my bets, I would say you will stay with Ella and Sid. Am I right?" he asked. Violet nodded her head yes. "I love you, Violet, and nothing or no one can change that, but I will give you my blessing. And another thing I might want to add is, you will get so tired of seeing me visit you at the mercantile. I hear you are just about running that place." That brought a big grin on Violet's face. "You got a lot of your mama in you. As matter of fact, all my young 'uns do. I am very proud of my family and I promise to do the very best to make it up to you all. Me and Joe have almost got our new house built. Just a few minor details and I will be ready for my family to join me." All but Violet coming, they nodded in agreement. Caleb was about the happiest he had ever been. God had restored his family back to him. What Satan meant for his destruction, the Lord had turned it around to bless him.

Sal was watching at a distance. She could clearly see Martha Rae and her children belonged with Caleb, and she felt in her heart Caleb was a changed man. Edna Sue would be married next Sunday to her sweetheart Robert along with Rev. Avery and his fiancé Bess. A double wedding. Reverend Frazier was coming all the way from North Carolina to marry them. He was one of Reverend Avery Banks' close friends, and they had asked if he would do them the honors. He also agreed to marry Edna Sue and Robert as well. God had brought this mountain full circle. A prophecy that was given before most on this mountain was even born to fulfilling it today. She knew those that had lost family members to the alcohol poisoning were saddened today, and she would have to remember to pray and reach out to everyone involved. She heard Pap telling Caleb all the latest news from the mountain. He even mentioned asking Caleb to pray for him to regain his sight. He had heard the story of how the Lord restored the blind in the Bible. Martha Rae had given Caleb and his children some time before they all would go to their homes. He had them down at the creek, wading and catching crawdads. She was thinking, in a very short time she would leave this magnificent mountain. In some ways, she would miss it like crazy but was looking further down the road. God had spoken to her heart and told her she had work to do for him. Right now, she would need to start packing up what little belongings they had. Suddenly, the old familiar hymn came into her heart. "Amazing grace, how sweet the sound that saved a wretch like me. I once was lost but now am found, was blind but now I see." Yes God had brought this mountain full circle, thought Martha Rae, He proved his word was true and he was faithful to fulfill a prophecy from a long time back. She remembered God speaking to her and telling her he had work for her to do. I just wonder what my God had gotten for me and Caleb in our future. One thing for certain she knew she would never be the same nor the folks that took the walk this morning from up on Marley Knott's Mountain.

# ABOUT THE AUTHOR

Pam Nester Cloud began her new journey as a step of faith. God had called her to "write a book." After much thought and pondering, the novel *Marley Knott's Mountain* began pouring into her spirit. It came from her vault of memories that she had stored up listening to the old folks spin a yarn in her youth. Raised in the Appalachian Mountains of Virginia, she drew strength from those who had walked before her. Faith in God along with her family are very important to her. She and her husband Rufus live in the foothills of the Blue Ridge Mountains. They raised one son and are blessed with a precious daughter-in-law and three rambunctious grandchildren.

CPSIA information can be obtained
at www.ICGtesting.com
Printed in the USA
JSHW052346190222
22976JS00001B/4